Dylan's Devils

TOM FAUSTMAN

Blue Sky Ventures
175 Tryon Street
Glastonbury, CT 06073

Cover Design by expertsubjects

Manufactured in the United States of America

DEDICATION

To Nett, Nif, La La and K-man, nickname victims and the loves of my life.

BEGIN

Vincente gave a rare smile as he hung up the telephone. He was pleased: blind obedience, as planned. He was nearby, but not close enough to see his prey's house from the telephone booth on Lansdowne Avenue, in an upscale section of bustling Upper Derby. Although not worried about being caught, he was cautious, methodical. He moved into the shadows, began his silent assault. He always parked within short walking distance of his attacks. It was early summer. The sun had set. The old maple trees gave cover as he moved down the dim side of the street. His breathing became rapid, the excitement building. He moved behind a mammoth rhododendron when he saw headlights approaching. Had the police finally discovered him? Would this be the end of his pleasure, his relentless quest for revenge?

A small man, he crouched low, trying to become invisible. The car passed harmlessly. He rose up, reflected that his whole life he'd been mostly invisible. Since childhood, no one ever paid him much notice. Except to torment, beat or humiliate him. That thought enraged him. His breathing came in pants, his brown beady eyes darted left and right. Vincente hated being ignored, insignificant. Since he began his ritualistic life, he considered himself extraordinary. Shaking his head, he snapped back to the moment, realized he was moving too quickly, was overly excited. He came to a stop, tried to calm down. Breathing deeply through his nose, he closed his eyes, exhaled deeply and raised his little hands. He flexed his fingers, getting them ready for the delightful work only steps away. He moved forward, the lust building.

This was his favorite time in the ritual, the anticipation of the ceremony that would soon start. He would become the master, in full control, no longer ignored, bigger than life. His careful preparation would soon be fulfilled. He stayed on her lawn, careful to avoid noise, moved toward the door. Following orders, the front light was off. Part of the excitement was the uncertainty. Would the victim obey his commands? Would there be a flaw in his perfect planning? It took endless repetition and practice to concoct these perfect crimes, years of training to hone his gift, his magic. Vincente was nearing fifty. He hadn't been caught in twenty years of rituals. He felt omnipotent, a predatory giant, no longer a man the world overlooked.

He got to the darkened door, rung the bell. Chloe answered immediately, stood in the entrance, haloed by bright light inside, a fine-looking woman. She was voluptuous and divorced, his desired type. As directed, she wore nothing but a robe, bra and panties underneath, accentuating her sensual body. When Chloe looked at her visitor, her eyes opened wide. Recognizing him, her breathing heightened, she stood motionless. Vincente said simply, "I'm here. Let's begin." Chloe didn't argue, followed him. As he entered the house, took the symbolic candy cane from his pocket, sniffed it deeply, eyes glazed in rapture. He stopped abruptly, turned to her, "Turn off the lights, it's too bright." Chloe circled the living room, flipping each switch till the downstairs was almost pitch dark. He nodded approvingly. "Show me to your bedroom." They marched upstairs.

DYLAN

I was mildly famous after solving the Sylvan Skolnick murder case a couple years ago. Sylvan was a serial killer who preyed on lonely old woman. I stumbled on the case when investigating an insurance fraud case that didn't add up and involved one of Sylvan's victims. My curiosity almost got me killed, but eventually I lucked into a happy ending. The News of Delaware County did a nice article on me, wrote, "Dylan Frazier, the next Columbo?" The picture they printed wasn't so hot, my dark hair mussed, blue eyes kind of red, like a ghoul. Gun to my head, I had to admit: I enjoyed the fame. But it was impossible to get too cocky with my childhood friends around. When I went to the courts to shoot hoops, I was the butt of jokes for a week. Jimmer Keilmann, "the commissioner of the courts" had the best line. He stood with his muscular arms akimbo as I shot baskets, announced to all, "Hey, Dylan, I showed that creepy newspaper picture to my son. He thought *you* were the serial killer."

I soon settled back to my booming investigative business. With the new notoriety, I had multiple insurance companies feeding me work. Dave Hoban, at Voyager Insurance, gave me my start as an investigator; he always got priority. When I returned from Vietnam in 1971, it was tough getting a job. Most people worried you might be a burn out from Nam, gave polite rejections. But Dave Hoban hired me, trained me in insurance investigative work. Later, told me to go out on my own, start my own business. He said I could make a killing. I started

"Lookout Investigations," solved the Sylvan Skolnick case, and suddenly had a reputation. The money rolled in. Cheesesteaks everyday if I wanted, rotated hoagies in as needed. Throw in a soft pretzel and mustard for dessert. I was grazing big time.

My work was rarely boring. A weird case would always come along. I liked that uncertainty. One of my witty father's lines was, "Suspense kept you sharp: like being on the business end of a farting horse." Remembering that always made me laugh. As if reading my thoughts, I got a call from Dave Hoban at Voyager. When I got off the phone, I was still chuckling. Hoban liked my warped sense of humor, called whenever something funny happened. Often gave me files that weren't technically noteworthy but had comic value. This time, Hoban said he was reading the daily attendance report that stated, "Rita Greene won't be in work till later. The lock on her bedroom door broke off, and she can't get out till someone knocks down the door." I volunteered to go over, but Hoban doubted the story. Opined that Ms. Greene was probably the victim of too much Ernest and Julio the night before.

Hoban changed topics, said he did have a file for me. Said a female employee of Container Corporation had been assaulted a few months ago, was still out on mental and nervous disability. The company wanted to make certain she was not milking it. He added, "They said the crime was legitimate, but the company doctor thinks victims are better off getting back to work. That getting in a normal routine again aids the healing process." I didn't make any quip right away, had seen too many assault cases already where people never got back to normal.

Finally, had to comment, "Easy to say if you never had the shit beat out of you." I got no reaction. Promised to drop by Voyager, get the details on Chloe Zubrisky.

VINCENTE

Vincente Candido was always busy on Mondays. His thriving business left him little spare time—except for his "ritualistic ceremonies." Selecting his next victim again dominated his thoughts. He was always on the hunt. But they had to meet his strict criteria: younger, divorced and living alone. Oh yes, and buxom, almost Rubenesque. Fortunately, his occupation gave him access to many people and lots of bored women. From the outside room he heard his wife answering the telephone, scheduling another appointment for next week. There were always people with so-called "emergencies." He got them in but made them wait as long as possible. He enjoyed seeing people upset. But his caring expression fooled them, showed otherwise. They adored this kind little man.

The only person who knew his total lack of empathy was Rosa, his diminutive wife of two decades. Vincente arranged the marriage to Rosa through an Italian wedding broker in South Philadelphia. He went through many pictures and biographies before settling on Rosa. He had her transported to Philadelphia from Puglia- the ugly duckling with no hope for marriage or a decent life in her native village. The Philadelphia church, St Christopher, housed her for propriety sake- grateful for Vincente's generous contributions. They were married after a few weeks. No one attended the private ceremony except the priest who conducted the service.

From their first meeting till now, Rosa wore her long, mousy brown hair in a tight bun. She had three large moles on her chin, almost forming a triangle, each sprouting a medley of dark hairs, a large gap in her front teeth. Rosa was pencil thin, maybe ninety pounds. She had a classic aquiline nose, but that didn't save her, it made her muddy eyes look crossed. Rosa was very homely, just what Vincente wanted. But he was pleasantly surprised to discover she was smart. Vincente taught her English every night. She worked diligently to eliminate any accent, and her grammar was impeccable, almost robotic. She didn't like to make mistakes, was a natural with mathematics and organizational skills. After two years, Vincente fired his office manager, installed Rosa as his able assistant.

To the outside world, they appeared a normal couple. But it was a loveless marriage, as Vincente intended. He was never cruel to Rosa, treated her well. She was resigned to the emotionless arrangement, preferred a relationship without passion. She was ascetic by nature, reserved. Vincente relied on her to tend home and office, gave whatever she needed. Rosa realized he was joyless by nature. She wasn't being singled out. Whenever homesick, she remembered her hard life in the Puglia town of Ostuni: meager meals, humble house, surrounded by prosperous villagers and tourists enjoying the scenic Adriatic village. Now she had a beautiful house in Drexel Heights, ate whatever she wanted, watched TV every night. Her favorite show was Bonanza, liked watching the old-time freedom and simplicity of ranch life, so different from her coastal village. Yet she missed the majestic beauty, musical language, Italian lifestyle and magnificent food. Rosa shook her head wistfully: Puglia is only for the rich. Maybe I will return one day as the wife of a rich man? She had thought frequently about that, was having trouble shaking the longing.

But this idle musing usually passed quickly. Her life had changed for the better, no more poverty, scratching for existence. More than anything she loved office management, it gave meaning to her life. She had contentment, if not pleasure. Just then, from the nearby room, she heard Vincente ask, "Have you organized the personnel files for this week?"

She got up, silently walked to his doorway, "The files are alphabetized by each day of the week, as you like them."

Her cheerless husband raised his eyes, nodded; gave a faint smile. "You are always on top of things, Rosa. I couldn't run this place without you. Why don't you take off early today? I may stay late to review the files."

Rosa shook her head. "I will have dinner waiting for you whenever you return." As she walked away, Vincente thought: loyal, just like a pet dog.

DYLAN'S NEW CASE

I thought about Laura while driving to retrieve the file from Hoban. The love of my life had decided to become an architect, a discovery she made while studying in Paris. I recalled the joy in her eyes as she explained her epiphany, "I found myself spending every spare moment wandering the streets of Paris, in awe of the beautiful buildings. Then I started looking at them differently, wondering how they were made, how they lasted so long. They seemed so timeless. Pretty soon I was going to the library to study their history, looking at the way they came from nothing but the mind of the architect. It hit me hard. Why am I studying to be an Math major?"

So, my beautiful fiancée switched gears, enrolled at the University of Pennsylvania School of Architecture, was now studying in London. Before she left, she helped fight my demons still lingering from my time in Vietnam. When I returned from Nam, Laura wanted to get married right away, but I told her we should wait till her schooling was less intense. What I really meant was till I felt certain that I adjusted back to normal, or at least my form of normal. With my mischievous mind, even with the Palomar telescope, that singular moment of maturity might be a tough thing to spot. Mostly, I was worried about the flashbacks. I never dwelt on my demons. Most time I was full of fun and mischief. The disturbing behavior just appeared occasionally: sometimes in nightmares, sometimes in spontaneous fury. The anger was subsiding, but still troubled me.

I shook my head, snapped out of that pensive train of thought. The sturdy brick Voyager Building loomed on the corner of the regal Parkway, not far from the famed Philadelphia Museum of Art. It was tough finding parking spots in downtown Philly, you always felt lucky when an opening popped free. Today was apparently one when fortune smiled. A big space was free near the front door, over an hour left on the parking meter. Plus, there was a hotdog and soft pretzel vendor on the corner. I started savoring lunch choices after seeing what Hoban had for me. I patted my belly, thinking about lunch. My stomach was still firm after daily basketball or judo routines. I was a nut about physical fitness, but the Philly treats were often irresistible. Or should I get a cheesesteak?

I climbed out of the elevator on the seventh floor, made my way to Hoban's office. On the way down the aisle, I looked to see if Rita Greene had freed herself from the bedroom. She gave me a big smile when I asked about her unplanned incarceration. "Damndest thing, know what I mean, Dylan?"

I nodded sympathetically, said, "I hate it when I get locked in my bedroom. Happened to me as a kid all the time." I paused, "Except it was my usually my mom doing it on purpose." She giggled as I headed to see her boss.

I knocked on Hoban's door, he waved me in. "Glad to see Rita made it in, did you have to post bond, or did her cat burglar skills save the day?"

He shook his head, "Don't get me started."

He grabbed the claim file for Chloe Zubrisky, opened

it as he laid it in front of me. "This is a sad case, really. She got assaulted about six months ago, still hasn't shaken it off. I can't blame her really, the sick bastard tied her to the bed, must have toyed with her for hours. According to the latest medical form, she's still a mess."

I let that sink in. "Why's Container so hell bent to get her back to work? Seems like this might be a waste of time. I'm assuming her Doc still ok's her disability, right?"

Hoban shook his head. "Her doctor says she's still not shaken off the trauma. That it might take a year or more before she's functional again."

I grabbed the file, put in my briefcase. Hoban smiled, "Fancy briefcase, huh? Things must be good. You used to carry the files in a paper bag when you started here."

I smirked at him. "It wasn't paper. It was an A&P plastic bag, more protection if it rained. You know I always plan ahead." We shot the shit for a while. Hoban was always dating different girls in the building. He couldn't settle on one that met his standards. I asked, "Found Mrs. Right yet? Or are you still working the Yellow Pages, hoping for a beautiful blind girl?" He grinned, waved for me to get going. I headed for the corner vendor, two soft pretzels smothered with mustard won the lunch contest.

I sat in the car reading Chloe's file as I munched on the pretzels, trying to keep the mustard from dripping, mostly failing. As normal, I was going to pay a surprise visit. The ton of napkins came in handy but hoped she didn't notice the sprinkling of yellow smudges on my shirt.

She lived in a nice section of Upper Derby, not that far from my apartment. Probably, the local males didn't have mustard gobs on their shirts. I pulled my tie wider. The file was somewhat vague on details. The cops didn't share any specifics about the assault—probably to protect her privacy. The attending physician listed "severe depression" as the diagnosis. Her "return to work" block said "undetermined." Still wondering why they were pushing her to return, I looked at her "occupation" block. It said simply, "distribution manager."

That didn't help much, so I finished my pretzels, went to the nearby telephone booth. I always looked in the change slot for bonus coins. A habit from my penniless days, sometimes you got lucky. Not today, so I called personnel at Container Corporation. After identifying myself, I asked the manager, Doug Grimm, what was really behind the push?

He was clear. "Chloe's a whiz at distribution." He explained she interacted with the warehouse workers and drivers. "The unions love her. She has a way of making them do those extra things that make this place run smoothly. The operation has been kinda chaotic since she left." He was silent before adding, "Plus we really like her, we think she'll snap back better if she's working. We're worried for her." I liked that answer, told the manager I'd drop over today, said I would convey how much they missed her. Maybe it would help.

I took the Schuylkill Expressway since it was off hours, wouldn't have any rush hour mess. Locals called it "The Sure Kill Expressway" since it was a total disaster in heavy traffic, no shoulder to use if there were accidents or breakdowns. It was smooth sailing today as I sped toward the short cut through Sixty-Ninth Street, the beat down area that was the suburban transportation junction into the city.

I passed the Chez Vous Building where Jerry Blavat disc jockeyed his way to Philly fame. My parents never let me go to his dances since there were too many "loose girls." I couldn't argue too much, since that was my exact reason for going. Being an obedient Catholic boy, I didn't fight my parents. That left no other choice: I had to sneak there. I pitched nicer clothes out my bedroom window into the azalea bushes, but walked outside in my basketball stuff, telling my parents I was off to the courts. Fun memories.

CHLOE ZUBRISKY

As I veered through the Beverly Hills section of Upper Derby, I rehearsed how I would gain admittance to Chloe's house. That Voyager was paying her a weekly check was usually clout enough. I had several lines I used, depending on the circumstances. I hadn't finalized my approach when I arrived at her address, decided to wing it. The house was large, only a block from busy Lansdowne Avenue, but totally quiet because of huge maple trees lining both sides of her street. I parked, got out, stared at the surroundings, a habit from my MP time in Nam. Typical of the neighborhood, her house was big, but relatively close to both neighbors. Her property was well maintained, but with the tree-lined street and lush shrubbery, it would be easy for a careful intruder to remain undetected.

With that rumbling inside my brain, I rang her doorbell, waited. After a short while, I heard footsteps. There was a small window near the top of the door. I saw a woman's eyes peering at me, asking in a halting tone, "Yes, what may I help you with?"

Told her I was from Voyager, checking to see if her disability checks had been arriving correctly. Before she could say "yes" and just walk away, "I can do this from outside if you prefer. Just talk with the door closed. I understand your need for caution. Your benefits are about to be renewed, but I need to update your file with any changes in your condition. Is it possible for you to answer a few questions?" To further assure her, "I spoke to Mr. Grimm at Container, he said to tell you how much everybody misses you, are anxious for you to come back and unravel the mess with the unions." That did the trick. I heard her fumbling with what seemed like a dozen locks. The door opened slowly.

An attractive but haggard woman stood looking at me. She was maybe late forties, would have been a real looker if she used some make-up and brushed her hair neatly. But I could tell immediately this lady hadn't seen a normal day since her attack. Her eyes were red, looked sleep deprived. Had the "deer in the headlight" look, hunched shoulders, very nervous.

To settle her down, "Your house is beautiful, what a nice neighborhood. I don't live too far from here, closer to the Drexel Heights border."

I saw her exhale. She was relaxing some. "Thank you, my former husband bought this, I got it in the settlement." And then a half smile, "I enjoyed sticking it to him." I gave her a big chuckle, watched her shoulders loosen more.

That made me think about Mr. Grimm saying getting back to work may be good for her. To Chloe, "You seem really popular at work, like you're invaluable. And by the way, isn't Grimm a bad name for a personnel manager? Isn't he supposed to work with people, keep them happy and all? That name's got to be a negative for his career. Right?" I didn't mean to blurt that out, but I saw her tiny smile. Taking advantage of the moment, "Sorry about that, weird things hit me, and I tend to let them escape without thinking. My mom says I'll never get a tumor because I never internalize." That got a wide grin. "Anyway, Mr. Grimm said the place has been a mess since you left. Said you had the unions eating out of your hand."

She gave a full smile this time. "You just have to let them think something is their idea. It works every time. Management tends to be too directive, never asks for the union's input before deciding things. I try to get to the unions before they hear about changes, ask their ideas. Most times they will be reasonable if it isn't forced on them. But if the conversation gets off track, I really just play referee." She got a sweet look on her face, "I do miss it."

I had my opening. "So, why don't you give it a try? Maybe that would be the best medicine for you." I regretted saying that immediately.

Her eyes suddenly fluttered, tears rimmed the edges. Nodding her head, said softly, "I just don't have the courage. The thought of travelling into the city and facing all those strangers on the bus is too much." She started to shiver. "And then to come home every night to this house, wonder if the creep broke in while I was away. It's just too much."

An idea popped into my head, "Is there a nearby co-worker you could car pool with? Somebody you know and trust. Maybe they could help you check your house out after work? Make sure everything was okay." I could see her thinking, trying to find a way, but she remained silent.

Changing gears, "Did they ever find the creep who broke in?"

At first the look on her face said I screwed up again, was too blunt, that she was agitated by that question. But then her demeanor changed slightly, her head rose up, "No, I don't believe they ever will. He was too clever. He left no clues. He had one of those nondescript faces. It was the perfect crime." I noticed Chloe said this without pause. Her voice was monotone, like it was memorized. Weird. Thought to myself: maybe it was her way of dealing with the painful memory, to create a story to give her peace of mind? But I felt bad for bringing up something so personal and traumatic.

Another idea came, "I'd be happy to pick you up myself. Do like a dry run. I'll drive you into work, take you home afterward." Her face still looked uncertain. I said quickly, "And I'll check your house out with you before I leave. It might be nice for you to see some old friends."

To my utter surprise, she said, "I'd like that."

I gave her my card and phone number, told her to call whenever she wanted to go to work. I stopped at a phone booth, called Mr. Grimm at Container. He was thrilled by my news. I told him I'd give him a heads up when I heard from her. Also said I'd stop by again if I didn't hear from her in a week or so. That we should strike while the iron was hot. On the drive back home, I felt myself get that itch. This was an interesting case. Maybe I could do some good. Rather than just push someone back to work, I could help a nice lady overcome her demons. And that made me think about my own periodic war torment. Maybe the distraction would help us both. As I was pondering that, Dr. Fran Philips came into mind. Time to visit my buddy?

DR. FRAN PHILIPS

I called Dr. Fran when I got home, arranged to have a beer at Schultz's Tavern. As I hung up, my stomach was barking. Had nothing to eat at home, so I went early, would grab a dog at the bar, shoot the shit with Duke the bartender before Fran arrived. Duke gave me a nice greeting when I got there. He owned this famous dump since I was a little kid, always treated the basketball players like royalty. Since I had been a decent player, I was well taken care of. He grinned at me, "Look what the cat dragged in. Ain't seen you for ages, Dylan. How's it hangin'?"

I shrugged, "I'm too modest to brag but I do get carpet burns when I walk around in my Fruit-of-the-Looms." Duke chuckled, poured me an Ortlieb without asking what I wanted.

I ordered a dog with pickles and onions, the only safe thing to eat here. Even the bar nuts and pretzels at Schultz's gave you the trots. I told Duke I was meeting Fran Philips in a bit. He frowned, "Ain't ever see him in here no more. I heard he become a doctor or somethin'. But I'll tell ya, that kid could play some ball." I agreed, Fran had been a terrific player in high school, had loads of scholarships, but was a shitty student, had to settle for playing in some school in Nebraska.

Fran got so homesick he quit and came back home for good at Thanksgiving. I remember meeting him at the airport after he left Nebraska. The first thing he said was,

"I could see buffaloes out my dorm window. Can you believe that?" I listened sympathetically, afraid to tell him I would love that view, was a huge bovine fan. But it wasn't time for my zany views. My friend was changed after that epiphany, got serious about studies, went to school year-round. To my surprise, he became a psychologist while I was in the Nam.

We had been close buddies since age ten, someone I trusted completely. Fran had always been easy to talk to, made the transition seamlessly to having therapeutic conversations for a living. Part of what made Fran a great basketball player was he never seemed nervous. Always appeared calm. That trait made him ideal for dealing with mentally and emotionally troubled people who poured out their miseries to him each session. Thinking about his daily routine made me grin. Had growing up with me been like on-the-job training? Made a note to ask if I deserved some credit. I could picture him shaking his head. But now my friend got paid for his natural empathy, business was booming. I wanted to ask his opinion on Chloe Zubrisky, see if he had any insight that might help her heal faster. Maybe I'd slip in a few comments about my Nam flashbacks while at it. Fran wouldn't bullshit me.

As I swallowed the last bite of hotdog, I spied Fran entering the murky bar. He was wearing khakis, penny loafers, a tweed sport coat and a freshly starched blue shirt. Always a dapper dresser, Fran now looked like a real professional, someone to tell your woes. I liked clothes too, but my occupation called for blending in versus getting noticed. I apologized for my appearance. "Sorry about the shitty duds, Fran, in my work, if I look too prosperous the bad guys won't open up."

He smiled, "You do kind of melt into the bar scene. I couldn't spot you till I got close."

I nodded, "Most of the knuckleheads I see almost feel sorry for me by the time I leave them. Like one loser to another loser kind of relationship. Works like a charm."

Duke brought Fran an Ortlieb, asked if he played ball anymore. Fran shook his head. "I haven't touched a basketball for almost six years. I lost the desire. It seems so pointless."

Duke had no comment for that. Raised his eyebrows like he was considering taking the beer back. How could anyone not love basketball seemed beyond his comprehension. I jumped in, "Fran doesn't know this, but I signed him up to play on my Narberth team this summer." I swatted Fran under the bar, signaling him to stay quiet.

That seemed to appease Duke. He walked away, muttering, "Glad to hear yer snappin' outta it. I mean, who doesn't love basketball? That's the craziest shit I ever heard." I looked at Fran. Spread my hands, a gesture that true wisdom had just been bestowed on us.

Fran laughed, "You always were fast on your feet. I almost forgot where I was. Schultz's is the mecca of basketball."

I nodded, "Thought Duke was going to pass out. Now that I think of it, isn't that like you telling your patients what their saying sounds crazy?"

He smiled again, "You have a point." And then, "So, what can I help you with?" I explained the whole story of Chloe Zubrisky, wondered if there was some way I could help her. That maybe she needed a push. Fran smiled. "You haven't changed much since you were a kid, Dylan. Always attracted to lost causes." I started to protest, he raised his hands, "That was a compliment. You might not remember, but you were the first one to tell me I had a gift for conversation. That I could do this for a living." He looked at me sincerely.

Could see Fran was thinking, I didn't say anything for a few minutes. Let him digest what I said about Chloe. I watched his head bob up and down. He told me I needed a lot more information. That getting the details of the assault would help him understand the degree of trauma. From there, we could work on a plan for recovery. I mentioned Frank Merlano was a police detective who might be a resource. That we used to play ball against him in high school. I had a relationship with him, could get some details they wouldn't generally give out. Then Fran and I went through a list of things I should find out. Told him I'd call when I got them.

As we were leaving, he asked how I was feeling after returning from Nam, that he was in the middle of a project for soldiers with adjustment problems. I swallowed hard, "Funny you should ask." We stood talking for over an hour about the cause of my nightmares—Percy Price.

VINCENTE

Rosa had done a flawless job organizing his new candidates. He sat in the quiet office and let his mind drift. He always savored the selection of his next target. As his eyes closed, he pictured Irma, his beautiful but stern mother. Since a toddler, she taunted him incessantly, "Why did you have to be born? You ruined my life." His father deserted Irma before he was born. He apparently thought Irma's family was wealthy, soon learned their perceived wealth was all show. She got pregnant, and dad was gone, never heard from again. Irma blamed Vincente for the break-up, made him feel he caused her miserable life. She made Vincente suffer as she had. His mom did not abuse him physically. She withheld love, showed him nothing but loathing. To survive, Vincente withdrew, created a fantasy world.

A loveless home was bad enough, but school was worse. Vincente Candido never grew, was brutalized since fifth grade when his classmates sprouted tall, and he stayed tiny. He also had the misfortune of a strangely shaped head on his scrawny body. His head was long but narrow, almost triangular. But his hair was the crowning touch on the misshapen pate—piled high with kinky brown fuzz. The favorite school torment of his mean classmates was grabbing his head, twirling him till he dropped from dizziness, all the while calling him "candy ass." But he was extremely bright. Excelled in every subject, but this too labeled him for grief. His teacher in fifth grade, Mrs. Crouch, praised his flawless math score. "Vincente, you have perfect grades. Maybe we have another Einstein in the making."

As he walked to lunch that day, Dickie Swift grabbed him, spun him mercilessly. As Vincente fell to the ground, Dickie said, "You might be smart but yer' still a shitty midget."

All this ran through Vincente's mind as he sat peacefully before his stack of potential victims. He blinked rapidly, shaking off the sour memories. He wondered whatever happened to Dickie Swift. He was one of fourteen kids in the Swift household, all big and stupid. Their last name seemed a glaring irony. He remembered fondly in eighth grade getting the last laugh on Dickie. He put an anonymous note on the teacher's desk about Dickie's disgusting habit of rubbing his head and collecting dandruff on his desk. Capping this revolting act, Dickie would stoop over and suck it into his mouth. Vincente was the only pupil attentive enough to spot this vile habit. Mrs. Crouch was wily. She took her time, watched his repulsive act for herself and humiliated him in front of the entire class. The nickname "Dickie-the-dandruff-eater" stayed with him for years. Smiling at his ploy from long ago, Vincente went back to his study.

DETECTIVE MERLANO

Following Fran Philip's suggestion, I had to get more information on Chloe Zubrisky. After a nutritious breakfast of Coco Puffs and Yoo Hoo, I drove to the police department. Had called Frankie Merlano that morning, told him what I wanted. Merlano was one of my high school basketball competitors. We had some of the same aggressive quirks as players, got along well. We rekindled the relationship when I started my insurance investigator career. He had been instrumental in solving the Sylvan Skolnick serial killer case. Like me, he got lots of press that helped his career immensely. I reminded him constantly that he "owed me." Last time I said that he replied, "Frazier, you're like a case of jock rash, you never go away." Merlano cracked me up, even when he was serious.

I parked my watermelon-looking car in the busy lot. Voyager Insurance sold me this bomb for almost nothing when I resigned. During my insurance training with Dave Hoban, I was advised that the pathetic car would help me maneuver through dicey neighborhoods without drawing attention. Hoban was right, most people felt sorry for me when they saw it. One feisty old lady on disability from Honeywell asked, "Who'd ya piss off to get that piece a junk?"

I remember chuckling, telling her, "It does keep me humble."

She finished with, "Ya might want ta check yerself

out for crabs." I never worried about anybody stealing my wheels.

I walked into the bustling police station, went to the desk sergeant, asked for Merlano. The grizzled old cop, Sgt. Bonner, asked, "He expectin' you? Ole' Frankie don't like to be surprised."

I nodded, "We've been friends since high school. I used to beat him like an old drum on the basketball court. Back before he became a big shot."

The sergeant smiled, "He does have a case of self-importance, now thatcha mention it." So he buzzed Merlano, told him I was here. I heard Merlano yell into the phone, "Don't believe any of the bullshit Frazier says about me. That dude ain't right in the head."

As I was let in, the sergeant smirked at me, mumbled, "Pot callin' the kettle black, huh?"

I spotted Merlano talking to a bunch of cops in the detective area. Frankie Merlano was about six feet, maybe 185. He had brown, liquid eyes. His bottom lip hung low, like his mom tied a roller skate to it as a kid. The lip gave him a perpetually puzzled look. Like everything he heard was a surprise. Plus, he was hyperactive, arms and hands always moving. He was a good basketball player. We had many battles. Both of us liked to talk while we played. Remind the other one when we did well. But we had a grudging respect. Neither one of us would quit, despite the score. I liked Frankie Merlano. He had something I learned to value in Nam, grit. Someone you could rely on in tough spots.

Frankie spotted me, told his fellow cops. "Hey guys, here comes Frazier. The guy I was telling you about." He paused a few seconds. "You know, my nomination for asshole of the year."

The cops chuckled, but I added quickly, "You won that contest last year, right, Frankie? So, they let you nominate your successor, that how it works?" That got a bigger laugh.

Merlano shook his head, "You never are at a loss for words, are ya Frazier?" The other cops walked out, and I settled in to explain the Chloe Zubrisky case. Told him I wanted to help her get back to work, needed some details to discuss with Fran Philips, who was now a psychologist. Merlano shook his head, "Man, that Philips could play. I thought he'd be a big college star. It surprised me when he quit playing."

I shook my head, "Fran could really play. He just suddenly realized he had a gift with people, wanted to help them, couldn't do both, so he quit."

Breaking the memory walk, I asked if he had a file I could review. He pulled open a drawer, handed me a thick folder. "You can't take it, but you're welcome to review it here. Take as long as you need." As Merlano stood up, "The weird thing is, I've worked other cases just like this. I mean, they're exactly similar, but the creeps doing this are all different. Almost like it's a ring."

I stopped looking at Chloe's file. "What do you mean?" Frankie explained there were other brutal assaults in the Delaware County over the past eight to ten years where women got molested, but none of the guys looked anything alike. But the MO was the same.

Merlano summarized, "Every victim was attacked by a different perp. Each victim gave good descriptions, none even close." He added, "The only thing in common was the woman were all lookers, lived alone. And all the cases are still unsolved. Frustrating, huh?"

Merlano showed me to an office. I sat down to study. Chloe's file didn't give me too much I didn't already know about her. She was actually forty-two, much younger than I'd guessed. The trauma had aged her. Was divorced for five years, had lived at her home on Harper Avenue since she and her husband bought it after their marriage. But the file did give details of the crime. It was tough to read. When the police arrived, they found her bound to her bed upstairs. She had on nothing but a bra and panties. The attacker did not rape her but had urinated in her face and all over her stomach. She was gagged, but apparently awake during this whole desecration. The police said she gave a clear description of her attacker—white male, tall, thick blonde hair, piercing blue eyes. The police file said after giving this description, Chloe went into shock, didn't speak another word.

I found myself breathing fast as I read this horrible information. I took a deep breath to calm down. Shook my head. What drove people to do such horrendous things? Had always wondered if some people were just pure evil? Maybe Fran Philips could shed some light on this inhumanity. I sat thinking, wrote every detail from the crime file. What did they signify? I kept looking at the

Current Status block. It said simply "unsolved."

Right then said to myself, "Not for long." Something ate at me, infuriated me. Maybe it was meeting Chloe and seeing what a nice person she was, how this shithead had ruined her life. It really pissed me off. But what could I do about it? And then remembered Chloe told me her attacker had a nondescript face. The file said he was tall, thick blonde hair and piercing blue eyes. That wasn't exactly nondescript. I made a note to follow up with Chloe.

I thought about Merlano's comments of similar crimes, but with drastically different perpetrators. Could there really be a ring of these lunatics? I wandered out, found Frankie hanging up the phone. He looked up at me. "Makes you sick, doesn't it?"

I looked at him hard. "It makes me want to beat the piss out of the guy who did this." He nodded.

I asked about the other files with similar MO's. He repeated that the perverted acts were identical, but the witness descriptions totally different. I asked to look at those files too. He squinted, "Why do I think I should say no?"

I grinned, "Because I'm now a famous detective, and you're intimidated by my wisdom."

He chuckled, "Sit still, I'll dig 'em out. Might take a while."

And so, I went through the five other horrific case

files. The pictures were chilling. Merlano was right. Each victim was abused the same way. None were raped, just tied up and humiliated in exactly the same manner as Chloe. All were woman in their forties and attractive. All were divorced and living alone. I noted one other characteristic: all the victims were smaller and very well built, bordering voluptuous. Was that why he picked them out? I was surprised Merlano didn't notice that. There was another similarity. From my early days as a delivery boy for Solomon's pharmacy in Drexel Heights, I knew all the victims lived within a few miles of each other in and around Upper Derby. I wrote all the names and addresses, visualized where they lived in this crowded community. How were they selected? Then I wondered why I hadn't read about this in the newspapers. Shouldn't women be warned about this maniac?

I wandered back to Merlano, asked about the lack of publicity. He had a good answer. "Each victim insisted their crime be kept private." I asked if that was unusual. He shook his head, "Not at all. Even most rape victims don't want anyone to know. It's like they're embarrassed. Kinda like if they don't talk about it, it will go away. Each victim here had that thinking."

I let that sink in. "I get that. It must be horribly humiliating." I clenched my jaw, felt my cheeks flush. "It just makes me sick. Whoever the bastard is, he's going to pay."

Merlano stared at me for a few seconds. "You kinda have the same look on your face as when you were chasing Sylvan Skolnick. You didn't know who it was yet. But you were like a cat chasing a mouse. Wouldn't let go. That how this is headed?" I walked from the police station thinking Merlano was right. I felt that irresistible itch.

I went back to my apartment and organized my notes. Since the famous Sylvan Skolnick case, I acquired a flip chart that was used to list similar categories of facts. Seeing them together helped me see patterns. Sometimes things jumped out right away. Sometimes they left nagging questions. Sometimes I got nothing. Today was one of those, no breakthroughs. It troubled me that so many assaults had occurred in my home area, and apparently no one but the police were aware of it. I went to my street map of Upper Derby, noted the locations of the six cases within the past few years. They were all on the western side of the township. Some of the victims lived on the eastern side of the nearby town of Drexel Heights, where I grew up.

But if I drew a circle, none of the victims lived more than three miles apart. All this carnage happened in my neighborhood. And that made me worry about the women in my life. They weren't safe and that scared me. I sat for a long time and reviewed my chart. I looked again at my notes, hoping for insight. No answers came.

THE INCREDIBLE CASE OF BERNIE NUDLEMAN

Hoban called early next morning. Not being a great morning person, I mumbled my name, asked who was calling. Hoban said, "Am I speaking to the illustrious Bernie Nudleman?" I recognized Hoban's voice, asked what the hell he was talking about. He explained, "I have a fifty-dollar bet that you're the Bernie Nudleman who's been writing different people at Voyager over the past year or so." I didn't answer so he continued. "At first, I just chucked the letters, thinking it was another crazy claimant wanting to bust my balls. But the letters kept coming, got weirder and weirder, and pretty soon other managers got them too." He paused for a bit, waiting for me to talk.

I said, "Still got no clue what the hell you're talking about."

Hoban was quiet for a while. "Can you come in this morning? I have a few files needing investigation anyway but want to see your face when I show you these odd letters."

Since Hoban was my prime meal ticket, "If it's important to you Dave, I'll be there in about forty-five minutes. Is that fast enough?"

He mumbled "Okay." I waited for more chatter, but Hoban hung up. Was already shaved and dressed, so I wolfed down a bowl of Captain Crunch, headed outside. Hoban had been pretty chipper on the phone. I figured this was one of those funny files he found amusing but needed to chase down for some reason. In general, the insurance industry had no sense of humor when it came to paying claims. A claim was either legitimate or not. Since the real world isn't that pure, my livelihood came in checking those gray area situations. The best part of my job was seeking clarity in the shit storm called life. And that was fun.

As I drove, I wondered if the funny letter culprit was Bob Amalfitano, an editor for Houghlin Dictionary. At Hoban's request, I investigated Amalfitano over a year ago while he was on extended disability with eyesight problems. Rather than sitting idle while disabled, Amalfitano wrote bizarre letters to fellow editors. He basically found all their factual errors and persecuted them over their slipshod work. The letters were hysterical and very witty. Of course, if you were the recipient, you didn't see much humor. I remembered he asked one peer if in the next dictionary update he would include the trendy profanity like "asswipe", "shitbird" and 'mo-fo." I still laugh whenever I think about that. I liked potty mouths.

As I got to Hoban's office, I noticed he watched me carefully as I sat. Raised my eyebrows, "Why the skunk eye, Hoban? You look like Perry Mason about to question a murderer."

Hoban shook his head, "Just making sure you really aren't about to get a case to investigate yourself. I mean, when you read these letters, you'll have to admit you pop to mind. It's kind of got your sick mind written all over it."

I threw up my hands. "I'm innocent." Hoban shook

his head, disbelief oozing. He then showed me a stack of letters almost two inches thick. "These started coming around two years ago." He stared at me, "About when you left to go out on your own." The pregnant pause seemed endless.

I waved for him to continue. "They come to me mostly but Bernie sprinkles in letters to others occasionally." I still didn't get it, took the pile from Hoban, asked where I could read them. As he led me to a nearby conference room, he added, "Bernie writes to me like we know each other well. One of the weird things is he says I'm Jewish but have hidden that from everyone." Hoban started to grin. "But he didn't just do that to me. Bernie claims everyone in this office is Jewish, grew up with him, and still hangs around with him. Like we're all pals."

I gave my Catholic friend Hoban my best deadpan, "Are you Jewish?" He chuckled, told me to use the conference room as long as I needed. He said to keep the letters as long as I wanted.

I pulled the top letter, began to read:

Hoban:

Our old pal, Morty Elkman (Shlomo's cousin) has come up with something that has me really worried. It concerns the ancient prohibition on mixing meat and dairy. In five-thousand years you would think the greatest Talmudic minds in the world would have fought it all out and settled it. Right? Here's examples of historic debates we pondered in Synagogue:

1. *A hamburger and a glass of milk—no way and everyone agrees.*
2. *A juicy leg of lamb with blended mint sauce and sour cream? A double no-no.*
3. *A cup of coffee with non-dairy creamer and a hot dog (kosher) —fine, but the real strict guys say that you're probably violating the spirit of the law.*

Now Morty Elkman says all the Talmudic scholars are wrong! His verdict: Not one sip can you take in any of these examples. He says, "Big trouble if you do!"

Here is Morty's theory:

The milk came from a cow and passed through the cow's udders during the milking, and, in so doing, it is scientific fact that some of the cow's molecules MUST BE in the milk. Ergo, ingestion of milk is a violation of The Law. MILK IS PART MEAT!

I say to Morty: "Moses didn't know for nothing about molecules. To Moses, molecules are schmolecules. Moses says that milk is milk, and if you take it straight, you have nothing to worry about."

Morty says: "Okay, just 'cause Moses doesn't know from molecules doesn't make it right. No eating meat with dairy. No eating milk with nothin'! Law is law!" He throws up his hands like the discussion is over.

Now, I think Morty is way out there, but this still worries me.

So, I take it to my rabbi and he takes a typical American liberal Jewish view: "Milk is milk, drink all you want. Tell your pal Morty he's a putz." But I'm thinking back to the old days, a problem like this would be debated for a hundred years. But my guy gives it maybe two seconds of thought. But then he gets mad when I say I'm going to submit it to the big wigs back in Israel. But I tell him the molecule thing is driving me nuts. Guess what the rabbi says to me? "When they start getting Scotch out of cows, then maybe I'll worry about it." Can you believe this guy? I've switched to having Pepsi with all my meals. Just thinking about milk gives me the goose bumps.

Call me at the store… you've got the number.

Bernie

P.S. Hoban, tell your squeeze Rachel to give my Rivka her kugel recipe! We're nuts for it.

By the end of the letter, I was almost hyperventilating with laughter. I scanned a few others in the pile, found a similar theme. This character Bernie Nudleman acted as if he knew Hoban intimately, like they hung out together and were related. He accused Hoban of being a Jew masking as a Protestant. He mixed in enough true facts to make it somewhat plausible. Hoban started to keep the envelopes after the letters kept coming in. Amazingly, the letters were mailed from all over the country but mostly from Chicago. In fact, Bernie Nudleman claimed to own a shoe store in an integrated section of Chicago. He accused Hoban of moving to Philadelphia to hide his ancestry. I again thought of my investigation of Bob Amalfitano, the gadfly at Houghlin. But how would he get so much history on Hoban? And why would he want to pester him? I didn't think Hoban was really serious about the case but put the letters in my new briefcase. I headed out promising to read the rest, give him my thoughts. Hoban smirked at me.

I was studying the hilarious Bernie Nudleman letters that night when the phone rang. My sweet mom was on the line. "How's my mischievous son? We haven't seen much of you lately. What have you been up to?"

I didn't want to tell her about the maniac on my radar. "I've been busy helping the less fortunate and walking old ladies across busy streets. You know how well you taught me, mom."

She chuckled, "And I've been out helping your dad sell sandboxes in Saudi Arabia." She got back to her real reason. "Dr. Power's office called. You have a physical exam next Monday. I told his wife you don't live here and gave your new address and telephone number." I thanked mom, told her I'd call Dr. Powers tomorrow. Explained I needed a physical to renew my investigator's license.

I heard dad in the background. He obviously heard about my physical, took the phone, asked if I would continue using Dr. Power. "Probably, he's treated me since I was a kid."

My zany dad, "Good move, it's hard to find a doctor with small hands. I mean you don't want a doc with catcher's mitts for hands giving you a rectal exam, right?" Dad could paint a picture with words. I laughed aloud as he hung up.

VISITING FRAN PHILIPS

I had an early appointment with Fran to discuss what I learned from Chloe Zubrisky's file. It still felt weird thinking of Fran as a psychologist, someone who healed troubled minds. We had grown up together, had been a successful basketball backcourt since eighth grade. We shared a lot of things fighting our way through the mysteries of high school and college. At one point, we both probably qualified as "not serious." But I trusted Fran, knew he changed his life dramatically, was now a gifted therapist. But I didn't let him off the hook, still needled him relentlessly. Walking in his office, I asked his secretary, Beverly, "Does Dr. Philips still wear that silver snake ring?" Beverly looked at me funny, trying to see if the question was serious. I continued, "Fran wore a snake ring his grandmother gave him that she brought over from Ireland. It was supposed to ward off evil spirits. Kind of like St Patrick did to chase the snakes from Ireland." Beverly was still speechless. I said, "Her grandmother thought I was a bad influence on Fran and gave him the ring for protection."

By now, Fran heard me tormenting Beverly and came to save her. He stood in the entrance, "Beverly, Dylan has an incurable sense of mischief. Pay him no mind."

As I walked into Fran's office, I said to Beverly, "If Dr. Philips' grandmother calls, tell her the ring didn't work."

Beverly started to chuckle. She said, "I wish we had

more visitors like you. We don't get to laugh too much around here."

Fran went to a leather chair, pointed for me to sit in the chair facing him. I looked at him, "Is this where the crazy people sit? If so, I'm sitting elsewhere. I don't want any crazy ju-ju seeping into me. Got enough wacky genes already."

Fran grinned, "I think you're out of luck. Crazy people, as you call them, sit in all these chairs. It's what I do all day. Remember?"

I finally settled in the original chair, explained what I'd learned from Merlano about Chloe Zubrisky. I told him about the perverted acts, that there was no rape. Fran thought a bit before he rendered an opinion. "Sounds as if it's more about power and control. In psychological terms, mastery is what this sounds like. Sigmund Freud went into great detail about mastery in "Three Essays of Sexuality." I'll spare you the minute detail, but it relates to the anal stage when the child is structuring his personality as he gains muscular control over fecal matters. In some cases, this childhood stage leads to anal eroticism, and ultimately sadism and hyper aggression. This can turn into mastery over an object or person as the psychic equivalent of the sphincter muscle." Fran paused to see if I was following.

All I could say was, "Holy shit." Paused, "No pun intended."

Fran shook his head, moved on. "But there is also a possibility this is a case of dominance. It is hard to distinguish between them without in depth discussion and analysis." Fran could see I was lost. "It is hard to define the differences, but basically mastery is aimed at excitation, and dominance is more an instinct that involves an object or person." He paused again before making matters more complicated. "There is also the possibility that this is a classic case of cruelty, which is also an instinct. And if that is the case, then the individual derives great satisfaction from the act of cruelty."

I stared at Fran, "I'll admit I only understand about half what you're saying, but if you had to pick, what do you think drives this nut?"

Fran sat back, pondered a minute or so. "I'd bet it's a case of mastery. This individual displays all the symptoms."

To keep my head from exploding, I asked some simpler questions. "Why do you think he chose Chloe?"

Fran shrugged, "It could be random, or it could be she fits a certain profile that triggers this out-of-control desire. She might have been in the wrong place at the wrong time and became known to the perpetrator." I thought about that some. Remembered Merlano's other unsolved cases with similar MO's and almost identical physical traits in the victims. I explained to Fran about the other unsolved cases, the vastly different descriptions of the attackers. Fran's eyes opened wide. "That really is interesting. So many cases in this area with identical rituals and widely different descriptions." After a few seconds, "It seems unlikely there would be a ring. It sounds like the same individual. Perhaps the victims were too traumatized to give accurate details. Or maybe some coping mechanism forces them to want to forget. They want to purge the experience as if it never happened. Or maybe they concoct a story that gives them the most peace of mind. I'd have to interview them to pinpoint which."

Fran just gave me the information I wanted to hear. I nodded, "That is exactly what I think."

Fran then asked me something I hadn't thought about. "Do you want me to have a discussion with Chloe? I do have expertise in treating traumas like this."

I shook my head, uncertain. "I really don't know. It seemed like I made a connection with her." I told Fran about my offer to drive her into work to give a comfort level.

Fran smiled, "That's remarkable that you developed that level of trust so quickly. Usually, female victims are timid around men till they fully recover."

I grinned, "Maybe it's my boyish charm and a kind of magnetic chivalry I give off."

Fran laughed, "Maybe I should start treating you for delusions of grandeur." But then he got back to the point. "I think you should follow up quickly with Chloe and take her into work. It sounds like she's taking that tough first step to recovery." Fran asked me to let him know how it went afterwards. He would weigh in later on next steps.

I got up to leave but Fran raised his hand. "I thought we were also going to talk about the flashbacks you mentioned at Schultz's?"

We had spent over an hour on Chloe's case, so I told Fran we could do it another time. I'd already outworn my welcome. He had a living to make. Smiling, added, "I hate to be the one between you and the loonies."

He frowned, "Dealing with you will get me warmed up. I allocated the whole morning to you. Let's get at it, my friend." When I protested he shook his head, "I'm actually treating a few Vietnam vets with persistent stress problems, so you're helping me out in a way. I hate to admit it, but I've made almost no progress with my patients, and the army isn't too helpful in releasing information. So, my friend, you are helping me as I try to help you. Okay?"

I smiled, "How can I say no to someone who has an army of nuts at his command?"

Fran grimaced, "You might be beyond help."

That's how my sessions with Fran began. We talked years ago when I got home from Nam, but I didn't give many of the gory details. Was frankly a little embarrassed about not dealing with it myself. But that was clearly a bad plan, the flashbacks continued. Now, I decided not to hold back, told the story of the traitorous team of MP's, and how a few of us survived murder attempts. How I went months looking over my shoulder expecting to get fragged. I explained our Green Beret buddy Nut was assigned to the case in Nam, caught the traitors, but the MP Percy Price was never convicted as part of the conspiracy. I felt certain he was one of the ringleaders but was so crazy that the alleged mastermind, Colonel Mullen, was afraid to rat him out. Mullen worried Price would escape from prison and kill his family. Fran never spoke during my narration but listened attentively.

When I told him that Percy had in fact escaped, he grimaced, "Oh no."

I nodded, "It's been over a year since the escape, not a trace of Percy. Nut's been hunting him but has no leads."

Fran looked at me intently, "How are you dealing with that?"

I told him the truth. "I try to put it out of my mind. Most of the time, I'm successful. But I keep up my training at Jimmer's judo classes, try be prepared if Percy suddenly shows up." He asked me what Nut's opinion was on Percy. "Nut thinks he went to Mexico or maybe the Caribbean. Percy's mother was from Jamaica. He could blend in there pretty easy."

Fran seemed to weigh that carefully before asking, "What do you think?"

I didn't hesitate, "I think he'll eventually come after me. He's flat out insane, blames me for getting sent to jail. Plus, I nearly killed him, and he won't be able to let that go. It'll tear him up. One day he'll show up, be standing in front of me."

Then Fran summed up what I already knew, "And that's why you still have flashbacks. Until you can reconcile the threat with Percy, it will be hard for you to have peace."

I nodded at my long-time friend, "That's why I have

to be ready." Fran looked concerned, stayed quiet. I could almost see his mind at work. How to fix the unfixable?

It surprised me, but I did feel better. Told Fran it helped to talk about it, that I wanted to continue meeting once in a while. And then asked about the other Vietnam vet problems he mentioned. He pressed his lips tight. "Combat Stress Reaction is the term the military uses to describe acute behavioral problems as a result of the trauma of war. Sometimes you'll hear "combat fatigue" or "shellshock" as a euphemism for what is post-traumatic stress disorder. You didn't start hearing about it in clinical terms until after World War 1. That horrific war was when trench warfare was common. At least ten percent of your fellow soldiers got killed and over fifty percent wounded, usually right before your eyes. And because the battles were prolonged, the bodies often stayed beside them for days. Can you imagine that?" I exhaled. The thought of that was overwhelming. Unable to fathom that horror, I waved Fran to continue. "I don't think the military is intentionally hiding anything, I think they believe that shellshock is just the normal after effect of war. It simply can't be avoided. War is truly hell, always has been."

I told Fran I had to get going, thanked him for his help. Left thinking that I didn't have it so bad as World War I vets. I just had one sadistic devil to deal with. My whole life was ahead of me. That sick jackass Percy wasn't going to rule me. Maybe Nut was right, that Percy wanted to disappear. I made a note to call my Green Beret friend to see how he was doing. Nut chased lunatics like Percy for a living. How did he deal with it? I bet Nut had a long list of criminals who wanted to kill him. The fact he was a world-class wrestler and freakish physical specimen probably gave him comfort. I mean, who the hell would mess with Nut? As I got into my hideous car, I thought about calling Jimmer to ramp-up my judo training. If Percy ever showed, I'd be ready to kick his ass.

TORMENTING HOBAN

After I left Fran's office, I headed downtown to Voyager Insurance. Whenever I got too serious, I played practical jokes to get my mojo back. Reading the Bernie Nudleman letters inspired me. Hoban was always a fun target, so I thought about using a bizarre medical letter I saw in one of my files. I knew with creative photocopying, I could make a bogus claim form look valid. All I needed was some help from one of Voyager's human resources specialists. I thought of Doris Flood, she always liked me, found me funny. I stopped the car, called Doris, and explained my joke. Doris listened quietly, started to chuckle when I hit the punch line. I told her that no one beside Hoban and us would be involved, so it wouldn't violate his rights or anything. Doris made me promise that our circle would be tight. After I swore to her, she agreed to help. I told her I was on my way.

Doris was waiting for me in the HR department. She handed me a couple forms, led me to her conference room for privacy. I gathered the required information and thought of a few more touches to fine-tune my masterpiece. The gist of the prank was filing a bogus medical claim on Dave Hoban. At Voyager, if you had a medical bill, you had to give it to HR, along with the appropriate explanations. To keep people's health problems private, they had a special unit to process the bills. The processors were told not to talk about their fellow employees' personal matters, or they could get fired. Naturally, they yapped to their friends, you often heard about weird illnesses or treatments. Despite threats, people liked to gossip, especially if the tidbit was juicy, and about someone they disliked.

I completed the appropriate forms, faked the required information. I used the original bizarre surgical notes I'd pirated, but whited-out the real name, added dicey touches, and then typed in Dave Hoban's name as the claimant. I photocopied an old document with his signature to hide the manipulation. I laughed out loud as I worked. To make the claim look real, I needed Doris's name on the bottom to make it official. For any employee claim, you had to have HR approval before your medical bills could be reimbursed. The last step was for Doris to call Hoban to ask if the information on the form was accurate, since it seemed so unusual. While I watched, she dialed Hoban and asked him to drop by to verify the claim form she was about to sign for reimbursement. When Hoban said he had no idea what she was talking about, she held her hand over the phone as she gathered herself and delivered the speech flawlessly.

She hung up, looked at me, "He's on his way up." I hid in her conference room to listen.

Doris composed herself, greeted Hoban as he sat down. She handed him the forms, told him she wanted to make certain he wanted this personal information to go into the claim unit, or if he wanted more privacy. I almost swallowed my tongue. Doris was a born actress. I peeked out, watched Hoban read the following:

Dr. Romig- Surgeon

Diagnosis: External Hemorrhoids (Huge)

Patient: David Hoban

Procedure:

> *The patient has enormous hemorrhoids located at three, seven, nine and eleven o'clock on his swollen rectum. Needless to say, even sitting is uncomfortable. Fecal elimination is like entering Dante's Inferno. Removal was mandatory to return patient to normal living. Under spinal anesthesia, with the patient in the prone (jack-knife) position, the anal canal was dilated. It took ten fingers to create sufficient room! (In my time as a surgeon, this is Olympic record material.) Each hemorrhoid was identified (using clock positions) and frozen for a total duration of two and a half minutes. The patient was then returned to rest-and-recovery in good condition. (If you can call a rectum the size of a Wilson basketball good condition.)*

> *# Medical lab analysis available upon request.*

Signed,

Victor Romig, MD.

At first Hoban started to protest, insisted this wasn't his form. But when Doris started to laugh, he got quiet for a few seconds before saying, "I'm going to kill that God damned Dylan!"

After an appropriate delay, I came into the office, looked hurt, "Why did you think I had anything to do with this. It was all Doris's idea. I just happened to be visiting her."

Hoban made us give him the forms, which he tore to shreds before he went back to work. I had forgotten all about Percy as I went back to my car.

VISITING CHLOE

I figured I'd better call Chloe quickly. Strike while the iron was hot. She answered on the first ring, sounded animated as I asked when she wanted a ride to work.

To my surprise, "How about tomorrow?" I agreed, told her I would call Container to say she was dropping by. Wanting her to be comfortable, I asked when she wanted to leave. "How about nine am, traffic should be lighter by then. Will you stay with me, or go back to your work and pick me up later?" I wanted to make this painless, so I asked what she preferred. She was quiet a few seconds. "Why don't we see how it goes?"

That was what I hoped. "I'm at your disposal, things are slow for me, so I'll let you decide." Knowing the harder part was returning to her empty house afterwards, I added, "Plus, I'll check your house thoroughly when I drive you home." She didn't say anything, but I heard her exhale, relieved.

Next morning, I got to Chloe's five minutes early. I parked out front, honked twice as we agreed, walked to her house. I could sense her on the other side of the locked door. This was a big step for her. Seconds later, the series of locks opened, and a smiling Chloe Zubrisky stood before me. She had a look of triumph.

She said simply, "It feels so good to do something normal." We started our journey to Container Corporation, in the sleepy mill town of Manayunk, just outside Philadelphia on the Schuylkill River. I stayed quiet while we drove, waited for her to talk. After a few minutes I heard her exhale, "It will be so nice to see the old gang. Since my divorce, the girls at work were my social life. We used to go to the movies, see plays sometimes, go shopping. All those simple things I took for granted."

Driving was tricky in Manayunk because the surrounding roads were so hilly as they descended to the Container plant on the river.

I kept my eyes on the road but finally said, "Maybe you can get more back to normal if you can get comfortable leaving the house."

She was silent for a few seconds. "I hope you're right."

Changing topics to something I planned to suggest, "Have you thought about getting a roommate? You have that big house with four bedrooms. Any chance one of your friends from work would move in with you? That way you could commute together, not worry about being alone. None of my business, just a thought."

I glanced over. She had a smile on her face. "You really are a helpful-Harry aren't you Dylan?"

I laughed, "My mother always says I stick my nose where it doesn't belong."

Chloe grinned, "This time, I think you have a great idea."

Turned out Chloe was a big celebrity at work. After

an hour or so, it became clear she didn't need me following her around. We made plans to pick her up after lunch. I killed time by going home and reviewing the police file information from Merlano. Remembered I needed to ask about her "nondescript" attacker comment. Had rehearsed being gentle with my questioning. I pulled into the Container entrance at two pm. Chloe had a spring in her step as she came outside. I let her yap about her great day.

She surprised me with, "Guess what? Elaine McNulty is going to move in with me. She never married and still lives with her parents, not far from me. Elaine and I were always close, very compatible. I mentioned it to her over lunch and she jumped at it. She can move in next week. You can tell your mother your nosiness finally paid off." She noticed the note I had on my dashboard to call for my doctor appointment. "Do you go to Dr. Powers?"

I nodded, "Since I was a little tyke. He's a nice guy. My dad likes him because, as he says, 'he has hands like a munchkin'." I left out the rectal exam part.

Chloe chuckled. "Now I know where you get your sense of humor."

While she was in such a good mood, I talked vaguely about my work. That I was the type who noticed little things that nobody else cared about. I used that as a preamble to what I planned next. I asked if I could ask one question about her case. She didn't agree right away, sat thinking. Reached a conclusion. "The doctor says it's best to discuss it. Go ahead." I told her the discrepancy between her statement to me and the one to the police.

I was watching the road, so I couldn't see her expression but could hear her voice change. "He was tall and blonde with blue eyes but other than that was non-descript. There was nothing remarkable about him. I don't think they'll ever catch him." I didn't push it. Asked about her plans for work. Her voice got animated again. "I'll be going back when Elaine moves in." We pulled up to her house and parked. After walking into every room and making sure everything was secure, Chloe took my hand, looked me in the eyes, "Thanks for the push. I think everything will be okay." I drove away happy but still troubled by her answer about the attacker.

PERCY PRICE

Percy Price sat in his dilapidated room thinking. Detroit was getting on his nerves but was a safe place to disappear, just another black face. He thought about his violent past and what brought him to this hellhole. He was convicted in military court for nearly killing another MP. His history of violence was irrefutable, both as a grunt and then as an MP. The charges against him had been much worse, but he never admitted to the murder of a Vietnamese papa-sahn and attempted rape of his wife. Because there were no American witnesses to the more heinous crimes, he was given a relatively light sentence of fifteen years, with possibility to parole after ten of trouble free incarceration. Survival was something Percy had done since birth, the bastard child of a Jamaican mother and black GI who knocked her up while on temporary duty. Percy's father was from Chicago, deserted his unplanned family when transferred back to the states. Desperate, Percy and his mother trailed dad to Chicago, but he was nowhere to be found. Dad's family wanted nothing to do with these strangers from Jamaica.

Percy's mother was resourceful. She found a thriving community of Jamaicans had settled in nearby Evanston. She quickly found work as a domestic in a mansion near Northwestern University, and became their cook when her exotic cuisine captivated the wealthy couple. She and Percy shared an apartment with another Jamaican family but moved out after a year when her income allowed. Percy was a bright kid, but because of his Jamaican accent got picked on at school, was beaten up almost every day. The more he got beaten up, the worse he did in school. His early promise as a student plummeted. But he got better at defending himself. He learned to hit first and ask questions afterwards. And then he started boxing at the local YMCA, became a Golden Gloves sensation by age twelve. But his rage overcame him. He punched an opponent senseless during a match, got thrown off the boxing team. Percy fell in with a nearby gang, learned different fighting skills, and dropped out of school. By age seventeen, he got into the army rather than being sent to jail. Vietnam was raging; the recruiters weren't picky.

Before being sent to Nam, Percy finished his GED, got excellent grades. But his violent nature was well suited for Vietnam. He was a gifted, remorseless fighter and bright enough to make the Green Berets. At first Percy thrived in Vietnam. His ferocity was expended on the VC, or any other enemy he confronted. He got promoted to sergeant after a series of successful missions. But he had trouble with authority, and soon ran into a Green Beret lieutenant who learned Percy never took prisoners and didn't distinguish between VC or civilian's casualties. When confronting Percy, the Lt. found himself lying on the ground with Percy pummeling him. Percy avoided court martial but was sent to the infantry as punishment. Again, his brutality was an early asset in the battlefield. But when out of the bush, if subjected to what he thought was something stupid, he'd snap. After beating another grunt near death, Percy was assigned to the MP's in Quang Tri. As it turned out, many of the MP's in Quang Tri were soldiers considered "too violent for the infantry."

Keeping peace on Quang Tri base was rough. Soldiers coming out of the bush were so worn out and shell shocked, they caused relentless trouble blowing off steam. Thus, the military thinking was you needed really tough guys to be MP's. Percy was the prototype they wanted in the MP's at that time. Percy Price had found a home. He met Colonel Mullen and Sgt. Burton during his second tour. Mullen was the Provost Marshall of Quang Tri, had almost limitless power. Burton was a financial wizard, knew how to hide money. Eventually they formed a conspiracy to make a fortune from dealing in drugs and prostitution.

And that was when Percy encountered Dylan Frazier. None of the conspirators thought the inexperienced MP would become their undoing. He blamed Frazier for getting sentenced to Leavenworth. Now that he was free, he would pay Frazier back. It was almost time to get moving.

PHYSICAL

I finally called Dr. Powers to confirm my appointment. Thought randomly while the phone rang: Dr. Victor Powers. Sounds like a made–up name for a tough, Hollywood star. His wife answered on the forth ring, breaking my musing. She was very business-like, gave me the time, and what would be covered during the visit. "It will entail blood work, urinalysis and full check-up. You haven't had been in for years, so it should take about an hour," was her prediction.

I remembered that Mrs. Powers was the office manager and very efficient. Trying to lighten her up, "What if I'm an Olympic athletic specimen? How long will I take then?"

She paused slightly. "I forgot you were comical." She opined, "Your parents are so pleasant, but they never make jokes."

I was about to mention dad but decided to let it pass. My dad preferred to remain a closet comedian. I heard a small chuckle when I said, "My brother says I was adopted from a Korean family." Promised to be on time, hung up.

THE AMAZING GATOR

Bill Light was one of my favorite people, truly unique and off beat. He got his nickname years ago "because he had a few extra layers of teeth," according to Jimmer, the bigger than life personality who ran things at the basketball courts where we grew up. Gator was a few years older, went to Vietnam before me, attended law school after returning safely. Despite a zany personality, he overcame the quirks and was now a successful lawyer, mostly because he was extremely bright, with insatiable curiosity. He was unorthodox and unpredictable, but that was his strength when defending or prosecuting a case. Opponents never knew what he would do next. Naturally, our personalities meshed perfectly. I loved the guy, had worked with him to help solve the Sylvan Skolnick case, and now wanted his opinion on my new strategy for Chloe Zubrisky and the other victims. It occurred to me I might be invading some privacy laws.

He picked up on the first ring. Snorted a laugh when I said, "Too cheap to hire a secretary or did your quano-breath scare her off?"

Gator was never at a loss for words. "My wife says I should avoid you, that you're a bad influence on me. Kind of like a nasty zit." No point in arguing that. Gator's wife was a very sensible woman. I confirmed agreement with her verdict; we were bad influences on each other but knew neither of us cared. In fact, it made us closer, kindred spirits. Got to the point of the call, told Gator about Chloe's case, that there were a few other cases I wanted to poke around in. He laughed that I didn't want to get tossed in the slammer for invasion of privacy. He asked a few questions I couldn't answer. We agreed it would be best to talk face to face. I suggested Schultz's Tavern for a happy hour meeting. He agreed enthusiastically.

Looked at my watch, almost four o'clock. "How about now?"

Before he slammed the phone down, he bellowed, "Now you're talking."

Duke was pouring some guy a Bud, when I wandered in and sat beside the visitor. I knew this customer wasn't a regular since Duke poured Ortlieb beer for friends. Duke wandered over, made an eye gesture toward the new visitor. "Asshole asked if we had any Yuengling on tap. I says to him, "Ya think this is some kind a German beer hall or somethin'? We got Bud and we got Schmidts. Fuckin' hillbillies from Reading drink Yuengling." I chuckled, felt sorry for the poor sap. New people didn't often fare well at Schultz's. Not what you'd call an inclusive crowd. Just then, Gator came storming in, disheveled as always. Gator was always out of breath. Like he'd just run a marathon. His enthusiasm was one of his greatest quirks.

I waved, "Hey shithead, over here. Don't stand by the door. You'll scare off the customers. They'll thinks someone's dying of Tourette syndrome, the way your shaking and jumping around."

Gator sprints over, hops down hard in the next stool. "Glad you gave me an excuse to get out of the office. I've got a real tedious case going on. Some ass-wipe wants to sue EJ Corvette for putting too much salt on the sidewalk last winter. He says the salt killed his expensive shoes, got eaten up by the corrosiveness. Says that his toes are all red and itchy. Nothing can heal them. Can you believe this shit? It's like I'm making it up." I could believe it. If I had a weird case, Gator would be the man to call. His whole life was an adventure.

Before I could react to Gator's story, a big lug started taunting the new guy sitting beside me. "Whataya mean ya never heard a Herbie McGee? He's better than any a them guards in the Big Five. The new guy looked scared, said he never heard of Herbie, that he didn't mean any harm. But the lug grabs his glass of Bud, throws it in the poor guy's face. And half the suds fly all over me. I jumped off my stool, stood beside the drenched newcomer.

I pointed at the big guy, "Lighten up pal. You heard the guy, he meant no disrespect; not everybody follows Textile hoops like you."

The big lump wasn't happy. "Stay outta this, dickhead. If I wanted the peanut gallery opinion, I'd a asked fer it." Then he grabbed the newcomer's shirt, was about to punch him when I chopped down hard on his exposed forearm. Electric shocks sent blinding pain to his muddled brain. As trained, I hit a nerve center. My extensive judo training helped me react instinctively. Just as I practiced endlessly, breathed deeply, steadied myself for the next step. The knucklehead wasn't done. He righted himself and bull rushed me. I pivoted, leaned away from him and hammered his exposed stomach with my left knee. The bruiser fell to the ground, puked all over Duke's wood floor.

Gator looked at me, deadpanned, "Can't I ever come in here without you beating the shit out of someone?"

By that time, Duke came to investigate, leaned over to see the big hulk on the floor, covered in vomit. Not knowing why, I felt kind of embarrassed. The last time I got into a fight here, I enjoyed it. I had never been one to pick fights, but since returning from Nam, I'd had my share of scuffles. The fights were nothing I planned, just spontaneous reactions. I'd kept up with my judo training because my work took me to dicey areas. When Percy escaped, I doubled the lessons. Despite a rough start in judo, I was actually a good fighter now. Even the smaller warriors in Jimmer's dojo had a struggle striking me. Jimmer was trying to get me to enter competitions, but I wasn't interested. Just wanted to defend myself.

All that ran through my noggin as Duke looked at me. "You obviously been keepin' up with that jujitsu shit, huh? That crazy fucker Jimmer trained you good." Then he got practical. "Can you and Gator drag that slug outside? I'll get a mop and clean that shit up."

That's what we did. Gator and I dragged the guy through the door, returned to resume our conversation. When I gave him all the facts, he looked serious. "You can't approach these women directly. You'll get Merlano in a world of shit for letting you see their files. You need their consent."

He was right. We talked about getting Merlano to approach them, letting me come along. A better idea hit me. "Maybe I tell Merlano I'll try to get Chloe to talk to them after he gets their okay. That meeting as a group could help trigger some clues." Something else hit me, "Maybe that will help them heal faster. It can't be any good keeping that bottled up. It's got to help talking it over with someone who went through the same thing."

Gator stared at me a while, nodded his head. "You are a complicated guy. You beat the piss out of that fat bastard and now all you're worrying about is helping these ladies." He smirked, "Interesting." He knew me well. I was drawn into hopeless causes. Was that way since childhood. It got me into trouble sometime.

The poor schlep I pounded wasn't there when we left an hour later. Gator said he probably wouldn't even remember it. I shrugged, "Only if he normally wakes up on the sidewalk smelling like puke."

Gator laughed, "Probably not a stretch with that dude. He was a sorry sack of shit." I got into my car, turned on WIBG, listened to Hy Lit spin tunes. Gene Pitney started to sing, "The Town Without Pity." It made me wonder if that's what these poor women thought about living in Upper Derby. Did they feel betrayed by their town? I thought how afraid they must be every night. They had to be reliving this nightmare every time it got dark.

I could feel myself getting worked up again, just like the Sylvan Skolnick case that put my career in high gear. Something wasn't adding up, and I knew it would be impossible for me to stop till I resolved it. When I couldn't stop thinking about something, but was getting nowhere, I grabbed the New York Times Crossword puzzle to distract myself. There was nothing like trying to remember if a gyrfalcon is larger than a peregrine falcon to settle your mind. Last time that happened, I called my smart dad.

Without much thought, he said, "The gyrfalcon rules. He's an apex predator. That's one bird not to mess with." That thought got me laughing. Got ready to hit the sack. I went to bed wondering if it was a good sign I regretted getting in that fight. Made a note to mention that to Fran Philips.

But another flashback ruined my sleep that night. We were on the edge of Khe Sahn watching a convoy of ARVN trucks, teeming with tiny soldiers, pouring into Laos at the beginning of another Tet Offensive. My best MP buddy McCarthy turned to me when the last truck disappeared. "Do you think they know they're about to get slaughtered again?" My usually chipper friend was in a dour mood. The last Tet Offensive from Khe Sahn in '68 had been a total disaster; thousands had died.

I knew Mac was looking for reassurance. "Think happy thoughts, Mac. Maybe the second time is the charm." Just as I turned for his reaction, a devastating blast tore the jungle apart… I jumped out of my bed in peaceful Upper Derby, realizing I had a long way to go before I healed.

VINCENTE

The office was very quiet. Rosa was doing the accounting work for the monthly billings. Oddly, Vincente was not haunted anymore by his tormented childhood. He liked to recall his early trials as a way to increase motivation. He sat back in the comfortable chair, drifted into the past. The worst treatment started as a freshman in high school. Because of brilliant schoolwork, Vincente won a scholarship to St John's Prep School in Philadelphia. Irma was happy because Vincente would be away more than if attending nearby Upper Derby High. The only difficulty was riding the trolley and subway every day. His scholarship included transportation, so the money wasn't the issue. The problem was the perils of riding the El into the city each day and getting hassled by the tough inner-city kids. Vincente's odd appearance made him an irresistible target, a defenseless suburban kid.

Most times, the gang of kids from the city schools targeted his anvil-shaped head, smacked it pretending to be blacksmiths. Sometimes, the punks would throw his books to the floor, taunt Vincente while he scrambled to collect them, barely missing his stop. But one spring day heading home, a more brutal crew pulled Vincente off the El, threw him to the ground, formed a circle. The leader of the thugs whipped out his dick, pissed all over him. The rest of the crew relieved themselves as Vincente struggled helplessly. Laughing, the sadistic boys ran off, hopped the next train, leaving their victim drenched on the platform. Vincente tried to hide the mess, but Irma caught him putting sopping clothes in the hamper. She looked at her son. "You pathetic little boy. Fourteen years-old and you still pee your pants. Such a sissy."

It got worse. This same gang started looking for him each day. Vincente successfully dodged them most times standing by the conductor. One day he wasn't so lucky. When the conductor went to the bathroom, the thugs swarmed him. They dragged him off the next stop, threw him down the steps into a dark alleyway full of trashcans overflowing old food. They stripped his clothes off, four kids held his arms and legs, while the other punks smashed rotten garbage all over his chest and face. They threw his clothes and schoolbag over a tall cyclone fence with barbed wire on top. Laughing, the hoodlums took off. The only way Vincente could retrieve his things was to exit the alley, walk naked down the busy street until the opening where his clothes lay. From that day on, Vincente stayed late at school, road home with the older commuters leaving work. Irma never asked about his coming home late, never noticed the changes in her bedraggled son.

DYLAN VISITS

After thinking over Fran Philips' suggestion, I agreed it was good for him to meet with Chloe. Fran had a way about him, a calm. Since Chloe hadn't returned to work full-time, I called and told her about Fran. To persuade her, I mentioned he was helping me overcome flashback problems from Vietnam. I told her he was a friend since childhood, that after one session I had already noticed a difference. The personal story helped seal the deal. Asked if I could take her to Fran tomorrow morning. Bright and early next day, I went to her door, waited patiently as the series of locks were opened. She was completely groomed. Her eyes not so red, looked much younger. I got a rare smile, "This feels so normal. To be getting up, rushing to get dressed and eating breakfast. I can't believe I miss the routine so much."

I threw my hands out, "As Chief Halftown says, the early bird gets the cheesesteaks." Chloe frowned.

On the ride, I gave more background on Fran, told of his stellar basketball career, but that an epiphany led him into psychology. Said he had a gift, promised he would be helpful. She nodded, didn't say much. I briefed Fran on a few discrepancies in her story, asked him to probe further. It occurred to me I didn't know much about her life. I used the ride there to dig some. Learned she was Catholic but hadn't practiced since her divorce. I asked about her husband. "I dated a lot but never found the right guy. Had reconciled I'd be single but then Sam came along. We met at work. He was a labor leader. Swept me off my feet. Everything went well until we found out I couldn't have children. I offered to adopt but he 'didn't want someone's cast-off.' He didn't believe the doctors opinion about my fertility, said it was doctor mumbo jumbo. Things were never the same after that. He wanted me to quit work and concentrate on getting pregnant. From there, everything fell apart quickly."

We walked up the stairs to Fran's office, entered his wood-paneled office. Beverly gave me a big greeting. "Dylan, I checked with Dr. Philip's grandmother. She claimed that she also got a snake ring for you, but you threw it away because it scared the girls." Beverly chuckled at her own joke.

Chloe looked at me quizzically. I opened my hands, "It's a long story about St Patrick, and it doesn't end up making me look too good. We'll drop it."

Beverly looked at Chloe. "In this profession, we don't get too many jovial visitors, so Dylan always gets us wound up."

Chloe smiled, "I haven't known him too long, but I'm getting the picture he's a character, full of funny stories of his past."

I jumped in, "Wait till I tell you about Bernie Nudleman, he's hall of fame funny." Both ladies looked quizzical. Before I could elaborate, Fran came out of his office.

He looked at Chloe, "I see Dylan has already tried to

corrupt you. Let's see if I can undo some of the harm. Come on in."

That's how Chloe started her treatment. She was quiet on the ride home, but a good quiet. She seemed at peace. I knew it went well when we arrived home and she declared, "This is the best I've felt in months." As I started to walk her up, she waved me off. "I can do this by myself. It's time I took back control of my life." I watched her walk confidently to the door, quickly maneuvered the locks. When done, she turned, waved goodbye like a normal person. When I got home, there was a message to call Fran. Got him on the first ring.

"Chloe is an extraordinary woman. I think your instincts were right on the mark. She can get this trauma behind her with work, which she wants to do." He paused a second, "But she's still repressing the actual event. Just as you said, she completely changed her demeanor when recalling that night. She recited the description of the attacker like reading a script. Very telling. I'll have to break through that before we get full progress." He was silent again. "But we can fix her."

HOBAN

I got a call from Hoban around eight am. "Bernie
Nudleman struck again. If you get a chance, drop by and
I'll show you the latest letter. I have a few other files
needing your touch anyway." He started laughing, "This
one is priceless." Agreed to come over later that morning.
I was starved, drove to McCormick's Deli to get a pork roll
and egg sandwich. The McCormick brothers were a few
years younger. I coached them in CYO basketball, and
they treated their old coach like royalty. The shop was
hopping, hungry people wanting a travel sandwich before
getting the bus into Philly. Deli and hoagie shops always
attract colorful local characters in Philly. McCormick's was
no exception. One of my childhood boogiemen, Wick
Slick-the-lunatic, stood outside the front door, bouncing
from foot to foot. Wick was a local handyman who lived
in a garage on Mason Avenue, near St Tim's Church.
Neighborhood gossip was, in exchange for living there, he
did chores for the owner. Wick soon expanded his services
to almost everyone on Mason Avenue.

That would have been fine except Wick hated kids.
Since I walked down Mason Avenue everyday going to St
Tim's, we had a few run-ins. I named him Wick Slick-the-
lunatic after he chased me with a big rake. In fairness to
Wick, I did mess up his leaf pile a little. But a grown adult
chasing a little kid with a rake is a little much, right? His
nickname stuck as he chased any kid not to his liking.
Wary kids soon avoided Mason Avenue at all cost. All that
ran through my mind as I approached McCormick's. I saw

him eyeing me as I got near, could almost see him puzzling to identify me. Taking the offensive, "Hey, Wick, how's things? Business good? We had a humongous leaf season last October. You had to be in fat-city, right?"

He squinted harder, couldn't place me but knew something was off. He mumbled, "What's it to you?"

I shrugged. "I'm a tree lover, am crazy about leaf season. Still go to the Tyler Arboretum all the time. No big deal, I'm just checking is all."

I got through the door uninjured from a sneak rake attack, shook my head at such immaturity. Wondered why I was so juvenile. Nothing came in response, decided wordlessly to blame my dad. I scanned the deli, smelled the grilled meats. Neither of the McCormick brothers was in so I waited in line. When it got my turn, "Scrambled eggs and crapple on rye."

The bored kid looked at me, "You mean scrapple, right?"

I feigned ignorance. "I thought it was called crapple. Kind of looks like a squashed dog turd, right? Have I gotten it wrong all these years?"

The kid pulls out the wrapper, shows me, "SCRAPPLE."

I nodded, "I'll be damned." The kid throws a big slice on the grill, cracks a couple eggs, and fusses with them till they were just right. He tosses a couple pieces of rye bread on top, lets them warm and moisten. It was a heavenly. I grabbed a big coffee, yelled to the kid, "Thanks for the Scrapple lesson." Wick was still outside as I walked to my car. I said to him, "Did you know it's not called crapple?" He grimaced as I got in my car.

I could amuse myself, was still chuckling on the drive into center city. While dodging traffic, I thought about Chloe's situation. She was a really nice lady who had her life ruined. Would she ever recover if she didn't confront her fear? Was I just butting in where I didn't belong? Chloe seemed to want my help, was starting to snap back. But the bigger problem was this sicko had attacked other women in my area and wasn't leaving any clues. Plus, the cops didn't seem to be actively hunting him. Merlano was right. This case had my juices flowing. Not knowing why, I believed I could solve it. Just had a gut feeling, some odd premonition. Thought I had a shot. And really had nothing too interesting going on now, would work this in my downtime. Deep down, knew I was deluding myself: this hunt would dominate me. I continued driving. The parkway was around the corner. Began looking for the incredibly elusive Philadelphia parking spot. Today I was lucky, a taxi pulled from the curb as I slid in.

Hoban was busy on the phone, waved me in. He pushed a letter to me, motioned me into the conference room. After a few sentences, I was laughing out loud. Worried I'd bother Hoban; I got up and shut the door. Sat down again, was belly laughing harder in seconds. Here is what the letter said:

Hoban:

Forget about being a big executive for that insurance company. Forget about being a top-level shoe salesman at my store. Bernie has come up with a deal for you that you simply won't believe!!! Let me say this first—I'm your agent for forty-five percent of gross; second, I guarantee stardom for you (your picture in People Magazine; interviews in Rolling Stone; substitute host on the Carson Show. I can hear Ed now… 'And heeeeeere's Hoban!! Your clever repartee with Letterman, Rickles, blah, blah…)

Look Hoban, everyone knows you and I are tight. It's common knowledge. So, out of the blue, I get a call from this big shot from MTV. He wants to know if I have the authority to act on your behalf. I say sure, what's the deal? This big shot (his name is Hal Shapiro, incidentally) says that this chick singer, Charo, wants to do a video with you. She turned down the Big Three (Jagger, Jackson and McCartney) and insists on Hoban. Charo says you "gots the fire." I figure it must be also your classic profile and smokin' wardrobe. Who, besides you, wears capes anymore?

Hal Shapiro says the video will feature her new song, "Nigerian Lover." I told Hal, "Hoban ain't a schwartzie, he's a nice Jewish boy." Hal said, "So what, did you see what we did for Dustin Hoffman in 'Little Big Man'?" The make-up guys will have him looking like Harry Bellafonte when they get done. Besides Hoban has naturally kinky hair." So, I nod my head. Hoban, he's got a point, now you see why the guys a successful producer. He's got vision.

We haven't decided yet on who will do the back-up music. A lot of possibilities. If you have input, call me at the store (you've got the number.) So far, this is what they got:

1. *Charo likes a nice Latin beat- bongos, cowbells, maracas, the whole schmear. Okay, I'll buy it. It's her style. So, I ask, "How about getting Desi Arnaz out of retirement and get his old Cuban band together? That gets us to the whole crowd who grew up with "I Love Lucy." Hal's thinking it over. What's to think about already?*

2. *How about this for a background scene. A bathroom- basic decorations circa late 1940's. A schwartzie lad, maybe nine to ten years old, is looking at the ladies' foundation garments section of the Sears catalogue—his eyes are bugging out- they look like fried eggs.*

3. *In the foreground, Charo is really belting it out—a percussionist—maybe Carlos Santana's brother—is going crazy on the cowbells. The camera, on the eyes of the little tyke, zooms in and out, in and out, on the sexy corset. FADE TO NEXT SCENE.*

4. *Switch to the water fountain in front of Lincoln Center. You're decked out in a white Bill Blass original. I mean WHITE, whiter than white!!! The contrast to your darkly made-up skin is stunning. You command the camera. After all, you are the Nigerian Lover so the contrast to your skin is breathtaking.*

5. *At last, Charo appears. For the first time, Charo is not wearing a ponytail or her hair pulled back tight. Instead, she has her hair buzzed out in a giant Afro, ala Elsa Lancaster in Bride of Frankenstein. (We grab the sci-fi crowd; get it.)*

6. *Next comes a split screen shot. The bongo man is playing like he just had a heroin shot in his femoral artery. Then bang—out pops Charo again doing that cuchi cuchi wiggle she is noted for. In the background, they flash to Xavier Cugat, his tongue is dangling like a slobbering hound dog…*

That's all we got so far. Wild, huh? Anyway, if you run into Dylan Frazier, tell him mazeltov for me. The guy is a legend—one day he's investigating transvestites, next day he bags a serial killer. Prior to that he was a gas station attendant who thought his world was ending when self-service became the rage. From shmuck to hero. Pow! Anyway, that's it for now. Call me at the store. You've got the number.

Bernie (the Video Mogul)

By that time, I'd almost turned blue laughing. Turned, saw Hoban entering the room grinning at me. "What are you so happy about? Didn't you notice Bernie now has you on his radar?

I grinned, "That's what I like the best. This guy is hysterical. Now, I'll be really motivated to find out who he is. I mean, I'd like to hang around with him. Can you imagine the time it took to write this? Plus, he's got to be doing research work on me to find out that stuff. I really did work at a gas station. How would this guy know that?" I thought for a minute. "I did tell *you* that was one of my worst jobs. Who did you tell? If we can figure that, we may have a clue."

Hoban stared at me. "I'll bet I repeated that to ten people. Maybe more. It comes up when I tell the story of you hiding the guy's car around the corner when he put the pump on automatic and went to take a leak. How the guy was freaking out when he came out, and you just stood there scrubbing the other customer's window, acting like nothing happened."

Hoban had a point. I'll bet I told fifty people that story. In my defense, the guy threw garbage on the ground every time he filled up. Half eaten sandwiches, French fries, soda cans all over the place. The guy was a slob. Looked at Hoban, "I see what you mean. But Bernie must be someone who either works here or has a friend who works here. Plus, it has to be someone with a really weird sense of humor. Bernie seems to know a ton about the Jewish culture. Is he Jewish?" I thought for a while. "Most of the letters are mailed from Chicago. How does he do that? Is he in Chicago all the time, or does he send the letters to be postmarked from there. This is such an elaborate joke. Why does he go to all the trouble? And what does he get out of it? When I do practical jokes, I want to witness it, or have someone who tells me the details. Otherwise, what's the fun in it for him?"

Hoban stared at me. "Now you know why I thought it was you. You're the only one I've ever met who has that devious a mind." I shook my head, taking his comments as a compliment. I left Hoban with the legitimate cases to investigate, but the Nudleman letters tickled my curiosity. It was like solving an obtuse puzzle in the Times. Last week it took three days to realize "a Down Under nether world denizen" was a Tasmanian devil.

VISITING DR. POWERS

Like most people, I hated visiting the doctor. After Nam, hated the visits even more. I had to give lots of blood in Nam, usually in steamy hot weather. Got no orange juice, soft music and couches afterwards. Vividly recalled getting blood drained, marching into a wall of heat, and feeling woozy for hours. Visiting Dr. Powers brought that all back. I wondered what drove people to pick that career. Who wants to be someone you can't stand? It baffled me. I'd been going to Dr. Powers since a toddler. He didn't live too far from our house, which was a great draw for dad, who wasn't big on giving rides. The other allure was Dr. Powers was straightforward, nothing fancy. My pop wasn't keen on big medical bills. I remembered getting my nose elbowed playing football, maybe broken. Dad came on the visit, suggested to Dr. Powers a crooked nose made me interesting looking. Dr. Powers didn't laugh or argue the point. He looked at me, "You have a very practical father. There's too much vanity today." I knew I was screwed.

That history ran through my noggin as I climbed the steps to his office door. Doctor's offices have a unique smell. The combination of nervous sweat, urine and sick people didn't make for a nice greeting card. My nose puckered up as I adjusted. Mrs. Power's desk was at the end of the large reception area. She wasn't at her desk, so I scanned the room. There were comfortable chairs and an assortment of magazines to wile away your wait time. I always went for National Geographic. It struck me odd they could get away with pictures of naked African women, but Life magazine would get sued if they showed the side of Ann Margaret's boobs. Didn't the League of Decency censors see the knockers on those Watusi girls?

My thoughts were disturbed as Mrs. Powers rounded the corner. She worked as receptionist and office manager. She spotted me. "Ah, Dylan Frazier, always on time. Just like your mom and dad."

I nodded, "The Fraziers, we aims to please."

She half nodded, trying to determine if that made sense. She continued, "The doctor is with another patient who ran a little late. Please make yourself comfortable."

I noticed a jar of peppermint candy on her desk. "I thought sugar was bad for you, makes you fat and all." She didn't respond, blinked rapidly, before deciding silence was the best strategy. I retreated, giving up on my failed attempt at levity. If I pissed her off, she might rat me out to Dr. Powers, who might accidentally re-break my nose, which had healed straight. Chuckled to myself, as I realized that was unlikely. Dr. Powers was just like his wife, always to the point, wasted no time on triviality.

I sat in the chair near her desk. Not wanting her to notice my interest in Watusi women, I studied the room. The walls had lots of leather-covered books neatly placed on library-like shelves. There was volume after volume on anesthesia, visualization, naturopaths, yoga and other unusual topics. I asked Mrs. Powers about them. She got a serious look, changed her tone a bit deeper. "The doctor is always looking for the best way to help his patient's pain.

His hobby is studying ancient medicine." She paused, "His patient's wellbeing is foremost."

I decided to be mature, "He's a prince of a guy. My dad always says that." Didn't mention dad's other quips. She raised her cheeks, almost a smile.

I thought about his research. The worst part of being sick or injured is when something really hurts. Guess the doctor who found a way to make treatment less painful would make a killing. He was a smart to dig for creative treatments. I heard footsteps, Dr. Powers' door opened. Out walked a woman chatting away to the doctor. "That was the most painless procedure I've ever had. My head is a little sore, but I don't have that nauseous feeling like after anesthesia. I do think you're on to something." The attractive lady noticed me, looked embarrassed. "Sorry I was jabbering so much. My mouth isn't working completely right yet. Was I being too loud?"

I waved her off. "No problem, the nuns at St Tim's always said my mouth was working too well for my own good. They even talked about demonic possession."

She smiled. "I'll have to remember that one for the girls at our next bridge game."

Dr. Powers interrupted the merriment. He turned toward me, "Well, Dylan, we haven't seen you for a long time. Come on in. Let's see if you've kept up your health regimen." I entered his tidy office, could still smell what was probably the woman's perfume. Inhaling deeply, I prepared myself for something less pleasant. Dr. Powers had me hop on the table, went about exploring my inner sanctum, mumbling observations. "Things look good. Have you been exercising regularly?

I nodded an affirmative. He told me to step down and drop my trousers for the rectal exam. As I did that, flashed back to the army physical as I entered basic training. The army doctor had looked at me with a crooked grin, "Bend over and smile. The train's about to enter the tunnel." I didn't have a twisted response today. Dr. Powers, a true professional. He wore a nasal mask and rubber gloves when he worked. A precise man.

Finally done, Dr. Powers told me I was in excellent condition, to keep up my health program. He looked at me, "Your parents are German and Irish, correct?"

I shook my head, "I'm a hybrid of both races."

He said seriously. "You should be thankful; the Germanic races have always had superior health. It's part of why they've remained a dominant breed throughout history. More cultures have succumbed to diseases all tracing back to mistreatment of their body."

That struck me as odd, but I looked at the small man, figured he was probably envious of powerful people, decided to stay noncommittal. "Just the luck of the draw, I guess."

He frowned, "So it is, so it is." He walked me out to his wife's office, gave her the forms. I left with a clean bill of health and completed paperwork to renew my license.

PERCY

Time to leave Detroit. On his walk to the bus terminal, he thought about his escape. The first year at Leavenworth was spent being a model prisoner. He talked openly to his counselor about a tough early life. Appeared remorseful, as he blamed his violent army behavior on shellshock from multiple tours in Vietnam. His anger at Frazier was an early theme, but after many therapy sessions, he told the counselor he forgave Frazier and all others involved with his incarceration. Percy looked sincerely at the army counselor, "The only one to blame is myself." The naïve therapist bought the act. Percy continued being an obedient, docile prisoner, and soon won the trust of his guards. After months of exemplary behavior, he was given lighter duty and the opportunity to help the guards and supervisors. His native intelligence allowed him to adapt to a variety of chores and services. With innate talent for paperwork, he was soon doing clerical work for the warden, and had access to army files. All the while, Percy did research.

Working for the warden, he learned of a construction project outside the prison, was the only volunteer for the strenuous assignment. Percy smiled at the warden as he squeezed his ample belly, "Could use me some exercise." He didn't have to wait long. From his office assignment, he knew the prison's weekly routines: delivery of fruit and produce always passed by the side entrance where he worked the construction site. As expected, the construction guard was bullshitting with the deliveryman as Percy ambled up. He suddenly karate chopped the guard senseless. In one motion, Percy turned to the stunned driver, punched him unconscious. He pushed the guard inside the truck, stripped off his uniform, grabbed cap and wallet, and dragged both bodies to the rear of the truck. Driving slowly, he exited Leavenworth, dumped the still unconscious men in a wooded area, and made his way to Kansas City, only twenty-five miles away. He abandoned the truck at a convenience store, walked to the railroad station, and boarded a train departing for Detroit. He melted into oblivion as another faceless resident of the Motor City's homeless shelters.

Percy knew the army would come after him but figured they would lose interest after a few months. Weekly muggings got him enough cash to get by. He hated Detroit but bided his time. He moved frequently between shelters, made certain he didn't stick out. At Leavenworth, he spent every second planning his revenge. He wasn't worried about Frazier, but his friend, the huge Green Beret captain was another matter. He played the waiting game for almost a year. Eventually, his anger and lust for revenge overcame caution. He hopped a bus to Charleston, South Carolina, and a reunion with his wife Gardenia Smith. When they married, she reluctantly agreed to keep her maiden name, so she would be almost impossible to find if someone came looking for him. He gave a rare smile, thought to himself, "Had my thinkin' cap on that day."

Defying logic, Gardenia and Percy co-existed

peacefully. She was also a survivor, raised by a mother on the poor side of North Charleston. A bright girl, Gardenia ran the laundry service on base, and met Percy when he was stationed at Fort Jackson. She wasn't frightened by his hyperactivity or mean streak.

She told Percy, "My mama's the agitated type. I be used to lots a action. Yo ain't so bad to me." She married this surly soldier hoping he'd mellow, thinking almost anything better than her sullen life with mom. After Percy started his scams in Nam, he sent home more money than she ever dreamed of. Per Percy's orders, she quit her base job and started a laundry business in Charleston. The business prospered. While not in love with Percy, Gardenia was loyal. He lifted her from a bleak existence.

She knew of his escape and wasn't at all surprised when he walked through the door of her laundry. Gardenia eyed him, "Ya'll got fat." Looked some more, "And hairy."

VINCENTE

He selected his new victim weeks ago. The grooming process was exciting because of the uncertainty. His business was unusually hectic and forced delays in the meticulous ritual routine. He needed to focus, or mistakes could occur. Thinking of Angelique settled him. She was responding to treatment perfectly. This was her sixth session. It would be the last until he visited her, late one night. He wasn't a jovial man but smiled as he thought of her mentioning mild pain after her recent visit. Vincente whispered, "If she only knew the real cause of that pain." Of all his victims, Angelique reminded him most of his mother. It was almost as if they were sisters. He wondered if Angelique was as promiscuous as dear old mother. He shook his head, probably not. Angelique had been divorced for almost seven years, never mentioned a boyfriend when he had her in his thrall. One thing he was meticulous about: no surprise boyfriend showing up on the day of the ceremony. He visualized Angelique. He started to pant, thinking of what lay ahead.

Her uncanny resemblance to his mother was unsettling. The memory made him relive her endless series of boyfriends. Mother always had her suitors. After dad left, she was determined to marry well. But marrying the beautiful Irma was one thing. But inheriting the gnomish Vincente was another. Whenever mother found a suitable husband, she pulled out all stops. His childhood was an endless nightmare of his naked mother performing sexual favors for these would-be daddies. The plan never quite worked. When the heat was turned up, mother always got the same answer. "If that creepy kid is part of the deal, I'm outta here."

Mother never did find Mr. Perfect. She always blamed Vincente. "Why did I have such an ugly little troll?" She was a bitter, cruel woman. But Vincente survived. And plotted revenge.

THE DU MONDE CASE

Hoban called yesterday to say he needed an investigation done quickly on Pierre Du Monde. Since Hoban was my primary cash cow, I gave him priority. I saw Mr. Du Monde just over two years ago when he first went on permanent disability from Goliath Chemicals. Permanent disability investigations were mostly rubber-stamping a claim for someone seriously ill. If a company was willing to pay hefty premiums for permanent disability, they were usually for important executives, or key performers who had vital skills. Because of this assumption of disability, I hadn't read much of Mr. Du Monde's file before making the drive to rural Chadds Ford, pricey horse country, miles from bustling Philadelphia. Remembering that first visit made me smile: rolling fields with horses grazing, pastures lined with ancient stone fences, classic Pennsylvania countryside. The beautiful terrain reminded me of childhood treks with dad to nearby Longwood Gardens; arguably the finest ornamental gardens in America according to my green thumb father. Chadds Ford was magnificent.

But on that long ago visit, I wasn't prepared for the splendor of Mr. Du Monde's property. Nearing the gated entrance, I slowed to a halt. Double-checked to make certain I had the correct address. I perused the file. Holy Shitoly, Pierre Du Monde was the President of Goliath Chemical, one of the richest chemical companies in the world. I swept my hand over my shirt and tie to make certain I was presentable. I always wore a suit. It made me look more serious, countered my large, athletic frame. Hoban always teased I had a mildly menacing look. Like I was waiting to smack someone if they got out of line. Sometimes that look came in handy, but I doubted it would be needed with this wealthy gentleman. I glanced in the car mirror, no spinach dangling from my pearly whites. Breathed heavily into my palm. A trace of the lunchtime hoagie? I grabbed a mint lifesaver.

I proceeded down the crushed stone driveway, lined with English Poplars. I slowed up, rolled down the windows, drank in the woodland smells. And came to a quick stop, as two incredible peacocks wandered majestically near the driveway. I kept my foot on the break. Figured Pierre Du Monde wouldn't appreciate whacking his exotic birds. These were the first peacocks I'd ever seen up close, so I got out of the car, stared. They were magnificent, almost from another place and time. I heard a noise behind me. Sitting on a bench was an older gentleman, dressed casually, but with an elegance that couldn't be hidden.

He broke the silence. "Aren't they spectacular? They are actually peafowl. The male is the peacock and the female the peahen. But the males are the more flamboyant. Their showy train is truly a wonder. I imported them from India. Normally, they don't thrive in this climate, but these two aren't your normal breed." He nodded, "Meet Napoleon and Bathsheba. These two are mated for life."

He laughed when I said, "If I were a bird and my wife looked like Bathsheba, why play around?"

That was my introduction to Pierre Du Monde. He

asked me to help him up. We walked the rest of the way back to his house. Well, technically, it was a mansion. But it was so tastefully done it didn't come across as huge. I made that comment to Mr. Du Monde. "You have a good eye, young man. That is exactly how I designed the house to be perceived, an old French chateau with a colonial American twist." He added, "The kind of place Thomas Jefferson would have liked, large but homey." I didn't make any wise quips, enjoyed listening to this refined man. We entered the house; the floors were old hearts of pine planks. The kitchen was huge, but appeared designed to mimic an old colonial style, but with updated appliances. It had an enormous fireplace, big enough to walk into. He saw me notice. "We cook bread there in the winter." I was going to ask about hotdogs and marshmallows but opted for silence.

I had identified myself when we met in the driveway. Told him that Voyager required a yearly visit to make certain his benefits were going smoothly. He shook his head in agreement, "Can't be too cautious when you're paying out a quarter million a year, can you?" I nodded, fighting off a gulp, when I saw we were paying twenty-five thousand a month. Mr. Du Monde went on to tell me his heart condition ran in the family. "None of the Du Monde men live long lives." He wasn't complaining, just stating a fact. Like it was important for me to understand. He sat back in a comfortable chair near the antique dry sink, started talking. He had a pensive look on his kind face. It occurred to me I still hadn't seen another person since arriving. Wouldn't a place like this require lots of help? As if reading my thoughts, he told me his story. While he spoke, I wondered why he chose to pour out his heart.

He said he married the granddaughter of Goliath Chemical's founder, chanced into the president role when none of the other heirs wanted to dirty their hands in business. He looked sad as he added, "My wife's family view themselves as aristocracy. I've never been truly accepted as worthy enough. Tolerated, but only so because I was useful. Since my stroke, my value has diminished. Now that it's obvious I won't be going back to run the company, I am persona non-grata." He said aloud, as if purging a demon, "How could a family abandon their own daughter? Me, I understand. But how could they totally cut her off?" He didn't want a response. It was as if saying it to a stranger might provide some plausible answer.

He continued, shaking his head, "After I got sick, the family cut off family funds. So, that disability check is all that keeps this place going. I had to let the groundskeeper and most of the housemaids go, too expensive. I hire help when the place gets too overgrown during the summer months." He looked at me blankly, "My poor wife is at wits end. She was not raised to do domestic work." He got quiet. I sat for a few minutes, but it was clear Mr. Du Monde was done. I left, pondered his tale on the ride to Philly, realized once again money can't make you happy. I kept wondering why he told me the sad tale about his family. I wasn't sure why, but it made me feel good that I somehow lightened his load. Made a note to give my family an extra hug when I saw them.

*

When I returned last year for the routine check, Mr. Du Monde was not around. I left my card on the door, came back a few times to get his signature on the disability form. I never got a call. Finally, on my fourth attempt, I met an older woman who identified herself as Elise Du Monde, Pierre's wife. She had an aristocratic air but seemed slightly careworn. She didn't have the natural dignity of her husband, even if allegedly from American nobility. I shook off that observation, should give her the benefit of the doubt, she married such a nice man. Quickly, another thought ran through my head: it must be tough taking care of a sickly husband and being shunned by her family, a tragic turn to a fairytale life. I should cut her a break. When I asked after her husband, she told me Mr. Du Monde was ill, would not be able to see me. Said she would take the form, mail it to me after signing it. The form arrived a week later.

All that history ran through my head, as I made this new journey toward Chadds Ford, this idyllic corner of Pennsylvania. I was anxious to see the peacocks, er, peafowl. They weren't around on last year's visit. The property was as beautiful as ever but no peafowl to be found. Disappointed, I parked my innocuous green car, ambled to the back entrance. After banging loudly, an elderly woman answered the door. I identified myself as a representative from Voyager, asked for Mr. Du Monde. She looked confused, but then said she hadn't seen him since she started working here a few months ago. That she thought he might be in a nursing home. I asked to see Mrs. Du Monde, was told that, "Mrs. Du Monde no longer meets with the public, she has retreated from daily life." Thinking that strange, I asked if she could tell me the name of the nursing home where Mr. Du Monde was staying. That seemed to throw her. After a long pause, she said, "Wait here, I'll see what I can do."

As she walked away, I moved toward the back door, hoping the peafowl would surface. I noticed a man mowing the lawn near the formal gardens. Everything looked in tip top shape. I wondered if Mrs. Du Monde had been welcomed back into the family. Thought it likely she had been restored her former family status after her husband went into the nursing home. That rattled around my noodle as the elderly housekeeper returned. She walked up, said succinctly, "The Mis'ess said to leave the form, we'll mail it to you." I was disappointed since I liked Mr. Du Monde. When I asked where he was staying, that I wanted to visit. She looked at me, crinkled her brow, "That won't be allowed. Mrs. Du Monde said to stop pestering her. In the future, just mail the forms or she'll call your superior." She pointed to the door, her way of saying, "get the hell outta here, pond scum."

I walked to my car, irritated, but not sure what to do. I moseyed to the guy cutting the grass. When he saw me waiting, he cut the motor, said hello. I told him I was a friend of Mr. Du Monde, was wondering if he knew what nursing home he was in.

He looked puzzled, "Ain't know nothin' about no Mr. Du Monde. The Mis'ess is the only one I ever see." He then frowned, "Except that old biddy done run the house. Now, that is one unfriendly cuss."

I shook my head, "Know what you mean, she could piss off the Good Humor man." He chuckled, said goodbye, and walked back to the big mower. As I ambled to my car, I glanced back, saw a curtain on the top floor pulled slightly aside. Noticing me staring, the curtain quickly closed. That didn't strike me as too odd, just annoying. They were probably making sure I left, not wanting the riff raff to loiter. People like Mrs. Du Monde didn't think the rules applied to them. I drove toward my next stop in the quaint town of West Chester, home of the famous teacher's college. I let the encounter percolate.

I got home that night and pulled out the file on Mr. Du Monde. I paged through the paperwork till I found what I wanted: the attending physician, Dr. Aaron Armstrong. Next morning, I called Armstrong's office, told them I was investigating the disability claim for Mr. Du Monde, needed the nursing home name to get some forms signed. Got an answer I didn't expect. "We haven't seen Mr. Du Monde for over a year, we don't know anything about him being institutionalized." They mentioned they'd been calling Mrs. Du Monde periodically, but never received a call back. They wondered if a new heart specialist was involved. When I said I'd gotten the same cold shoulder, the nurse said off-handedly, "That Mrs. Du Monde is a cold fish. It's too bad. Mr. Du Monde is such a sweetheart."

When I called Hoban, told him what happened, he said to back off. "Goliath already got a call from the old lady that you're harassing them." Before I could protest, Hoban interrupted, "Don't sweat it. The personnel manager at Goliath said to wait for the forms, if they aren't signed to go out again. Apparently, she's a major pain in the ass. They don't mind you messing with her some. Just don't overdo it." Hoban chuckled, "I know that will be a challenge for you. Subtlety isn't your strong suit."

Not liking Hoban having the upper hand, I said. "Okay, Mr. Suaveness, tell me the difference between an Indian and Burmese peafowl? Which one is bluer? Let me see how sophisticated you are, smart guy." He hung up without answering. I really did enjoy amusing myself.

But Hoban was right. I was kind of irritated, wanted to mess with her. The signed form came in a few days later. The signature was almost illegible; so, I thought it might be fun to play with, maybe have another visit to force a better signature. I paged through the file, went to the original form with Mr. Du Monde's application for disability. What I found caught my eye. Mr. Du Monde's signature was very neat, distinctive. The current signature was no semblance of the original. Interesting. I scrolled to last year's form. Huh. It was exactly the same chicken scratch as the form that I just received. I went through the entire file. Every signature except the last two years were in Mr. Du Monde's refined penmanship. I wondered what had changed. Even his signature six months after the stroke was clear and strong. Must have been trained by the nuns. Shoddy writing got you a ruler on the knuckles.

I thought for a while. Decided to call Dr. Armstrong's office to get advice. The friendly nurse listened to my tale of the signature change. Told me to wait a second while she looked at her file. A few minutes later, came back to the phone. "You're right, he has great handwriting." She added, "Even after the stroke his handwriting was quite steady. I wonder what happened?" I asked what would be the likely nursing home he would be in. Figured with their money, nothing but the best. She told me to hang on, that she would check with Dr. Armstrong. After a few minutes, she came back. She told me there were only three likely locations that would handle someone with severe cardiac issues. All the nursing homes were within a manageable driving distance. I wrote them down, told the nurse I'd let her know when I found him.

None of the nursing homes had him as a patient. I called Dr. Armstrong again. Told them my news. The nurse agreed it was odd. I asked if there were other cardiac specialists that might be treating Du Monde. That maybe they placed him in another more remote facility. She said she'd call back. Rather than wait around, I went out, did a few routine disability investigations in West Philly. I had to pay the bills, couldn't get carried away with my desire to bust Mrs. Du Monde's chops. Later that afternoon, checked in with my new nurse buddy. I listened to her surprising information. "No other physician in this area is treating Mr. Du Monde. They were under the impression that Dr. Armstrong was still the AP." She added, pride in her voice. "Dr. Armstrong is nationally renowned. That's why the Du Monde's picked him." I thanked her for the help, again told her I had to think some, but would let her know when I solved the mystery. I went to my flip chart, wrote down the facts I knew. I added a few pieces from my initial meeting with Mr. Du Monde, like not being accepted by the wife's family. I looked at the charts, said them out loud. Nothing came to me.

As I had done since a kid, I went to the nearby basketball courts and did my shooting drills. The slanted court befuddled most players, but I grew up here, I adjusted easily to the up and downhill shots. I remembered great college players being frustrated after not making a shot the entire game. When I was in high school, one college star asked me what the trick was since I had made every shot in a hotly contested game. Straight-faced, "You just have to adjust your algorithm to neutralize the time-space differential." When he squinted at me, I added, "Unless it's windy. In that case, you're screwed."

As I did full court lay-ups, I laughed to myself. I realized I'd never grow up, didn't really want to. In that mindless moment, I got a really weird thought. Heading home, I thought I'd discovered where to find Mr. Du Monde.

The next morning, I called Hoban, gave him my theory. At first, he thought I was joking. But when I assured him I was serious, he agreed to call Goliath, tell them we might have a problem. We needed their support to force the issue. It took a few days to unravel, but it turned out that Mr. Du Monde had been dead for over a year. There was a quiet burial on the grounds. Apparently, no relatives or friends were notified. Needing the money and unable to reconcile with her family, the desperate Mrs. Du Monde kept cashing the checks. Not wanting a scandal, Goliath Chemical decided not to press charges since she was from the founding family. They agreed to reimburse Voyager the fraudulent funds for agreement to keep quiet. The personnel manager said Mrs. Du Monde claimed she was confused, never meant to do anything illegal.

Since I needed the Voyager's business, I agreed to keep my mouth shut. Voyager was elated I saved them a fortune in disability payments and gave me a bonus check for a thousand dollars in appreciation. Or was it to keep me quiet? What did I care? Maybe I could afford a better car now. Nah, it was better to let the people I investigated think I was worse off than them. Gave me a sympathy edge. But something nagged at me. I couldn't let the case close this way. Drove out to visit the Du Monde home one last time. I scanned, but no peafowl. Knocking on the door, I wondered if they sold the rare birds for money. As I puzzled that, Mrs. Du Monde opened the door. I saw a look of surprise, then of recognition and pure loathing.

About to get blasted, I put up my hands. "I'm not here to bother you. I just want to explain that I really liked your husband, that I was worried and wanted to make sure he was okay. That's why I was so persistent. We only chatted that one time, but he really impressed me. There was a dignity about him. I just wanted to make certain he was alright." Her eyes blinked rapidly, I could see that took the wind from her sails. Tears trickled down her cheeks as she closed the door.

PERCY

Percy was getting on Gardenia's nerves. She'd gotten used to living on her own and liked it. The laundry business was booming. She enjoyed the feeling of success, thrived on the friendly customer interaction. But losing it all worried her. Part of Percy's original plan was having a legitimate business to show the government if they discovered her large savings accounts in Bermuda and wondered where they came from. Gardenia learned the corrupt MP, Ben Burton, had set the Bermuda accounts in her name, so funds wouldn't be tied to Percy. When Percy and Gardenia got married she kept her maiden name. At the time she didn't like it, but Percy was unbending. "Look woman, you jus' do as you told. Got me a plan and you a big part of it. So, hush up." Gardenia did stop complaining after the money started pouring in. More money than she ever dreamed of. Livin' high on the hog.

Now Percy was back, laying around getting drunk, and bitchin' about some dude named Dylan. He said to Gardenia at least once a day, "That motha'fucker gonna pay. Pretty white boy's gonna get his. Percy's a comin'." When she asked what he'd done to him, he slit his eyes. "None a yer business, woman. Never you mind." Gardenia knew better than to hassle Percy when he was drinking. Percy was mean sober. Drunk, he was a vicious.

She would always nod when he was in a mood, "Jus' makin' conversation is all."

One day she came home from the laundry, and Percy had their bags packed. "We makin' a trip to Bermuda, woman. Got us tickets for tomorrow's flight. Got all you gonna need in this bag. We gonna make a nice, big withdrawal. Time fer Percy to settle some debts." Gardenia was used to his mercurial moods, but this time she was scared. She said nothing to Percy but thought: somethin' bad's a comin'.

Unknown to Gardenia, Percy had used his time in Charleston to gather equipment to help his hunt. With military bases so nearby, it was easy to buy "lost material" on the black market. When he was in Nam, Percy had gotten assigned to a special group in military intelligence that tracked drug activity in the army. His job was to find and eliminate local drug merchants who sold heroin on the bases. It wasn't hard for these Vietnamese gangsters to believe Percy was a corrupt, merciless bastard. While doing this work, he got access to the latest radio tracking devices. He'd plant the device in the bag of money then follow the sellers to their headquarters. Percy could still picture the puzzled looks on the drug dealers faces when he pointed his stolen AK-47 at them, demanded the money back. Sometimes he let them live. Most times he unloaded the full clip. He shook off that pleasant walk down his past. He thought about the task at hand, nodded to himself: the tracking device from Ft Jackson would be helpful. His cold eyes blinked at his next thought: and the Colt 45 pistol.

Getting even with Frazier consumed Percy when he was in prison. The money he got for stealing army munitions was never the important thing. He got involved in the conspiracy to lash out at the army. They made him a killing machine but turned on him when he got too good at it. His chaotic train of thought had him also wondering how his ole partner, Colonel Mullen, was doing in prison. That ole piece a shit wasn't cut out to do time. I'll bet that sumbitch is dead by now. He closed his filmy eyes, drifted to the past. He relived their last discussion before getting caught. It didn't take much effort to convince Mullen he'd kill his family if he snitched on him. Maybe killin' his pal Ben Burton made him take me seriously. Don't fuck with ole Percy. He breathed deeply, came back to the present. Shifted his troubled mind. Now he had his focus on different prey.

Thinking about Frazier made him smile, as he boarded the US Air flight to Bermuda. He had a bounce in his step, things were finally startin'. Gardenia complained at first, but after getting someone to run her laundry business, seemed to enjoy the idea of a vacation. He knew he was gettin' on the ole gal's nerves but didn't care. Once he got done his mission, he'd settle up with Gardenia, one way or t'other. Now he needed her to get the money. It was all settled. After he killed Frazier, he'd disappear. Maybe go to the Caribbean; melt away. He settled into his seat, didn't pay attention as Gardenia chattered on about how nice it was to be going back to Bermuda. Years ago, she made a trip there to establish her credentials, and came back once to make a large withdrawal to start her laundry business. She remembered how nice it was to stay at the Hamilton Princess. Wouldn't her mama be proud? She mentioned that to Percy, but he didn't respond.

She said it louder, but Percy shushed her. "Be quiet woman, I got some thinkin' to do. Gonna toast me some white bread pretty soon." Gardenia didn't show any reaction, but that statement alarmed her anew.

DYLAN

I kept close tabs on Chloe. Her new roommate Elaine, and the return to work, invigorated her. I dropped by weekly to see how she was. She and Elaine had become best friends. They did everything together. During the last couple visits, I'd been asking if she'd like to meet my friend Monsignor Pugh. Got polite nods but no commitment. On this visit, Elaine answered the door, gave me a hug as I entered. Chloe was upstairs getting changed after work. She pointed to a chair, offered something to drink while I waited. Elaine was plain looking, very slim, had light brown hair. That ordinary impression disappeared when she started to speak, she lit up. Her voice was crystal clear, had a raspy edge to it. There was warmness to the tone that made you sorry when she stopped talking. I found myself inventing questions to keep her chatting. She was about forty-five years old, had the kind of soft features that would let her age gracefully.

I mentioned that natural youthfulness to her. She blushed, "Honestly, Dylan, you should have been a used car salesman. So full of the blarney." I grinned, was hoping that gift would help me sell Chloe on a couple things: meeting Monsignor Pugh and speaking with another assault victim so we could see if any clues would surface.

My strategy was to elicit Elaine's help in convincing Chloe. I hit her with my plans. "Elaine, I know Chloe has been dodging me on visiting Monsignor Pugh, was wondering if you would help."

She grinned, "Are you trying to convert Chloe. You know she's not a practicing Catholic anymore, don't you? Hasn't been for years. Her incident didn't exactly restore her faith in God." I could read people. She was sincere, not giving a lecture.

I was prepared for that rebuttal. Looked at Elaine, "Well, now that you mention it, hear me out. If I reconvert a non-practicing Catholic, I think that qualifies me for a plenary indulgence. And if you don't know what that is, let me assure you it's a big deal. It basically means I can screw off the rest of my life and still go directly to heaven." I gave her my most mature look. "I'm begging you for help. Since you've gotten to know me, you might have figured I'll need a huge push to make the pearly gates."

Elaine was laughing now. I raised both hands. "But the real reason is Monsignor Pugh has an air about him. He's a regular guy but has this holiness and serenity that makes you feel everything's going to be all right. I really think Chloe would find him helpful in her healing."

Elaine sensed my sincerity. "Okay, let me think it over." After a few seconds, "Don't get too optimistic, neither of us is too keen on religion."

I switched gears as Elaine sat down "But here's the hardest one. I need you to help get Chloe to speak with another victim who was attacked by this heartless bastard." She started to argue. I asked her to listen. "What you don't know is there are at least six other victims who had the same horrible things done to them. And what makes it even worse is that none of the victims will talk or file charges." Elaine sank into her chair, considered that as I continued. "It's even worse. All of these attacks occurred within a few miles of here." That got her attention. "And if we don't catch him, this will just continue. I met with my buddy Fran who's a psychologist. He said sickos like this never stop till they're caught. If no one is chasing him, he'll keep doing it." I hit her with the knockdown punch. "Do you want that on your conscience? Knowing we sat around doing nothing when we could have helped stop this?"

Elaine looked defeated. "I'll help but let's start with Monsignor Pugh first. Then I'll mention the other similar victims, see if Chloe comes to the conclusion herself without us nagging her. She's doing so well, I don't want a setback." I didn't either, agreed to start with the Monsignor. Just then I heard noise on the stairway. Chloe came down the steps briskly. It was amazing how much more animated she'd become.

She was a sharp woman, realized we had been in a conversation about her. She looked back and forth between us. "So, what have my two-favorite people been plotting?" Before I could answer, she pointed at me. "You'll be happy to know I haven't forgotten you want me to meet this Monsignor Pugh you raved so much about." She shook her head, "But I'm still wary and want to go slow. The last thing I want is some stranger trying to convert me. I'm a staunch agnostic now, you know."

Elaine chuckled when I said, "Did I ever tell you about plenary indulgences?"

VINCENTE

Tonight, was the big night. Angelique lived on a dark, heavily treed street near the Waverly Theater in Drexel Heights. Although there were many nearby commercial businesses, the huge elm trees muted most noise, and all but swallowed the streetlight. He parked his car amidst other vehicles, innocuous if the police happened to patrol. He didn't need his equipment, so carrying his customary gear would not be a source of attention: just a citizen out for a stroll on this balmy summer night. Vincente stayed inside the car till the area was absolutely quiet. Satisfied, he emerged from the vehicle, indoor lights turned off, so he wouldn't be spotted. With his small stature and black clothing, he again became invisible. Most of the time, this obscurity enraged him. But on the nights of his rituals, he embraced the blandness. He got a contented look, as he realized he would soon be shining like the brightest star.

He learned from the sessions with Angelique that she was a night owl, rarely asleep before midnight. Watching Johnny Carson was part of her routine. A random thought came to him. Instead of the moronic Ed McMahon barking: Heeeere....'s Johnny, Angelique would think Heeeere...'s my Master. The power pleased Vincente. Moving toward her house, the third from the corner, he paused. He stood motionless, doing a three hundred and sixty degree sweep of the surroundings. No one. Not even a dog barking. He got in front of her house, looked around, and then moved behind a gigantic azalea bush. The nearby houses were all enormous. Angelique's dead husband had done well, left her wealthy after his fateful cardiac arrest. Not that Angelique needed his inheritance. She was a named partner in a successful accounting firm, filthy rich. He breathed in, felt the surge of adrenaline. This was one his favorite moments. Would all his preparation work?

Satisfied he was alone, Vincente bent low, and almost crawled toward the door. He breathed deeply: the moment he'd waited for was nigh. Instead of knocking, he circled the house, looking for the den where Angelique watched her endless series of TV shows. Her mathematic simplicity, the black and white view of the world also reminded Vincente of dear old mom. He crinkled his brow as he thought: my father must have been bright and clever. Otherwise, where did I come from? He'd often considered hunting down his philandering father. It would be fun to repay his years of childhood torment. Vincente shook his head. He had to focus. Moving stealthily, he spotted the brightly lit den, just off the kitchen. He crept closer, nose almost touching the window. Watching Angelique giggling, unaware of what awaited her, gave him immense joy. He exhaled. It was show time!

Retracing his steps, he went to the front door, rang the bell. He listened to the melodic chimes. Ding, dong, ding, dong. Ding, dong, ding, dong. Ding, dong, ding, dong. On the fourth melodic set, the front lights came on. He watched Angelique looking through the small window at the top of the door. He could see her register surprise. But as expected, she opened up for the familiar face. He could see her mind form the words: what a surprise, I wonder what he wants? Without letting her say another word, Vincente performed his much-rehearsed wizardry.

To his delight, Angelique stood taller, stared at him, waiting for instructions. He entered the house, told her to turn off the lights, and to proceed to the bedroom. She did as ordered.

He watched her dutifully walk the grand hallway steps. He followed close behind, drinking in her scent. Chanel? Vincente mused that she was probably the wealthiest of his chosen. Did that make this better or worse? He couldn't decide as he entered her bedroom. It was very neat and feminine. Her housekeeper was to be commended. He knew Angelique did no housework. She stood beside the four-poster bed, waited for his command. In his practiced voice, "Take off your robe and get under the covers." He watched carefully. With no hesitation, she did as directed. Vincente's nostrils flared. He pulled out the candy cane, licked it sensuously and then her lips. He whispered, warm breath into her left ear. Angelique closed her eyes and fell fast asleep. Vincente watched her chest rise and fall, silently left her room. As he descended the majestic stairway, he felt very satisfied. He thought: next time is real.

BERNIE STRIKES AGAIN

I hadn't given much thought to the Bernie Nudleman caper. But another call from Hoban pushed him back in my pile of "to dos." I could tell immediately that Hoban was agitated. "You're not going to believe this, Dylan. I work for a new guy in Hartford, his name is Harley Burns, he's a real piece of work. I mean, no sense of humor, one of those fast track guys who wants to be president of Voyager before he's forty. Anyway, I just got a call from Harley that he got this weird letter from someone named Bernie Nudleman." I started to laugh, but quickly checked myself. I could tell that Hoban was irritated. "So, the letter got my new boss really wound up. The letter had Bernie's typical style, mentions my name, acting like we all know each other. That we're Jewish and grew up together. Harley's humorless, a total prick. He's going to hold this against me if it keeps up. Like somehow this is my fault. That I'm immature or something." I promised to come in for the letter, swallowed a laugh as I hung up the phone.

Hoban was out on a business call when I arrived later. His secretary gave me the Nudleman letters, turned back to her typing without any comments. Hoban must have threatened her not to kibitz with me. I went to my car, read them quickly; was soon chuckling.

Remembering I wanted to do something to keep Chloe upbeat, I called her at work. Asked if I could drop by to show her something, get some advice on how to handle it. She was about to leave work, agreed to meet. I

112

left Hoban's office, not wanting to bump into my surly friend. I drove home and went to Chloe's before dinnertime. As usual, Elaine answered the door. Chloe was trying to get the nerve to answer the door but was still reluctant. I followed Elaine inside. Chloe joined us in the living room as I explained the history of these crazy letters. I gave the background on Hoban's dour boss, Harley Burns, now in Bernie's crosshairs.

Elaine looked incredulous, "You mean this guy writes people he doesn't really know, claiming they're Jewish and are somehow related or grew up together?"

I nodded, "You got it."

Chloe cut in, "That's just stupid."

I spread my hands, "Also probably true but wait till you read the letters. They're hysterical." I was already laughing. Both ladies looked at me like I was a loon. And that made me laugh even harder. Pretty soon they started giggling. Having a hard time controlling myself, I handed them the Nudleman missives. Elaine volunteered to read aloud. Using her melodious voice, she explained:

There were two letters to Hoban's new boss, Harley Burns. The first one was on nice stationary, from "The James Messinger Mortgage Company." The letter was addressed to Mr. Harley Burns and read as follows:

Re: 18960 Birch Avenue

Country Club Hills, Illinois

Dear Mr. Burns:

This letter will serve to inform you that my company took the assignment of your mortgage on the above-cited real estate property. The mortgage was paid off on the sale of the property, and it appears that we are in possession of certain escrow proceeds in the amount of $1,592.45 to which you are entitled.

We were in the process of preparing an instrument of payment, when contacted by Mr. Bernard Nudleman; who asserts to us as follows:

1. *He is your uncle on your Jewish mother's side.*
2. *You owe him money in connection with certain advancements he made in your behalf to one Mr. Fielding.*
3. *You are originally from the Philadelphia area.*

Mr. Nudleman maintains that we can make the check payable to him and he will settle up with you directly. We are pleased to do so, but only with your specific approval.

By coincidence, I have a cousin named Harvey who is from Ephrata, Pennsylvania and he thinks he might know you. Did your family run a kosher poultry business in Philadelphia? Were you quite a soccer player?

Please call me at your earliest convenience to direct me on the disposition of the aforesaid proceeds and to shoot the breeze about old times.

Very truly yours,

James F Messinger, Jr.

I watched the lady's grins get wider. It had the Nudleman touch. I said they needed to visualize Harley Burns reading this nonsensical letter, a man devoid of any silliness. They should picture him frowning the whole time. Elaine laughed first, was soon joined by Chloe.

But the second letter was priceless, totally wacko. It was addressed as follows:

To: Mr. Harley Burns, BIG BOSS.

Dear Harley:

Are you guys totally nuts? I just called you and found out you were at the Big Bosses convention in Tucson. I didn't even have to pry; the gabby secretary spilled the beans. Can you imagine the sheer lunacy of having all the Big Honchos from Voyager at one place at the same time? You don't think the competition would like to bump off all the fat cats and send the Voyager stock spinning? But that got me thinking. Is this a big chance for Harley to be the Lone Ranger and save the day?

I'm willing to bet that not one of those Home Office guys has given the slightest thought to the enormous lapse of security that exists at the boss's convention. You guys would be sitting ducks. Harley, just consider yourself lucky that you get home safely this year. But, don't press your luck.

Here's what to do:

1. *Draft a detailed memorandum and give it a clever title that really grabs the attention, like, "How to Avoid Armageddon," a modest proposal for security at the Boss's Convention.*
2. *Begin with a Worst Scenario technique. In unemotional terms, outline the convention being air assaulted, everyone is massacred. SEC suspends all trading of Voyager stock, the corporation collapses.*
3. *But try to be balanced. Don't be all negative. Nobody likes a whiner.*

The new security plan is the following:

1. *A security force of fifty, with two officers. My suggestion is to get Israeli commandos, the same guys who smack Palestine around.*
2. *Gas masks. One at every boss's chair, an atropine injector attached.*
3. *Flak jackets. Mandatory for all meetings. Tell them you'll work with Hickey Freeman to get something light and tasteful.*
4. *Karate and Tae Kwon Do lessons. Only for the top echelon guys. They'll like that you think of them as elite. Pitch it that if the invaders make it past security, it may be left to hand-to-hand skills and they'll be ready to kick ass.*

5. *Counter-guerilla measures. Plant moles in all our competitors' operations. Equip them with cyanide pills should their cover be blown.*

6. *Convention situs. Forget the posh settings. Suggest the Rockies, in January or February when snow cover is heaviest. Set up an armed perimeter complete with tanks, howitzers, bazooka, the works. The invaders won't have a chance!*

Harley, believe me—this memo will send your career soaring, right to the top of the corporation. I can see it now, your name in lights. Harley Burns, Executive Chairman of Security. A word of caution, don't let anyone know your plans. Someone else will try to grab the credit. That's just a word to the wise.

Call me at the store. You've got the number.

Bernie

Mission accomplished. The two friends were still chuckling as I left Chloe's house.

DYLAN

I checked in on Chloe a few days later. It was obvious she and Elaine were now inseparable. Both had a vacancy in their lives that was now filled. It was hard for me to relate to being alone. I always had steady parents, nothing showy about them, but they were rock solid, were there if you needed them. Same with my close buddies; we were like brothers. They had my back if I was in any jam. My mother always said I was drawn to hopeless cases. Most of my friends had quirks. To me the eccentricities made them interesting. As I thought that, shook my head, smiled. Look at me talking about people with quirks. Anyway, it made me feel good to see Chloe adjusting back to a more normal life. I believed if we caught her assailant, she would snap back completely. That motivated me. My dear mom had it right. I liked to fix broken things.

I knew one thing would jump-start the process: getting Chloe to call another victim. From there, see if some significant clue would shake loose. I was no psychologist, but it didn't take Einstein to figure talking to someone who shared your same nightmare had to help. That revelation made me think about Dr. Fran asking me to meet with his vet group having adjustment problems. I tucked that away, would call Fran soon. Why did I think I was immune to help? I shook my head. Chloe came first. I had an appointment with Merlano to review the victim files again. Wanted to pick a victim closest to Chloe's circumstances. My earlier notes weren't detailed enough. Was lucky I clicked with Chloe from the start. The tip I got of how well liked she was at work gave me an in. That's what I needed now, a door opener. Needed to make sure whomever I picked would not withdraw. I chuckled remembering Hoban describing me as slightly threatening because of my size and smirk.

I pulled up to Merlano's headquarters. Always got a tingle when entering a police station: it brought back bad memories from Nam. I learned as an MP that desk sergeants designed their offices to intimidate criminals. Make them have no doubt who was in control. Ambling up to his huge, elevated desk, I saw Sgt. Bonner. I identified myself, asked for Merlano. Told him I had an appointment. Bonner scowled at me, I remember youse from last time. "Ain't you that hotshot investigator that caught the serial killer?" He blew out some air, "Merlano says you got lucky. That you're the kind a guy that stumbles inta shit, comes up smellin' like a rose. That true?"

I shook my head, "When it comes to shit detection, Merlano's an expert, he's like an asshole wunderkind, so I think you have to listen to him." I paused a second, "But on the other hand, you have to temper that with him being a total shithead. So, make your own judgment."

Bonner chuckled, called Merlano, told him I was there, mentioned I informed him about his shit expertise. My old hoop buddy was grinning as he came out. "You never let up do you, Frazier? Bonner's gonna be talking about that for weeks. Come on back so you don't give him more ammunition." Merlano's office was usually a mess but the victim's files were in a neat pile. He looked at me.

"It's amazing that you got this rapport with one of the victims. I mean, all of them shut down instantly when we questioned them. They weren't rude or anything, just shut up." He rubbed his chin, "So, if you can find anything interesting in these files, good for you. Have at it."

Told Merlano I was looking for another victim that might have something in common with Chloe, or even me, maybe school or something. He squinted his eyes, wanting to hear more. "I got lucky with Chloe, she trusted me right away. Chances are that won't happen again unless there's some connection to make them comfortable, get them talking."

Merlano licked his huge lower lips. "Makes sense. Sort of like the good cop, bad cop routine. The victim trusts the nice cop, starts yapping." But he added, "Since you were here last, I went through all the files. Their descriptions of the attacker are just so different. We can't even get our artist involved to give us someone to hunt. It's frustrating."

I looked at Merlano. "Solving that mystery is my starting point. Could it be possible that this is a gang of perverts? Or is this nut wearing disguises?"

One of the things I'd learned quickly as an investigator was eyewitnesses were almost totally unreliable. Ask people what color hair their best friends have, and you get widely different responses. People see color differently. And this is when someone is just asking simple questions in non-stressful situations. Add trauma to the equation and weird answers flow. Knowing that, I didn't hold much credence in the victim's descriptions. I went with the single attacker as a premise. Had to be. The rituals were too similar to be coincidence. Maybe there would be a couple victims who gave close descriptions and could collaborate on an accurate picture for the police artist. I took out my notebook, got ready to scribble thoughts as I read the files. Patterns, that's what I was looking for. Something tangible to help connect how these helpless women encountered this sadistic bastard. What was the link?

After I caught Sylvan Skolnick, the killer who preyed on older women on Medicare, I studied what they now called serial killers. Although this sadist didn't kill his victims, he did have some similarities to Sylvan in that he picked a certain type of woman. I wrote down what I already knew before attacking the files. Made a column for "victims" and wrote the similar facts:

1.woman in their forties

2. single or divorced

3. all on the short side

4. all busty

5. lived alone

6. attractive

7. proximity to each other

8. same perverted ritual

That was what I knew so far. I started reading the gory files. I read slowly, not wanting to miss something small that didn't fit with the rest of the cases. I thought back to my pharmacy delivery boy days. I drove all over the county, really learned the area. Because of that old job it was easy to gauge how close these victims were to each other. These atrocities had happened all around my old neighborhood. Couldn't be a coincidence. The attacker must live or work in the area. And that made me think again about how the pervert picked his victims. I started a new column for "Common Link Possibilities":

1. *postman*

2. *doctor*

3. *church*

4. *lawyer*

5. *stores (Pharmacy, food, etc.)*

6. *lawn services*

7. *deliveryman*

8. *school*

9. *plumber, carpenters, etc.*

10. *hospital*

I ran out of ideas after that. Made a note to drive around the area on the way home to see if there were other possibilities. The other murderer, Sylvan Skolnick, had been a pawnshop owner, eastern European women came into his shop to pawn treasures when things got tough. He selected his victims after determining their helplessness. Was there another pawnshop sadist out there? I doubted it but would see if there were any in the area.

Went back to the file review for the second time. My plan was to read these gruesome reports multiple times for anything I might have overlooked. Sometimes I'd read too fast, skim too quickly and miss a key word. Sure enough, I spotted something right off. On the oldest victims file, Gillian Bender, the investigating cop noted, "she tasted something sweet." Wondered what that meant, made an entry in my notes. Then decided to go through the files again to see if anything about a sweet taste was mentioned again. Bingo, on Ginger Spellman's file, the cop said, "she said she could taste something minty." I scoured all the reports but none of the other victims mentioned anything similar. I added "minty" next to my note on sweetness. Maybe it was just their toothpaste but I'd ask Chloe about it later.

Noticed that each victim had very specific comments about not catching the attacker; "he's too smart" or some words to that effect. Did the attacker threaten them somehow or frighten them into believing he would never be caught? I made a note on a separate piece of paper in bold letters: *DID ATTACKER TRAUMATIZE/MANIPULATE THE VICTIMS?*

I wanted to think more about that later. This point made me even firmer in my opinion it was one person. I remembered back to my discussion with psychologist buddy Fran Philips about mastery and dominance. Fran had picked the attacker as someone suffering from one of these illnesses but settled on mastery when I pressed him. He gave me a few articles on the subject, and the more I read, the more I agreed this was what the lunatic had. The attacker made it clear to each victim that he was in charge.

He was smarter than everyone and would not be caught. Somehow convinced them he was invincible. What type of person was prone to have this personality perversion? How would he manipulate them?

After reading all the files multiple times, I settled on Miriam Keller as the other victim most likely to talk with me. Miriam was the widow of an army pilot, a warrant officer killed in Vietnam. Shot down by the North Vietnamese Army in 1967. Miriam also went to St Tim's elementary school as a kid, same school as me. I wondered if she still went to St Tim's? If so, maybe Monsignor Pugh knew her and might help. I made another note to drive by her house on the way home. Maybe there was a way to get introduced based on where she lived. Was there a neighbor I knew? I sat back in the chair, exhaled. For some reason I felt better. The file review made me feel that I'd made some progress, that we would catch this bastard. I gathered the files, went to give them to Merlano, but he was out. I left a note thanking him, resisted making a note on his fecal acumen. I liked Merlano, he was a piece of work, but he was helping me, didn't have to. Why piss him off? I fought off the temptation.

I pulled out my SEPTA map and drew a line connecting the victims. Drew a circle around them all. Realized that Drexel Heights was almost in the exact middle of the circle. My family's house was at the center of the circle. Was my hometown where the killer met his victims? It was disturbing that my neighborhood was the hub of this circle of misery. I shook my head, tucked that somber thought away. Went back to finding a solution. Per my routine, I made a travel list, and would visit them in an order that got me closer to home when done. My friends teased I was anally organized, that I needed to loosen up some, be more in the moment. Always gave the same response. "Great suggestion, I'll put that in my monthly planner: be spontaneous on the fifteenth of every month." I admitted it was hopeless. I was a planner, didn't like things sneaking up on me.

As I drove toward Gillian Bender's house, the first victim, I noted her street was just a few blocks from West Chester Pike, a busy road that led from Philly to bucolic West Chester County. Gillian's side street was heavily treed and hidden from view. I circled the area, looking for anything that wasn't in her file. There were loads of small businesses and shops, but nothing that would be a shopping draw for the other victims. I did another wider loop. She wasn't far from Delaware County Hospital and numerous doctor offices. This was the closest hospital to all the victims, but there were numerous doctors and nurses working inside. It would be tough checking all the possible suspects if the attacker was in the medical world. I made a mental note to see if the victims had been to the hospital before their attacks.

The second victim was Cynthia Sutter. She lived on the fringes of Drexel Heights, near the Highland Park border, not far from bus and trolley lines. She lived less than a mile from Gillian Bender. Both were near the bus and trolley lines to Sixty-Ninth Street. They could pick either form of transportation to work. Hmm. Would that be a link? I added that to my page of possible connections. Margot Palmieri was the third victim. She lived in Drexel Park, a tony section of Drexel Heights. That got my attention. It wasn't far from my sweetheart Laura's house. Not too far from the trolley stop. A pattern? The forth unfortunate was Ginger Spellman. She lived off Township Line and Edmond Avenue, a major bus stop. I started to like the transportation angle.

I drove to Miriam Keller's house; the fifth victim I hoped would have a chat with Chloe and me. Miriam lived near St Dorothy's Church, on the far edge of Drexel Heights. There was no trolley stop nearby. But she was near the bus line. I wondered if SEPTA had drivers that ran both trolleys and buses. Could the attacker be a driver? I thought about Chloe's house, more in the center of Drexel Heights but not too far from either a bus or trolley. I let that settle. I made a note to call SEPTA to get information about drivers. I did a wider loop but ended back at Miriam Keller's house and parked outside St Dorothy's Church. From this parking spot, I could see all the businesses on this active area on Township line. I wanted to think. What had I missed? How would I connect with Miriam Keller?

As I sat there thinking, I needed to distract myself. Most of my better insights came when I thought about inane things. As my mind drifted, I realized many of my closest friends were from St Dorothy's, a parish on the edge of Drexel Heights. If Philly was famous for nicknaming people, then St Dorothy's kids were superstars. I mentally compiled a list of St Dorothy basketball players with the best nicknames:

1. *Frog (short and squat, bug eyes)*

2. *Cuda (lots of small, sharp teeth, like the fish)*

3.   *Stopper (had an octagonal head)*

4.   *Shark (had a big chunk out of his leg from a childhood injury)*

5.   *Wang (thick glasses which distorted his eyes)*

6.   *Snot (grayish skin, droopy face, yellowish eyes)*

7.   *Laz (moved slow, as in Lazurus arising from the dead)*

8.   *Weasel (long, rodent-like face)*

9.   *Helmet (flaming red hair, like a fireman's headgear)*

10. *Lipper (immense, drooping lower lip)*

11. *Earzo (giant receptors)*

12. *Pup (always had tongue hanging out)*

13. *Monk (waddled like a chimp)*

14. *Stovepipe (long, skinny neck)*

15. *Duck (pigeon-toed, waddle walk)*

By now, I was totally amused, hoped no one called the cops to report me as I idled outside the church. Most of these basketball players were nicknamed for a dominant physical trait but occasionally irony entered the fray. That's how I got the Dylan handle, an ironic tribute to the scraggly Bob Dylan, since I was the opposite, neat and groomed. Compared to most other choices, considered myself lucky. As I got composed, a plan started to unfold. First talk to Merlano again and then Chloe. I needed them to open the door to Miriam Keller. I drove home satisfied. No answers but more organized.

VINCENTE

The summer was a busy time for Vincente. He loved the summer traffic. Mom usually had to bring the kids along to their appointments. Today, lovely Monica Carey sat beside him with her fourteen-year-old daughter, Patty. Vincente had to force himself to concentrate as Monica leaned in to expose her ample cleavage. A bohemian, she let her charms hang free. Vincente fought for control. He couldn't let her know how much she bothered him. Rather than pant and draw attention, he breathed deeply through his nose, tried to center his thoughts. He turned his gaze to Patty, could see she would be a looker like mom. He blinked rapidly. Questioned whether he should alter his formula, include married women to his prey. It would add layers of complexity but would expand his possible targets. The possibility of broader horizons composed Vincente.

Looking at this budding adolescent made him recall his most painful childhood humiliation, the event that forged his ritual. While Vincente gave Monica his canned spiel, he drifted mentally to his youth. Liane Angell was the first attractive girl to ever pay him notice. She attended a private girl's school, Villa Goretti, the sister school to his St John's Prep. Vincente was in sophomore year, the academic star of his grade. He particularly excelled in math and science. Who would have guessed that the comely Liane Angell was also a whiz in the same subjects? They met when both schools sponsored a science fair. Each won awards as the best from their school. After the award ceremony, he remembered her giggling friends who pointed at him. When she wandered over to congratulate him, he expected the worst, but Liane was nice. An unlikely bond formed.

He never noticed her friends sneaking peaks as they chatted the next day after school. Unlike other girls he met, Liane said he was "interesting." She remarked on his voice. "You could be on radio, Vincente. Every word is so clear, it's very unique." Vincente blushed. He learned Liane was a wealthy girl, lived in the posh section of Drexel Heights. Although he didn't live nearby, she was only a few blocks off the ubiquitous trolley lines. After a few awkward failures at asking for a date, Vincente finally got the nerve to make the attempt. Asked if he could buy her an ice cream cone after school. To his delight she agreed but was disappointed her silly friends came along.

As they stood in line for the cone, Liane said, "We're having a party in a few weeks, do you want to come with me?" Oddly, the other girls chuckled. Liane grinned but seemed to ignore them. Vincente nodded yes, like an obedient puppy.

That perfect day got better. Liane asked if he wanted to ride home with her and the girlfriends. He eagerly agreed. The only trouble was it involved riding the subway and risking bumping into the thugs that persecuted him freshman year. He hadn't ridden that line directly after school for almost a year. He hoped they were no longer a threat. They walked to the subway. Vincente was vigilant, eyes darting left and right for danger. He held his breath, had a hard time talking to Liane, worried. He hoped she didn't notice his fear. But his fortune had turned. All went well. The punks were no longer around. Their first date was wondrous. She patted him on the head as they said goodbye. That first touch kept him company on the long trek to his decrepit neighborhood.

Tuesdays became their routine day to ride home together. But the giggling gaggle of friends was always there. He did his best to ignore them, was bewitched by Liane. Time seemed to stand still when they were together. He was encouraged when she said, "All the other boys I know think I'm an egghead."

Vincente could hardly breath. He wanted to say that she was a literal angel, that her last name was no accident. That she was straight from heaven. But he gulped out, "I think you're perfect." This brought a howl of laughter from her friends. Liane shushed them but was grinning as she did it.

Vincente was embarrassed, recovered as soon as she patted his oddly shaped head. "Just ignore them, they're immature." He wondered if she was ashamed of him but kept the dour thought to himself. He would give her whatever time she wanted. He was certain that Liane Angell would one day become his wife.

Some people are not destined for happy endings. Bad luck followed Vincente like a hungry dog. He was so taken with Liane that he never noticed being tracked. One of the malevolent punks from the subway noticed him riding blissfully with the pretty girl. It puzzled the punk. How could a little pussy like that get such a pretty girl? The next day he told his gang what he'd seen. The gang leader remembered how they'd stripped Vincente and pissed all over him.

He thought for a few minutes, "This time we'll do it right. That little shithead ain't gonna be dating that honey after we get through with him." The gang waited at the subway the rest of the week, but Vincente never showed. They continued the vigilance and patience was rewarded. The following Tuesday they spotted Vincente and a few girls riding the subway and trolley, completely unaware they were being stalked. The gang stayed far in the background, making certain they knew exactly how their quarry behaved. The gang leader was depraved but also cunning, street smart.

The following Tuesday, Vincente and Liane walked to her house. It was the only time they were alone since her friends stayed on the trolley to their stop. It was early November. Daylight was almost gone as they walked to her door. He got his coveted goodbye pat. Entranced, Vincente walked home dreamily. He always cut through Carlington Cemetery, the closest route towards toward his gloomy house. After he hopped the stonewall circling the cemetery, he suddenly spotted the four thugs who tormented him last year. The biggest one had a feral grin. "Remember us?" Before he answered, they tackled him, stripped Vincente naked, and tied his arms and ankles together. The bandana stuffed in his mouth kept him quiet. Vincente struggled hard, but soon became exhausted, went completely limp as the thugs lifted him, carried him toward their goal.

Decades later, he could still see the look of horror on Liane's face as she and her parents answered the doorbell, found him bound to the wooden pillar that supported their front porch. The perverted thugs weren't satisfied with tying him buck-naked to his girlfriend's entranceway. Vincente met his future in-laws for the first time while tied spread-eagle to their porch, his ass facing them with a huge candy cane stuck in his rectum. Scotch taped to his back was a sign with *THE CANDY ASS* in bold letters.

Although her parents helped him get free and covered him with a blanket, he knew it would be hard to overcome this first meeting. But he knew that kind Liane would empathize. He waited after school next day. Liane and her posse were chatting as she spotted him.

She darted at him, fire in her eyes. "Don't you know I was just jerking you around? You were my winning ticket to Villa Goretti's 'ugliest date contest.' I can't play the charade any longer. You make me sick. Get lost."

At first Vincente was devastated, heartbroken. Something snapped inside his puerile mind that day. He plotted to get even with those who consistently betrayed him—beautiful heartless women, just like his mother.

DYLAN'S PITCH

I called Chloe, told her I was coming over to discuss something with her that might sound crazy. That made her laugh, which was still a rare event, a nice sound. She promised to listen with an open mind. Her roommate Elaine answered after one doorbell ring. She looked at me sternly, "Chloe told me what you said. You won't say anything that will upset her, will you? She's made such great progress."

I held up my hands. "What I want is to catch this sick bastard. But I need her help. I don't think she'll fully recover till we put the piece of scum behind bars for good."

Elaine's look softened. "Well, then, you'll have my full support." After a few seconds, "I think you're right about getting completely better. She won't even discuss the attack with me. She just shuts down, so I gave up trying. I think she's pretending it never happened, but out of nowhere sometimes I see her agitated, like she's reliving that night. It makes me so sad."

Chloe had apparently overheard us from the living room. "Don't I get a say in this?"

Seizing the moment, I began my sales pitch. I told her about the other victims, all within a few miles from here. She started off very calm, but I could see her breathing more rapidly as my facts unfolded. I stopped talking, walked over and took her hand. "Chloe, it's going to be all right. You have to hear me through. I think I can catch this bastard." She started to shake her head, but I held her hands more firmly. "You have my word, I will catch him. You have to trust me."

Her breathing got shallower, she nodded, "Okay, I'll listen." I continued to explain what other patterns I'd found. That the women were all attractive, all early forties and divorced. I hit the punch line about the vastly different descriptions.

I shook my head. "There is no way this is a gang thing. It's got to be one person who either wears disguises or somehow clouds the victim's perception of him." I stopped talking. Chloe didn't respond, but I could see her thinking. Had I broken through her barrier?

I didn't want to lose momentum. I pulled out my map of where the attacks took place. Pointing at my circle, "As you can see, Drexel Heights is dead center, not far from right here." I let that sink in. "I think all the victims encountered this maniac at some common place. What I'm trying to piece together is what place or person all of you have in common." Her brow wrinkled, I could see her thinking. Continuing, "If we can narrow down the possibilities then I think we can catch him." Chloe's eyes were wide open. Hopeful? I went on. "From my last case, I learned that psychos like this have huge egos, they think they're smarter than everyone else, invincible." I let her consider that for a few seconds. "But that hubris is exactly what gets them caught. They think they won't make mistakes but that leads to carelessness." I paused for effect. "And that's when I'll find a clue that will put him away forever." By now even Elaine was nodding enthusiastically.

To lighten the moment some, "So, when I catch him, do you want me to beat him to a pulp first or hang him upside down for a few hours till the cops lock him up?"

I could see my joke went over their head. "Just kidding ladies, I will smack him around some, but then let the cops do their job, okay?"

Now Elaine was smiling. "I do like that beating into pulp idea, now that you mention it."

Chloe looked at me intently, "Just put him away forever."

I looked back just as firmly, "Count on it. I won't stop till he's behind bars." I closed the meeting saying that Merlano was going to speak with another victim, Miriam Keller, to see if she would be willing to meet with you and me. Chloe was nodding, so I added, "And then maybe we get in contact with the other victims, using the power of your group to help me find the clue we need to bust this." I walked away from Chloe's house hoping I wasn't delusional. Optimism doesn't solve cases, hard work does. And I was willing to do the work.

NUT

John "Nut" O'Hanlon was a force of nature. He was six-foot-three, weighed about 230 pounds but looked almost slim, panther-like, all muscle and sinew. When you looked at the intensity in his blue eyes, you realized he was no one to mess with. Between freshman and sophomore year in high school he grew into the greatest wrestler in Pennsylvania history. He would have been the Olympic champion except his passion to enter the Green Berets and fight in Vietnam prevented that from happening. Since the time Nut was a kid, and abused by his alcoholic father, he had dreamed of fighting for America, and freeing the world from bullies. Despite an Ivy League intellect, Nut entered the Green Berets after high school, and rapidly rose through the ranks to his current captain level. His language skills and brilliant mind led to inclusion into an elite unit in Nam that investigated corruption, whether internal or foreign. Through random chance, Nut encountered his childhood pal, Dylan, in Quang Tri, Vietnam, while investigating the case that ultimately led to Percy Price's incarceration.

Although they got Percy jailed for attacking Dylan and breaking another MP's leg, he was never convicted of the murder and rape of a Vietnamese couple. And they never definitively linked him to treason while part of a traitorous group who stole weapons and munitions. The other criminals in this ring hid money in offshore Bermuda accounts. All their money was recovered. But there was no trace of Percy hiding his share. Although the army lost interest, Nut never gave up. After intense research, he learned Percy was married to a woman from South Carolina, with the last name of Smith. He visited the Bermuda bank involved with the other traitors and put an alert on every account with the last name of Smith. The bank had been embarrassed to be caught harboring money for these war criminals and was now cooperative. Especially after Nut paid them a personal visit. While not noble, the bank knew fighting with the US Army was bad business. Saying no to the imposing Captain O'Hanlon seemed unwise. He had a look.

Years passed quietly, when out of the blue, Nut got a call from his bank source, Herbert Rollins. The proper banker said, "You asked us to notify you if any of the flagged Smith accounts made any large withdrawals. It turns out G. Smith has just asked to withdraw two-hundred and fifty-thousand dollars." Nut heard the banker clear his throat. "By the way, the "G" stands for Gardenia, as in the flower. She came in today and asked for the funds in cash, all twenty-dollar bills. All her paperwork was in order. Per our agreement with you, we told her it would take twenty-four hours to clear her withdrawal request and get that amount of cash. She just nodded agreement, said she would be back next morning." Nut thought rapidly, unfortunately he was on assignment in Japan, and would never be back in time to intercept Gardenia Smith in Bermuda.

After a short pause, Nut told the banker to find out as much about Gardenia Smith as he could without arousing suspicion. The banker started to mumble about this being against bank protocols, but Nut shut him down.

"Herbert, do you remember me? Do you think I'm the sort to make idle requests? I'm telling you to find out as much as you can, things like where she stayed in Bermuda, when she was leaving, where did she fly from, that sort of thing. Then we'll be able to get a better idea where she lives, and if she's going back to the same place. This is a matter of life and death. Gardenia Smith may not herself be involved, but her husband is a vicious murderer and is after someone very important to me. Have I made myself clear?" Before the befuddled banker could answer, "I'm going to ask you once again. Find out everything you can about Gardenia Smith. Have her followed but don't get spotted. Make certain you get some solid intel. I'll be there in person in a day or so and will be in to see you. Are we at an understanding?"

The banker, now almost breathless, whined, "Understood." Nut hung up forcefully, like he was smacking him.

As threatened, Nut arrived in Bermuda two days later, went right to the bank to see Herbert Rollins. The diminutive baker stared at the hulking Captain O'Hanlon, as he loomed in the doorway. Forcing a smile, Herbert said, "I think I have some good information for you, Captain. Ms. Smith informed me she lodged at the Hamilton Princess during her stay. The manager is a cousin. When Ms. Smith checked in, she gave Charleston, South Carolina as her residence. Her street address is here for you."

For the first time in forty-eight hours, Nut smiled. "That is very good work Mr. Rollins, very good work. That is exactly what I need." Nut looked at the information. Gardenia's address was 605 King Street, which she also listed as her place of employment, a laundry business. He rubbed his chin, absorbing the information.

As Nut was leaving, the banker added another piece of information. "My cousin had her watched, said she was accompanied by a Negro gentleman." That bit of information froze Nut. It couldn't be coincidence, had to be Percy after his money. He hurried to the airport, called his contact in Parris Island. He made plans to be picked up at the Savannah Airport. It was time to hunt.

*

Nut loved Charleston. He used to visit whenever he had leave from Parris Island. The drastic difference from military life was refreshing. There was elegance to the city, a true bastion of Southern gentility. It gave a peek into the simpler life of long ago. The parcel of land between the Ashley and Copper River was founded in 1670 and named in honor of Charles II of England. It soon grew into the cultural and architectural center of South Carolina, famous for beautiful gardens and courtyards. But this trip would not be a cultural visit. His instinct said Percy had returned home, and finally made the trip to Bermuda to cash out his stash from his treasonous activity in Vietnam. What he wasn't sure of was if he was going undercover with all that money, living out his days in comfort, or going for Dylan. His gut gave him the answer. And that was why he was on high alert.

He entered Charleston on Calhoun Street, followed to the intersection with King Street. The map said to take a left. Rather than go directly to Gardenia's address, Nut decided to cruise around the neighborhood to get his bearings. He was used to hunting human targets. It was best to anticipate escape route in case something went awry. With the psychotic Percy, nothing would be easy. He drove up and down King Street and studied all the intersecting streets. He always went by the principle: how would I get away? Satisfied he understood the terrain, Nut parked the car two blocks away. Fortunately, the Citadel wasn't too far away, so a man in uniform was a common sight. But a man of his size got noticed no matter how much he tried to blend. The combination of his extreme musculature and cat-like grace made him pop out. People's eyes got wide as he approached. He looked like Captain America. Realizing this, he stayed on the shaded side of Calhoun, minimizing his visibility.

Always attuned to his environment, he noticed three large guys loitering on the corner. His plan was to circle King Street from this direction but decided to alter course to avoid encountering anyone who might be a witness if things got messy with Percy. He turned back toward Calhoun, cut down an alley that would get him back on track. He heard them before he saw them. One of the punks emerged from a walkway, blocked Nut's path. He had taken a shortcut through one of the courtyards. His swarthy buddies quickly fell in beside him. The biggest thug pointed at Nut, "Ya'll one of them sissy boys from Citadel? Like ta play soldier and such? Didn't know they let gorillas join such a fancy school. Standards must be a droppin'.''

His smaller buddy added, "Shame ta mess up that pretty uniform, huh? Ya'll might have ta do some extra push-ups, er some shit."

The third guy added, "Bet the big gorilla is yella as those bananas he eats, huh?" They all chuckled, proud of their taunts.

As they moved closer, Nut put up his hand, "What's the closest hospital, fellas?"

That stopped them, the smallest punk answered without thinking, "Roper Hospital's is aroun' the corner."

Nut pointed at the leader, "That's convenient. Your two pals won't have far to carry you after I break your leg." The three guys froze. Nut continued, "Here's what I suggest, gentleman. Turn around and go about your business, or if you take one step closer, I'm going to put my size-twelve government issued boot solidly into his femur. And if you two morons try to intervene, I'll break your shoulders. By the way, they are all very painful injuries that take forever to heal." Nut settled into attack position as the morons let his warning sink in. Unfortunately, they made the wrong choice. The big punk hadn't taken a full step before Nut closed on him and swept his left foot with a lethal kick. You could hear the big bone break. The crunch was sickening, like a tree limb snapping in a windstorm. As the big punk fell to the ground, his buddies made a smarter choice. They ran like hell, never turning around to make the suggested trip to

Roper Hospital. Nut breathed in and exhaled, stood upright, and resumed his hunt for Percy without a wrinkle on his uniform.

He exited the alley, made a right turn. This section of King Street was once rundown but was being gentrified. All types of boutique stores had popped up. Gardenia Smith's laundry business was one of the nicest storefronts on the block. Large urns full of flowers guarded her meticulous entrance. The large front window flashed a neon sign: *GARDENIA'S LAUNDRY, PERFECT EVERY TIME.* When Nut had driven by earlier to case the area, he slowed to a crawl, waited till a customer had entered, so he could see who manned the front desk. Each time a spry black woman helped the customer with their order. On foot this time, Nut walked by the entrance, made sure there were no customers. He glanced inside; the black woman was well dressed, neatly groomed. She gave the appearance of someone who would do her work meticulously. He closed on his prey. When Gardenia looked up and saw the enormous soldier enter, her eyes gave her away. Her look said, "OH NO!"

Seeing her unease, Nut raised his hand to his mouth, signaling her to be quiet. Gardenia had stopped breathing. Getting close to her, whispered, "Is he here?" Gardenia finally breathed, shook her head. Looking straight in her terrified eyes, "Where is he?" She started to pant, unable to answer. Nut reached out his massive hands, softly touched her shoulders, "I'm not here to hurt you. I'm here to take Percy back. This can go easy or go hard. His choice." And then he smiled, "I'll make certain you're protected. I know Percy can be vicious. You have nothing to worry about."

It took a few minutes, but Gardenia started to calm down. She looked at Nut, worry on her face. All she said was, "Then you don't know Percy. He ain't gonna fergive and ferget. He'll be comin' fer me." Nut stared at her, trying to read all the information. Gardenia was telling the truth as she saw it. Percy would kill her if she helped.

In response, Nut said, "I'm going to put Percy away forever." He added, "Or I'm going to kill him."

Gardenia walked over to the door and put the *CLOSED* sign up. They went to her office and talked for over an hour. Gardenia said she didn't know any details of what Percy had done to get locked up. She figured the money he sent home and deposited in Bermuda was dirty, but she didn't ask questions. She looked at Nut, "Percy ain't the kind ta answer questions." Nut realized that the cash he gave her allowed the escape from poverty. She looked at Nut, "I ain't no saint but ain't knows he killed anyone or stole from the army. I knows Percy be bad binness, but I spen' my whole life arounds that type. Bad be normal here abouts." Nut believed her. Most people in her condition just want to survive. Putting up with Percy once in a while on leave was her price for salvation. She looked at Nut solemnly, "Figured Percy be dead pretty early. Mens like him die young." She shook her head. "And thens I be free."

*

As Nut walked to his military vehicle, he assessed what he learned. Percy had taken all the money and left Charleston the same day after returning from Bermuda. All he told Gardenia was, "I'm goin' north. Gonna toast me some white bread." When Nut heard that phrase, he knew she was telling the truth. Percy always called Dylan, "white bread." Now Percy had enough cash to avoid detection. He could stay in beat down motels under fake names. Dives like that didn't check paperwork.

Percy was crazy, but was smart enough to take some time, do reconnaissance before going after Dylan. Percy was a sadist, would enjoy stalking Dylan. Make sure he caught him by surprise. Nut exhaled deeply, he had to warn Dylan, had to get to Philly right away. As he drove to the Charleston airport, Nut never knew that Gardenia had forgotten to mention some key information, how much Percy had changed. He'd gotten fat and sloppy, sported a huge Afro. He looked totally different from the clean-shaven, wiry sociopath he knew from Vietnam.

DYLAN

The call from Nut was like a perfect kick to the goobers. As I heard the fateful news my mind drifted. It had been almost two years since Percy escaped. As time passed, I tried to convince myself Percy had traveled to Mexico, or maybe back to Jamaica, blended in with the locals. Deep down, I knew Percy was unforgiving, was the type that got even. He blamed me for getting caught and jailed. Most of all, he remembered I almost killed him. Had beaten him one on one. Percy would need revenge for that. He prided himself on being the toughest. It would consume him. After my brief reverie, I said to Nut, "At least I can stop looking over my shoulder, stop wondering if and when. Now, I know he's coming and can be prepared."

I tried to talk Nut out of coming back, but deep down I wanted him there. Was relieved when Nut said succinctly, "I'll be there by dinnertime. Stop trying to talk me out of it. We're in this together. This is army business we should have finished in Nam." After a pause, "This is personal."

I hung up after making plans to pick up Nut at the airport. He was on an Allegheny Air flight. Locally people called it "Agony Airline," because that's how you felt after flying with them. I needed to allow plenty leeway retrieving Nut. Navigating the Philly Airport was always an ordeal. Somehow or the other, you'd encounter something unexpected along the way. Philly is a friendly city overall,

people you don't know always chatting you up on the
street. But the staff working at the airport didn't get the
memo on "brotherly love." I remember complaining to
the baggage clerk when my suitcase got a big chunk taken
out of it. The clerk looked at me, "Shit, man, that ain't
nothing. One dude last week had the whole side of his case
tore off. Looked like it'd been in a wood chipper. Ya
should a seen all his shit flying around on the carousel.
Some funny shit there."

With the pleasant airport journey to look forward to,
I turned my thoughts to Percy. I had to be ready, had
prepared for his return. Did my judo sessions with Jimmer
religiously. His dojo was thriving. Although Jimmer would
never admit it, it was mostly because I mentioned his
training center in the Bulletin as the reason I kicked the
serial murderer Sylvan's ass. I knew Jimmer appreciated
the notoriety. He never charged me for lessons.

When I thanked him for the generosity, he shrugged,
"You're the kind of kid people want to take a swipe at, just
for fun. Wouldn't be right if I didn't protect you some,
being neighbors and all growing up." In all modesty, I'd
gotten very good in judo. Sparring with numerous
opponents my size or larger had helped make it more real.
No one had beaten me in over a year. But Percy would be
different. He would fight to kill, no rules, no fair play. I
thought back to Vietnam when he stalked me. That made
me shiver. I picked up the phone. Called Jimmer, told him
I needed to amp up my practice. When he asked the cause,
I filled him in on Percy. All he said was, "We'll have you
ready."

I called Detective Merlano, told him I wanted to review the victim files again. Heard him exhale. "You are a tenacious bastard, Frazier. What the hell are you looking for this time?"

I did have an ulterior motive. I wanted him to call Miriam Keller to see if she would talk to Chloe, to catch him off-guard. "No offense, Frankie but you're not the brightest bulb in the lighting store. I assume you must have missed some vital information and want to catch that before your boss does. I mean, I'm a generous guy, and we do have a long history together. You can consider it my act of human kindness." Paused, "No need to thank me or get all gushy."

Merlano was quiet for a few seconds. "Come on by. My mom always taught me to be nice to retarded people." He hung up abruptly. I chuckled all the way to McCormick's deli. I needed a juicy Italian hoagie to make me forget about Percy. Plus, I wanted some pungent garlic and oregano on my breath as I greeted the witty Merlano.

There was a specific point I was looking for in the files. I didn't want to discuss much till I was certain it was relevant. One thing that helped catch Sylvan was keeping an active listing of every fact about the victims. Following that past practice, I kept scanning what I listed about this psycho and the multiple victims. As I did that, it triggered something I'd learned about serial killers. There wasn't much information about these demented humans, but one fact was consistent in every text. A true serial killer has a hunger that can't be stopped. Many of them are extremely smart. They can act normally for most of the time. But eventually that lust to kill becomes overpowering. Each of these sociopaths had an internal clock. Once the alarm went off, they became a savage beast. Like a cornered animal, they went for the kill. Remembering that point, I let my mind drift on this predator. Were there any similarities between a serial killer and this lunatic? And that's when it occurred to me. I had never noted the exact date of the attacks. Was there a pattern?

Desk Sgt. Bonner greeted me as I entered Merlano's police station. "We'll ain't it the funny guy again. Frankie warned me ya was comin' in. He said ta put ya in a holdin' cell if ya said any bad shit about him."

I threw out my hands. "If I told you Frankie used to dress up like Roy Rogers all the time in high school, pretended he rode a broom called Trigger to piano lessons, would that get me in trouble? I mean, he did go to psychotherapy for a couple years, said they fixed him. At least that's what he told me. But my guess is he doesn't go around sharing much personal information. I think the shrink told him that he needed to have a more subdued fantasy life. That people weren't as open minded as you and me."

Sgt. Bonner got a big grin on his face. "Wait till I tell the guys at coffee break. Thinkin' about that hairy bastard Merlano dressed like a cowboy will kill everybody."

Just then Merlano wandered out, looked at the smiling Bonner, pointed at me. "Did that asshole say anything I should know about?"

I jumped in, "I just told the Sgt. what a good dresser

you used to be way back when." Bonner kept his head down, not wanting to rat me out.

Merlano lead me to his office, told me to take the files to the conference room. I figured I better ask him about calling the victims before Bonner went on coffee break. "I got another favor to ask, Frankie." He frowned at me, said nothing. "I want you to call Miriam Keller, see if she'll talk to Chloe about what happened. Tell her if they talk to each other, maybe some clue might pop up. I know I'm pushing it, but maybe you should call all the victims, tell them about Chloe, that she wants to talk with them. That her doctor said she needed their help to heal. Kind of like a support group thing." Merlano squinted at me, trying to decide if I had some other motive. Countering that, "After I have Chloe call Miriam, I'll have her mention she's bringing me along, that I've helped her a lot. I'm thinking if I listen in, might pick up on something we've missed. Pretty sure Chloe will do that for me. And then we'll call the others." As Merlano's frown got deeper, I added, "There's something here that might lead to the attacker, but we just can't see it. It's eating me up that this asshole is getting ready to strike again."

Merlano's face softened, "I'll call. But no funny business."

I organized the crime files in a neat pile. Took out my yellow note pad and lifted the first file, Gillian Bender. She was attacked eight years ago. I decided to make a listing of the victim's name, age, marital status, date of attack and exact description of the attacker. I filled in Gillian's details. Remembered to look for the mention of something sweet or minty again in the other reports. The next victim was Cynthia Sutter. Her attack was almost seven years ago, wrote down the remaining data. I flipped open the file for Margot Palmieri. She was more current, just over three years ago. Next was Ginger Spellman, even more current, just about two and a half years earlier. The last files were Miriam Keller and Chloe. I wrote down the information. Without realizing it, I had started to sweat, was breathing in pants. These poor ladies had their lives ruined by this sadistic bastard and I'd written it down so simply, like compiling a grocery list. I got up from the table, walked to the window, tried to gather myself.

I stared at Appleford Estate across the street, a beautiful arboretum and bird sanctuary. Thought about the incredible beauty it contained, and then wondered how such unspeakable evil could co-exist in the same area. I watched people walking mindlessly in this lovely nature preserve, peaceful walking trails, flower gardens and fountains. Would one of them become the next victim? Have their perfect life ruined by such malevolence? I realized that train of thought didn't help calm me down. I turned, walked back to the desk, read through my list. I flipped to a new yellow sheet, arranged every victim chronologically. I had already determined they lived in close proximity to each other. What else was similar? I circled the months and exact dates. Now that I had it laid out, I noticed that Gillian Bender and Cynthia Sutter's attack was actually less than a year apart. Looked at Margot Palmieri and Ginger Spellman. They were also less than a year apart. Before I verified it, I was already certain what I'd find with Chloe and Miriam Keller's dates.

I went from the conference room looking for
Merlano. His office was empty, so I went to Sgt. Bonner,
asked if he had one of those calendars that went back for
years. He could tell from the look on my face that I wasn't
in the mood to bust more balls about Merlano, so he sifted
around his desk, scanned his huge desk calendar that
tracked all activities for the police department. He nodded,
"This goes back ten years and goes ten years to the future.
Whatcha want it for?" I asked if I could borrow it for a
few minutes, didn't give him any reason. The amiable Sgt.
shook his head, "No problem, don't spill coffee on it er'
nothin'. Okay?"

I took the book to the conference room, scanned the
dates, and confirmed my theory. The oldest two cases were
almost exactly nine months apart. The next pair of victims
was also separated by nine months. Sure enough, Miriam
Keller and Chloe were attacked nine months from each
other. I flipped back to Chloe's date. If my theory were
correct, this lunatic would be after another poor woman in
a few weeks. Said out loud, "This asshole is on human
pregnancy cycle. What the hell does that mean?"

I returned the book to Sgt. Bonner, asked if there was
a way to get hold of Merlano fast. He needed to hear what
I discovered, wanted his input on what I was thinking.
Bonner said he'd radio him, to wait in his conference room
until he heard back. I ambled off, went to my yellow pad
to verify something else I learned on the previous visit.
Made note of the victim's exact words. Sure enough, each
victim gave vastly different descriptions and ages. But each
told the police clearly, they would never find the attacker,
"he was too smart or too careful" or some verbiage to that

effect. That last point nailed down my earlier observation. Somehow this pervert masked his identity and convinced or shocked them into believing finding him was hopeless. I stared out the window. Let that percolate. How did he do that? I kept asking myself how he altered his appearance? Did he wear disguises, or did he terrify them so badly they couldn't remember him? Was there another missing variable? As I'd already learned, witnesses to crimes are almost totally unreliable.

Bonner popped into the room, "I got Merlano on the line. Ya can take it in his office." I got right to the point. His answer summed up my feelings. "Shit, that can't be coincidence." I mentioned the "never catch him" consistency from victim to victim. Told him that we were dealing with one serial criminal, and that somehow, he manipulated his victims about his appearance. And then hit him with, "How can we catch him before he does it again? If I'm right, we only have a few weeks." His silence didn't make me confident. Finally, "There must be a common place where he interacts with these women. They are all in their forties and living alone, all divorced. Does he have something against divorced women? Is there some support group in Delaware County where he finds them, then stalks them till the right moment?" I didn't have any answers, stayed quiet.

Merlano ended with, "I'll put some manpower on this, see if we can shake a clue loose. I'll keep you updated. In the meantime, if you get any other ideas, yell." When he hung up, I sat in the empty office for a while, but nothing came. It pissed me off.

PHILLY AIRPORT

The unmistakable form of Nut exited the Agony Airline plane. The stewardess standing beside me stared at him as he ducked under the ramp doorway. You could almost read what she was thinking: he looks like Superman, thought he was just a cartoon superhero? My bigger-than-life buddy was no fictional character. He was a real-life fighting machine, a marvel of nature. Even before his growth spurt, he was freakishly strong, a fearless fighter. I said to the stewardess, "Don't worry, I'll get him in his cage pretty soon. The circus doesn't let him wander around without his keeper." She recoiled a little, so I smiled, "Only kidding, he's harmless, he just looks wacked. I've been his handler since birth, I know what buttons to push." She took a deep breath, held it as he walked up.

Nut reached where we were standing, gave one of his infrequent grins. "I'm glad to see you're still punctual, some things never change. You could always set your clock by your arrivals, never too early, always seconds before the promised time."

I nodded, "Wasn't something I had much choice in. Someone had to manage the other knuckleheads we grew up with. I mean, the zoo animals had to be kept on a schedule, or they'd go ape shit. Right?" He grabbed me around the neck, squeezed till it hurt, his idea of a hug, not big on normal shows of affection. I turned as we left, the stewardess finally started to breathe.

As we walked toward the parking area, I asked

questions about Percy. Nut shook his head, "Not here, you never know who's listening."

If I wasn't nervous before, that made me jumpy. I looked over, "Thanks for making me feel worse. You need work on your bedside manner. Marcus Welby you ain't."

We maneuvered through the bustling airport. I noticed no one seemed to get the basic concept of walking on the right side of the aisle. People mindlessly collided. This was one of those times when Nut's menacing appearance helped. Once people spotted him, they moved away. I could see Nut was completely focused. He was studying his environment. He had done that since a kid. I recalled when we slept out in my backyard tent one summer after seventh grade. The advice he gave me then was the same I got on my way to Nam. "Never relax, always plan what you'll do if the shit hits the fan. Always have an exit route. Hesitation gets you dead." Nut had a horrible family life. I never found out how bad till we were seniors in High School. People always thought our friendship was an odd pairing. We were totally different but had been inseparable since kids. He liked my sense of humor, my ability to joke in tense situation, the calmness of my family. Even though he never said it, my home was a resting place from his tempestuous home.

I parked in the cheapest lot, so we had to ride a dumpy parking van to the remote spot. As we drove in the dilapidated van, Nut settled down. He looked at me deadpan, "Could you have picked a worse spot to park? Did you inherit your dad's trait of driving to Timbuktu to save a dime?"

Not to be outdone, "My dad would have parked at the free lot at the Spectrum and taken the free shuttle they run to the airport. Count yourself lucky, I'm a spendthrift by comparison." Nut shook his head, frowned his version of a grin. The van finally came to the dingy lot. We hopped out, ambled to my crappy olive green Chevy.

Nut eyed it skeptically. "Still driving the same junker, huh? I thought catching that serial killer got you famous, would have helped your business. Guess not."

I gave the real answer. "When I drive into these craphole neighborhoods, the bad guys think I'm worse off that they are, don't mess with me. Maybe even feel sorry for me. Honor among thieves is alive and well in the city of brotherly love."

On the drive home, Nut filled me in on what he learned about Percy. "He had his wife establish the number accounts in Bermuda. She fell under the radar since she was registered as G. Smith, hard to pick up. The G turned out to be Gardenia, like the flower. She never took Percy's name after they married. She didn't ask many questions about where the money came from. She was from a poor family, had nothing growing up, so when Percy gave her the cash to start a laundry business, that was all she wanted to know. It was her ticket out of poverty. I can't say I blame her." I kept my eyes on the road, commented, "Plus she must at least have some screws loose if she married Percy."

Thought about that, "And if she didn't know he was loco, I'll bet she found out fast. Probably scared to death of him. Did whatever he told her." I could feel Nut nod agreement. Percy viewed the world through a very dark lens.

Nut told me he was staying with his mother while here. I pulled up to his house, wasn't too far from my parents. We agreed to meet later next morning to discuss Nut's strategy. He wouldn't give me any details, except: "I'll have eyes on you, but you'll never see me."

I scrunched my brow, "Better shower tonight. I might not see you, but I'll smell you." He swatted me.

As he got his duffle bag, "By the way, thanks for checking in on mom. She told me you drop by every few weeks. She said you didn't have to, but I can tell she likes it. My brother still lives with her, but they see each other at work so much it's nice to see a new face."

I waved him off, a "happy to do it." I liked Nut's mom. Much of her married life had been a living hell, was glad things were better. I waited till she answered his knock. Smiled watching as he picked her up, gave the most massive hug imaginable and carried her inside. She was the only one Nut never cheated on with his affection.

PERCY

It wasn't hard for Percy to find Frazier, or "Dylan" as everyone called him. When he suckered the assholes in Leavenworth into believing he was rehabilitated, he often worked in the administration office, had access to army records. Percy shook his head: a chump was born every second. It took months, but he finally was left alone long enough to research Thomas "Dylan" Frazier's file. He memorized the Drexel Heights address. He recalled this as he exited the plane at Philadelphia's bustling airport. Compared to the sedate airport in Charleston, this place was a madhouse. That pleased him, just another face in the crowd. He went to a newsstand in the terminal, bought a map, asked for directions to the car rental lot. Percy veered to a nearby bench, studied the map. Drexel Heights was just outside the western edge of Philadelphia, not more than 10 miles or so from the city. Percy looked to see how far away the airport was from Drexel Heights. His plan was to leave Philadelphia immediately after killing Frazier. He had already checked, daily flights to Puerto Rico, his place to disappear.

The car rental operation was apparently a couple blocks outside the terminal. He took his time maneuvering the airport, studied where to find the terminal he would leave by after killing Frazier. There would be no time for hesitation. He planned things carefully. Once outside, he saw signs for the rental car area, and started off. The man at the car rental counter was friendly, very helpful. He was apparently a veteran, spotted the Vietnam service patch on

Percy's army jacket. He dressed as a soldier to blend in with the myriad of soldiers always pouring through this airline hub. The friendly guy asked, "Where was ya stationed? Me, I done a couple tours in Pleiku. Now thems were some bad-ass times. I ain't even bullshittin' ya."

Percy decided to be more forthcoming, hoping to pump the guy for information. "Done most of my time in Quang Tri. Think Pleiku was bad? Ya shoulda seen Quang Tri. Was closer to Hanoi than Saigon. Some heavy shit went down, I'm tellin' ya." Added, "Sure is nice ta be home, huh? Fuckin' Nam could really do ya a job."

His fellow veteran nodded, "Ain't that the truth." Percy asked about Drexel Heights, places to stay. The black agent nodded, "Ain't many brothers in Drexel Heights. Might look ta stay in Lansdowne or Sharon Heights, not very far away and lotsa home boys around." Percy got another map from his new buddy. The map of Delaware County had street level detail for Drexel Heights and confirmed that Lansdowne was close. Percy left the rental lot, began his blood mission.

thinking. No one needed to convince me Percy was smarter than he let on. Couple that with street smarts and you had a formidable enemy. Nut broke the silence, "Dylan, can you wait outside for a couple minutes? I have some other business to discuss with the Colonel." When Dylan looked at him skeptically, Nut said, "Army business. Need to know only." Reluctantly, Dylan left them alone. After he closed the door, Nut turned to Colonel Lynam, said in a low voice, "Here's what else we're going to do."

DYLAN

Nut came out ten minutes later. Before I could probe him, he waved me off, "I'm staying here for a bit. Colonel Lynam is getting me a civilian car to use. And I'm going to meet the men he's assigning for duty, make sure they pass muster. I'll be in touch later today." And then he was off, not waiting for a reply. As I walked down Broad Street to get my car, something hit me. The drill Sgt. called the new troops "candy ass." That randomly triggered the image of poor Chloe being molested, the idle comments in two police report of a sweet or minty smell. Is that a clue, a key part of these attacks? Or is it something entirely different? Nothing else popped to mind, but I believed the sweet odor was relevant. Had to be of some meaning. After being traumatized, why would those ladies remember that odor? Grabbed my notebook, highlighted it with a big circle on the fact sheet. I got no other flash of insight.

Stopped at a pay phone to check in with Chloe at work. Merlano had gotten permission from Miriam Keller, and Chloe was to call her last night. She answered on the first ring, "Chloe Zubrisky, industrial relations, how can I help you?"

Her voice was enthusiastic, firm and confident. "Well, aren't you the model of efficiency. It's nice to hear you sound so chipper."

She anticipated why I called. "Miriam agreed to meet with me tonight. I told her I was bringing you along, and that you were helping the police to solve the case. She

NUT'S PLAN

Up early next morning, Nut evaluated his strategy, concluded that managing Dylan would be hard. His gung-ho friend would not like the idea of being followed covertly, so Nut decided to withhold some parts of the plan, misinform him of the real approach. His mom had already left for the day. He couldn't believe the change in her, no longer worn and bedraggled. Some of her youthful beauty had returned. There was a smile on her face, something he rarely remembered from his childhood. They had talked for hours last night. He didn't tell her about Percy. She had enough to deal with getting her nightmares to go away. "Just here to see my beautiful mom," was how he explained his visit. She offered to stay home from work, but Nut said he had some work to do with the local army location. "Training sessions, that kind of thing."

Nut heard a car pull up, looked at his watch, almost eight am. Dylan hadn't changed, less than two minutes early. He bounded out of his front door, looked left and right, saw nothing out of place, moved down the walkway. Dylan yelled, "Stop the Inspector Clouseau shit, let's get going. Some of us actually have work to do."

Nut hopped in the front seat. Without a hello, "One more favor to ask. Drive me to 401 North Broad. I'm meeting Colonel Lynam. He's going to help in the search." That address brought chills down Dylan's spine. It was the location Philadelphians reported to for the start of military life, the fun times at Fort Dix for basic training. His

Vietnam tour got him into this predicament with Percy. But Dylan was actually happy for a chance to see Colonel Lynam. When he returned from Nam, he suddenly figured out Percy's treasonous scheme. The Colonel believed his wild story, tracked down Nut in Nam, who arrested Percy and the others. This sad history ran through Dylan's mind as they drove.

He nodded at Nut, "Colonel Lynam will be glad to see me. Always felt I had a special place in that flinty heart of his."

Without shifting his gaze, Nut winced, "I think the Colonel's exact words were 'you're like a hemorrhoid that won't respond to treatment'."

Enjoying Nut's rare wisecrack, Dylan replied, "So, what's the plan funny man?"

Nut paused, seemed hesitant. Looking straight ahead, "Some of the plan I'll tell you. Some I won't. We can't have you acting unnatural." Caught his phrasing, "At least more unnatural than is usual for you." He made an attempt at a smile, "Anyway, here's a quick summary, rather than wait around for Percy, we're going to hunt him. Try to anticipate what he'll do. Obviously, he'll wait to catch you off-guard. You already told me your normal routines, but I'll track you for a day or so to make sure there's nothing else. I'll post Colonel Lynam's MP's in disguise at likely locations to watch for Percy. Rather than sitting still, we'll keep them moving, so they aren't obvious." Listening to this made Dylan anxious, he wasn't one to sit and wait. But he wanted to evaluate this approach before arguing. He made a mental note to get Jimmer to include "sneak attacks" to his judo training.

Said to Nut, "Sounds smart. I think Percy will look for a place where I'm relaxed." He thought more, "Like when I get a hoagie at McCormick's Deli for a late-night snack." Dylan shook his head, "I hadn't even thought about that, I do that at least three times a week."

Nut, an icy stare, "You never mentioned that. You have to be more thorough."

They parked the car on Broad Street, ambled into the military building. They spotted a fresh troop of recruits being greeted by a drill sergeant. The furious NCO marched before the line of young men. "Now, you are about the sorriest bunches of pussies I've seen in a long time. Are you sure you aren't enlisting at Arthur Murray's dance studio, and not in this man's army? Let me repeat, you are one worthless collection of maggot sucking pieces of shit. I can't wait to whip your candy asses into shape."

Dylan turned to Nut, "Ah, the good old days. Brings back such nice memories of humiliation."

Nut laughed for the first time all morning. Added, "He's just doing his job. First you break them down and then build them up again. Then they're stronger and tougher. There's no place for the tender hearted in the army. The world's a bad place." Dylan could tell he was talking about Percy.

Colonel Lynam wandered into the open hall, spotted them, and walked over. Doing something completely unexpected, Dylan gave him a crisp salute. Lynam looked at him warily, waiting for a quip. "I know I'm a hopeless smart-ass, Colonel, but Nut told me you're helping, and I really appreciate it. Like to think I can take care of Percy myself, but I'll take all the help I can get. Maybe this time we can put him away forever."

Colonel Lynam's face was stone. "He'll never see the light of day this time. If they ever had any doubt about his guilt, this escape fixed that. Life sentence, no question." Nut was standing beside the Colonel as he made this prediction. On Nut's face was a different type of expression. Fury? Hatred? Whatever it was did not bode well for Percy. Colonel Lynam turned, gestured for them to follow.

Nut spent the next half hour outlining Dylan's routine day, his plans for protection. When Nut mentioned Dylan's late-night deli runs, the Colonel had a unique take. "I'd do that every night from now on. Maybe park a little farther away than normal. That has to be the perfect time for Percy to hit—late at night, dark, nobody around, you're a little tired, a perfect time to strike. We'll get men out there today; reconnoiter the area. We'll anticipate his place of attack, set up a counter move." The Colonel paused, weighed what he'd just said, crinkled his brow, "I like it." Added, "Your other routine patterns are public. Not ideal for approach. Percy Price is a sociopath but he's cunning. I remember his file. He got high IQ scores in army tests even though not traditionally educated. He suckered all the doctors at Leavenworth. He'll strike when he has the best odds."

We sat still for a few minutes, no one talking, still

thinking. No one needed to convince me Percy was smarter than he let on. Couple that with street smarts and you had a formidable enemy. Nut broke the silence, "Dylan, can you wait outside for a couple minutes? I have some other business to discuss with the Colonel." When Dylan looked at him skeptically, Nut said, "Army business. Need to know only." Reluctantly, Dylan left them alone. After he closed the door, Nut turned to Colonel Lynam, said in a low voice, "Here's what else we're going to do."

DYLAN

Nut came out ten minutes later. Before I could probe him, he waved me off, "I'm staying here for a bit. Colonel Lynam is getting me a civilian car to use. And I'm going to meet the men he's assigning for duty, make sure they pass muster. I'll be in touch later today." And then he was off, not waiting for a reply. As I walked down Broad Street to get my car, something hit me. The drill Sgt. called the new troops "candy ass." That randomly triggered the image of poor Chloe being molested, the idle comments in two police report of a sweet or minty smell. Is that a clue, a key part of these attacks? Or is it something entirely different? Nothing else popped to mind, but I believed the sweet odor was relevant. Had to be of some meaning. After being traumatized, why would those ladies remember that odor? Grabbed my notebook, highlighted it with a big circle on the fact sheet. I got no other flash of insight.

Stopped at a pay phone to check in with Chloe at work. Merlano had gotten permission from Miriam Keller, and Chloe was to call her last night. She answered on the first ring, "Chloe Zubrisky, industrial relations, how can I help you?"

Her voice was enthusiastic, firm and confident. "Well, aren't you the model of efficiency. It's nice to hear you sound so chipper."

She anticipated why I called. "Miriam agreed to meet with me tonight. I told her I was bringing you along, and that you were helping the police to solve the case. She

immediately said it was hopeless." I heard Chloe inhale. She added, "It's funny. That is exactly what I think whenever you start asking questions." She went quiet.

I filled in the silence. "Chloe, I think that mindset is a clue. Don't spend any time worrying about it. That's my job and I'm all over it." We agreed I would pick her up at seven o'clock at night. I did mindless disability investigations the rest of the day, to kill time and earn money. All the sick people were legitimate, nothing slightly funny, no roof-climbing wizards with sprained backs. Too bad, I could use a reason to belt someone.

♦

I arrived at Chloe's that night, got there a couple minutes early, but delayed my doorbell ring till the appointed time. Nut had jabbed me that morning about my predictable punctuality. Habits are tough to break. While I walked Chloe to the car, thought: I better alter my patterns in case Percy trails me? No need to make it easier for him. I pledged right then to change, would start tomorrow. Shook my head, or would I? As we drove toward Miriam Keller's house, I told Chloe about all the St Dorothy nicknames. She chuckled when I told her I'd met Snot Vogelsong a few weeks ago at the movies, called him by that unsavory name. His girlfriend had looked at me funny. "Why did you call him Snot?"

Realizing that wasn't too flattering for her boyfriend,

I winged an answer. "Er, I didn't say Snot, I said, Slot." She frowned as I clarified, "Because of his cute dimple."

I explained to Chloe that Snot had no dimples, and this further mystified the babe. By now, I had Chloe laughing out loud. Was glad she was in a good frame of mind as we approached Miriam's door for our discussion.

Unlike the cautious Chloe when we first met, Miriam Keller opened the door widely, stood arms akimbo, the picture of confidence. With a strong voice she greeted us, "Well, I assume you are the do-gooders here to save me." I heard Chloe breathe in, taken aback.

Taking my cue from this aggressive start, I said, "No, but we are here to put the asshole away forever."

Miriam chuckled, "Maybe this won't be a waste of my time after all." With that, she looked me up and down, asked us to come in. Led us to her kitchen table. Told us to sit while she got her coffee. I looked closely at Miriam as she walked off: attractive, short, busty and seemingly brimming with self-assurance. She was physically similar to Chloe but a completely different personality. That made me think the psycho picked them purposefully for their appearance, maybe disposition had nothing to do with it. Looks seemed to be the only reason for selection, or was I missing something? I glanced at Chloe. She was also studying Miriam. I wondered what she was thinking. Made a note to ask her on the way home.

Miriam returned with her mug, never asked if we would like a cup. She looked at Chloe. "Why didn't you tell me this guy was cute and funny? I would have had him come by himself." She winked at me. Chloe didn't know what to say. I blushed, had no witty comeback. Miriam filled in the void. "All right, what can I do for you?"

I gathered myself. "We're here to give you some details about the attacker, to see if you can provide some clue the police have overlooked." I told what I'd learned, told her all the victims were divorced, forties and attractive. I left out the busty part.

Chloe interjected here. "And all the attacks were within a few miles apart, so we must have encountered him somewhere locally." And then I mentioned the nine-month cycle. That it was within a few weeks of the next possible assault.

Miriam squinted, put her arms on her hips as she said in a flat tone, "You'll never catch this guy. He's too careful."

Her eyes got wide when I said each victim said the same thing when catching the pervert came up. While she paused, "That can't be a random occurrence. Somehow this bastard has manipulated you, or somehow gotten you to believe he's invincible." That information jarred her.

She looked at Chloe, "I'm a tough woman, always have been able to take care of myself. Since the attack, I've tried to put it entirely out of my mind. Like it never happened." She seemed to think about that. "But now that you mention it, every time I think about that night, the first thing that pops to mind is, "They will never catch him." She looked at me. "I've come to accept that, can live with it. As I said, I'm a tough lady, and this asshole isn't going to rule my life."

Chloe answered first. "But all of us aren't as strong as you, and we need your help."

I added, "And we can't let him do this to other woman. He needs to be stopped." I could see this tough woman think about that, soften.

Miriam agreed to list all her usual habits, things she did almost every week or month. I said, "Like doctors, mailmen, deliverymen, grocery stores, that sort of thing. If you go to church, list which one. Try to think if there are men you've met who strike you as odd, particularly if you no longer see them since the attack. Thinking about my incident at the recruiting station, "Have you had any recent contact with military people?"

She frowned at me. "Now that's an odd question. What would I have to do with the military?"

Didn't want to bring up the "candy ass" connection. "Probably nothing, I just don't want to overlook anything. Even if it seems unrelated." Miriam agreed to make the list. As we walked to her door, she regained her sauciness. Looking at me, "I'll get this done tonight. Why don't you drop over tomorrow night and pick it up?" I nodded, saw Chloe slant her eyes at me.

Chloe was quiet for the first few minutes of our ride home. "You certainly made quite an impression with Miriam." She smiled at me. "I think you might need a chaperone."

I chuckled, "She sure wasn't what I expected. I believed her about being a strong woman. Maybe you ought to pick up the list? Leave me out of it."

She nodded her head. "Not a chance. This is going to be too much fun to watch." I let her have fun, was glad she had some enjoyment—even at my expense. She turned more serious. "Where did the military question come from?"

I felt Chloe and I had formed a bond, was owed an answer, "I was just wondering if the attacker's rituals could have something to do with a bad experience in the military." I told her about the "candy ass" comment, how that triggered the mention of sweet and minty in the two other victim's reports. She was quiet the rest of the ride.

As I walked to her door, Chloe said, "I'll think about the candy thing, but don't have any recollection like that." Quiet again, "It's painful to think about, humiliating, but I'll try to see if I can help you figure that out."

I knew that was a lot to ask. I patted her shoulder. "Thanks." Quickly added, "I promise we'll catch him."

She patted me back. "For the first time, I believe you." She went inside without another word.

♦

I fell asleep that night watching Johnny Carson. The

last thing I remembered was Don Rickles telling Charles Aznavour, "For a little cocker, you sure can belt it out. You're a spunky ole' frog." The bewildered look on the tiny French singer was priceless. I must have chuckled off to sleep.

My amusement was quickly replaced by a nightmarish dream. I was being greeted by an angry mob as I returned from Vietnam. The gang grabbed me as I deplaned in Philadelphia, started pummeling me with balled fists, calling me "baby killer." I looked at a woman holding a sign, hoping for mercy. Fury in her eyes, she lifted the sign, crashed it over my uplifted arms. I gasped in pain… The noise woke me.

Raised both hands to my face, no damage. It was just a haunting memory. I steadied my breathing, vowed to call Fran Philips in the morning. He had repeatedly asked to meet with his veterans. Fran mentioned helping the vets with a topic I knew well: hatred of Vietnam veterans.

PERCY PROWLS

He tracked VC in Nam, was good at it. Finding
Frazier's new address wasn't difficult. Found it right away
in the phone book. Different from what he'd memorized
in Leavenworth. He must have moved when he got back
from Nam. He shook his head in anger as he scanned the
Yellow Pages, saw Frazier's ad, growled, "Lookout
Investigations, my black ass. That white sumbitch gonna
look and look but ain't ever gonna find ole Percy. Cocky
motha' fucker." He was breathing hard, already worked up.
He did his first drive around Frazier's town, as it got dark.
When he found the right street, drove slowly past Frazier's
address, an old colonial that was turned into a two-floor
rental. He fought an urge to stop as he noticed lights on
the second-floor apartment. Wonder if that's him up
there? Should I fuck him up right now? Percy was no
dummy. He figured Frazier had been warned he escaped,
might be on alert. No need to rush things. Got me some
studyin' to do. He drove around the adjoining streets,
getting a feel for things. He drove to his Lansdowne
apartment, all worked up but satisfied with surveillance

When back in his room, he double-checked Frazier's
address. "Number 2." Percy thought: musta been him
ta'night. Top floor it be. Or would they have a bottom
apartment named Number 2? After a fitful sleep, he drove
by Frazier's place next day, late morning. He didn't want to
bump into him by accident, wanted to make sure he would
be at work. In daylight, it was easy for Percy to verify
Number 2 was the top floor. He was pleased, lots of trees

and bushes around, easy to hide if that was necessary. Percy already had doubts about attacking him at home. He wanted a spot where Frazier wouldn't be expecting it. He wondered if he had family nearby. He shook his feral head, recalled something. Wasn't he always yappin' about some honey back home. Hmm? Percy noticed there was a school across the street, had a view of Frazier's place. He saw a big parking lot, almost filled with cars. Perfect, a good place to watch without drawing attention. Then he remembered the rental guy's comment: "ain't too many brothers in Drexel Heights." Had to think some.

That night he returned to the school. Percy smirked when he saw the place was full of cars, lots of activity. He parked his car, moseyed in the dark to the dimly lit front door. Got happy as he read the sign: Drexel Heights Adult Education. He thought smugly: good place fer' studyin' me some white bread, won't be noticin' a brother in the dark. That started his deep surveillance. He angled his car, sat looking for action. He wasn't there long before Frazier came out his front door and drove off. He didn't follow immediately, watched if someone tailed him. No other cars followed, so he took off but kept back a couple blocks. He watched as Frazier parked, entered a small store. He drove by, studied Frazier's car for later use. Percy looked at the shop: McCormick's Deli. Saw a neon sign proclaiming, "Best Hoagies in America." Thought to himself: fuck's a hoagie? Must be a sandwich er some shit. Fuckin' Crackers.

Percy drove past the deli, stayed on busy State Road for a block, made a right turn and parked where he could see the entrance. After about ten minutes, Frazier loped out, carrying a brown bag. Rather than follow him, he sat and watched, still wary of his surroundings. Percy's nostrils flared. Frazier was a piece of shit, but he wasn't stupid. Remembering how Frazier almost choked him to death got him excited. He breathed in rapid pants. His eyes fluttered as he visualized how different things would be this time. When he calmed down, Percy pulled away from the curb, made another trip to the school parking lot. As he pulled in, he saw Frazier entering his apartment. He watched as the second-floor light went on. Percy smiled, said softly, "Gotcha." While he sat watching, a disturbing thought came to him: that car rental guy might remember me. It'll be all over the news after I kill Frazier. Maybe they put pictures of me on the news. Gots ta think on that.

After his reconnoitering, a plan formed. His first chore was planting the tracking device. Frazier had an olive-green Chevy. It didn't look like it got cleaned much, not likely to be found. He assumed Frazier had been alerted of his breakout. Captain O'Hanlon might be here looking for me. Percy crinkled his brow thinking of the giant Green Beret: O'Hanlon be one bad motha' fucker, gots to go easy. Most people underestimated Percy, but he didn't think O'Hanlon would. He remembered how the giant Green Beret terrified the VC. Had a reputation as a cold killer. He drove a few blocks away, got out of his car, made his way by foot to Frazier's street, stopped a couple blocks back. He started his slow approach, stayed on the lawns, vigilant for cars or noise.

Only one car came up the street. Unknown to Percy, there were two MP's inside. He watched the car come to a stop, sat idling with the lights out. He shook his head in recognition: guards. Staying in the shadows, it took another half hour to get close to the car. There were two large figures inside. He watched an orange glow come from the passenger seat. The dumbass is smoking. That pleased him, amateurs. He sat for a few minutes, was about to reverse course when the car pulled away. He sat still for another half hour, thinking. Did this mean the guards weren't on Frazier fulltime? Or were they trying to fake him? When Percy felt sure no one was watching, he came out of the hedges, planted the magnetic tracking device under the back fender. Disappeared back to the shadows. Checked his receiver to make certain it was working. He nodded when the green light went on. This would be easier than he thought.

DYLAN

I stopped at Jimmer's dojo before heading to work. Percy wasn't about to give me warning. Wanted Jimmer's advice on being better prepared. One of the things I liked about my childhood friend was bluntness. After explaining Nut's strategy, Jimmer frowned. "What if he's wrong, and the dumb ass MP's are waiting at some godforsaken place, and Percy decided to pummel your ass in broad daylight? Fuck that idea. How about some good old manpower to pound that fucker if he shows?"

I laughed, "You read my mind, Jimmer. You'd think Nut would have the juice to get me a bulletproof car, a ray gun or some other cool army stuff. Right?"

Jimmer didn't take the bait. "Let's get to work." We spent a few minutes practicing being assaulted from behind. Jimmer went through his technique in slow motion, explaining, "Once you feel contact, roll with the angle of the blow, but quickly shift sideways. That way you avoid the follow through power, which is usually lights out if done well."

He demonstrated the move, pushing me forward, then right, and then bouncing to my feet. Afterward, "Do I always shift to the right?"

He gave a logical answer, but one that added a load of complexity. "Not always right. It depends on the angle of attack. We'll practice attacks from every conceivable angle, try to get your reaction to be instinctive, without thought."

175

That's what we did for the next couple hours. We went through every type of attack and reaction in slow motion, gradually building speed. I understood the concept, but the instinctiveness wasn't there. Whenever I screwed up, Jimmer said, "Bang, Frazier's down for the count. Fights over."

I grew very tired of the taunt. "Time for some new material. It stopped being funny after the thirtieth time."

Jimmer didn't smile, "Trying to keep you on the right side of the dirt, my friend. This is going to take lots of practice. If you're serious, you'll drop by every day till this maniac gets caught." We called it a day. I promised to drill with him at least a few times weekly, thanked him for the help." Jimmer smirked, "What would I do for aggravation if I didn't have you around?"

♦

Exhausted, I went home for a quick shower. From there, I called the SEPTA telephone number to ask if drivers could operate busses and trolleys. I listened to the bored clerk chomping away on bubble gum as I asked the question. "We don't give that information out. It's proprietary. Get me?"

I wasn't expecting much, so I replied, "I get it. You're worried that Penn Central will figure out you have these gifted geniuses that are so versatile they can pilot multiple vehicles and they'll try to steal them, right? Kinda like what Oppenheimer did with the Manhattan Project, keeping it all hush-hush. Afraid the Nazi's would try to kill all our brainiacs before we got the A-bomb ready. Makes sense to me you wouldn't want your driver's expertise leaking out. I mean, who would ever believe someone could drive a bus and a trolley?"

The clerk listened politely. "Is there anything else I can help you with?" I hung up to her, "Have a nice day, thank you for riding SEPTA."

I knew there was a SEPTA office in the Sixty-Ninth Street terminal. I figured an "in person" appearance was required to get the secret answer. Parking was a nightmare in Sixty-Ninth Street. I pulled my old trick, parked in the Pep Boys lot just up the street from the terminal. Commuters often left their cars at Pep Boys for service while they rode the EL into downtown. The only trick with my ploy was making sure you weren't gone too long, or a vigilant attendant would call the cops, get you towed. Most times the attendants were busy, never noticed me slip near an open spot by the curb, far from the shop entrance. I wasn't lucky this time. Guy in greasy overalls wandered over as I locked up. "Help ya, Mac?"

I smiled, "Think I'm all set. Just have to check inside to make sure my lube job's all set." To distract him, "Whataya think about The Phils this year? Don't ya think Luzinski'd be better off with The Eagles? I mean the guys a load, right? Maybe play him at tackle?"

He chuckled, "They don't call him 'The Bull' fer nothin'. He can't play left fer shit is how I see it." I nodded, walked off toward their office. As the attendant headed into the garage, I veered toward my real mission.

The SEPTA offices were intentionally tough to find. If you didn't want customers pestering you, why would you make it easy to find customer service? I finally found the grimy door wedged between Nathan's Hot Dogs and Sweet Buns, which sold some melt-in-your-mouth honey glazed donuts. I recalled my dad's earlier advice that "you better be within running distance to a crapper if you have one of those honey glazed." Thinking of my zany dad put a grin on my puss, as I asked the receptionist to talk with the manager.

She said, "What's so funny? Most people comin' in here are honked off about somethin'."

I shook my head, "Was thinking about something my dad said. He's a bit kooky. Anyway, is there someone I can speak to about the drivers? I'm trying to find out if drivers can operate both busses and trolleys. I'm an investigator, it's important to a case I'm working."

The young receptionist seemed intrigued by my profession. "That must be excitin' work. Do you ever have to use a gun?"

I nodded sagely, "Can you keep a secret?" She shook her head. I looked around, as if checking for someone listening. Whispered to her, "Plugged a dude last week that tried to kill his wife for the life insurance." Her eyes got big.

Thinking I had her hooked, I asked again about the

drivers. She shook her head. "The unions don't allow us to give out any information on the drivers. It's in the collective bargaining agreement that any technical information about driver's qualifications is private. They're worried about getting sued in accident cases. You know, like the rider says the driver wasn't qualified. That kind a thing."

Trying to play my exciting job card, I said softly, "This involves a secret case of a serial rapist. Very hush-hush." Looking around again to insure secrecy, "How about we play twenty questions." She looked puzzled. "What I mean is, I ask questions, if I'm right you nod. That way you never "told" me anything. You'll be able to read in the Bulletin that I caught this guy, and you'll know you were instrumental in the arrest. Wouldn't that make you proud?" The receptionist beamed her assent. Minutes later I walked out after learning that it was possible to drive both, but currently there were none qualified for both. Dead end?

I exited the SEPTA office, was immediately entranced by the exotic smell of glazed donuts. Wandering to the counter, I spotted two scantily clad girls wearing skin-tight short shorts, thought immediately of the store name— "Honey Buns." These girls really filled them out, were a walking advertisement. Apparently, I was gawking as the nearest girl said, "Youse gonna stare at my butt all day er ya gonna buy somethin'?" The mood was ruined. Her thick Philly accent took off the edge of her attractiveness.

I recovered quickly. "If you're giving me a choice,

maybe I'll look at your butt all day."

Without missing a beat, "No buy, no look. Thems the rules at Sweet Buns."

I liked her spunk. "How many do I have to buy to stand here all day?"

Not impressed she countered, "One old perv stood here all day, bought 'bout three dozen. Betcha he puked all night. Hopes the thrill was worth it."

She winked, and I chuckled. "Okay, give me a couple. Don't want you to think I'm an old pervert." She scooped up the donuts.

As I paid, "Don't trouble yerself with guilt, youse just a young pervert." I laughed all the way to Pep Boys.

My luck held. They car was undisturbed. Driving off, I thought about what I'd learned. If the attacker had anything to do with SEPTA, he could be either a bus or trolley driver. The more likely culprit was bus driver since trolleys weren't near all the victim locations. Bus stops were. Still a long shot, but worth considering. To see if fresh insight popped up, I decided to drive to all the victim locations again. Since they were nearby, I made the entire trek in less than a half hour. Nothing new came to me. After that, I looked at the map again, looking for new ideas. I tried mentally tracing the sequence of attacks chronologically. Zip. I drove to the center of the circle, wondering if there was anything of interest. My path took me near McCormick's Deli, but I wasn't hungry. Those donuts were like weights in my gut. Why didn't I listen to my dad's advice? As I drove by my dentist's office, it reminded me I had a loose filling. Had to get that taken care of fast. I turned off the radio; let my mind rest as I continued home. Not knowing why, I didn't think the day was worthless.

♦

Early that evening, I stopped at Miriam Keller's house to get her list. My plan to avoid trouble with the feisty lady was still being formulated as I approached the front step. The door opened instantly, like she'd been waiting for me. Not a good sign? As if reading my thoughts, "Well if it isn't the interesting detective."

Trying to act official, "I'm not a detective, I'm just an insurance investigator. Dropping by to see if you got that list done, Miss Keller."

She frowned, "No need for the Miss Keller, call me Miriam. How are we going to be friends if you act so formal?" She stared boldly. I took a deep breath, hoping it wasn't obvious.

To keep my focus, "Sorry, just trying to be polite. I'm kind of in a hurry, got a meeting with the police in twenty minutes. Can I get that list if it's ready?"

Miriam lowered her brows, "Now that disappointing. I thought we were going to get to know each other a little better." She raised her eyebrows, "Don't I get a special reward for being such a good girl?"

Not wanting to shut down the flow of information entirely, "Maybe another time when I'm not in such a rush."

Miriam fluttered her eyelashes, turned away. Came back with a neatly typed list. "I'll hold you to that promise." Was in a mild sweat as I drove off.

PERCY

It took Percy a few days of surveillance to determine the car rental agent's schedule. When he arrived weeks ago it was a late morning flight from Charleston. He got his ticket with fake ID purchased from a street punk in Charleston. The ID worked perfectly, no trail for any future inquiry. He used the ID to rent the car but worried his face might be remembered. He waited patiently but never saw the helpful vet the first few mornings. After a week of watching, he expanded his surveillance till late night. Percy finally spotted his target. The friendly vet was working the late shift. Percy observed the energetic guy line up cars outside the checkout station. Trying to prevent check-in delays? Percy saw grateful clients often tipped him for this prompt service. The hustling attendant obviously figured he'd get more tips doing this courtesy without being asked. A smart, industrious man was cause for worry. Percy surmised all this from his hidden perch on the adjoining edge of the short-term parking lot.

After watching for a few days, Percy bided his time for the right moment. The pattern was consistent. Each day the busy time was around dinner, slowed down thereafter, another busy time around 9 pm. The car rental parking lot was huge, easy for him to hide, blend in. On Wednesday night Percy arrived around 6:30 pm, assumed his lookout post, waiting for darkness. His excitement built as the attendant scrambled deep in the lot to retrieve cars. The flurry of dinnertime activity died. It was a muggy, gloomy night. Percy grabbed his equipment, moved to the

TOM FAUSTMAN

edge of the rental lot. He wore khaki cargo pants with deep pockets. As expected, the attendant moved into the lot to line up future pick-ups. Percy let him get deep down a row of cars before yelling to him. "Hey, brother, remember me. Yo' helped me a couple weeks ago pick out a crib in Lansdowne? Me and you was in Nam."

The guy recovered from being startled, gave a smile of recognition. "Sho does, how's it goin'?"

To cover why he was in the lot, Percy said, "Just parked over yonder, goin' ta pick up my mother jus' comin' in from Charleston. Thought I'd mosey over, say hey."

The attendant smiled, "That's right nice." Percy reached inside his baggy pant pocket, gripped the handle. As the friendly vet reached to give the dap handshake, Percy swung the heavy metal bar and crushed his skull. The attendant gasped, the noise like air escaping a balloon. The attendant banged into a T-Bird as he fell. Percy beat him multiple times in the head, checked his pulse to confirm the kill. He fished his pockets, stole his wallet, made it look like robbery. Percy walked toward his car, thinking he'd throw the weapon in the swampy land that bordered the airport.

He shook his head, said aloud, "Philly sure is a dangerous place, crazy fuckers all over."

DYLAN PUSHES

I hadn't looked over Miriam list yet. Was about to do that when I realized it would be more revealing if I got lists from all six victims. Dialing Chloe, I asked if she would help me contact the other four victims. While she paused, "More chances to find a clue if there are multiple overlaps. There must be a connection for how he targets you. There must be a spot where you all intersect. No way this is random. You are all too similar."

I heard Chloe breathe hard. "Get me the numbers and I'll call. Can you come over when I do it? It'll make it easier. Plus, I can mention your involvement, maybe have you say a few words."

I liked that angle, agreed to drop over shortly. I hung up, went to my notes, retrieved the numbers, figured I better update Merlano in case they called to verify. The surly Merlano listened silently. When I was done, "You are a pushy son of a bitch, Frazier." Before I could protest, "I like it." He hung up not wanting me to get the last word.

I could see roommate Elaine watch me exit my car and approach their door. It was mid-August, a humid time in Philly. Lightning bugs filled the air. These sparkling creatures always made me feel like a kid, simpler times when playing outside at night was magical. And safe. Now, some sadistic ghoul prowled my neighborhood ruining women's lives. I shook my head, not wanting to get worked up and spook Chloe. Just then a hungry mosquito bit my arm, brought me back to other childhood thoughts.

To kill the pesky mosquitoes, Philly sent spray trucks through Drexel Height's streets to thwart the pestilence. Gangs of kids, me included, ran behind the trucks to disappear in the fog of spray. Each year, we'd wonder why we felt like a dead bug later that day. Couldn't have been good for you, right? Maybe that's why my childhood classmate, Randy Ritter claimed he was growing a prehensile tail. I chuckled, weird memories. Now, I was chasing a more violent strain of virulence.

Elaine broke my reverie. "Penny for your thoughts, Dylan. You look like you saw a ghost." The relationship with Chloe had also transformed Elaine. She let her brown hair grow out and wore a little make-up. Nothing extravagant, but it softened her, much more feminine than when we first met. She still had the clear, commanding voice. I really enjoyed her company. It was no wonder Chloe found her so comforting.

As if reading my thoughts, Chloe emerged from the kitchen with cups of steaming tea. She smiled, "You like black tea, if I remember correctly."

I nodded, "Got the taste from my Irish mom. It was always a way to spend time with her after school. At first, I just did it to get her attention but pretty soon got hooked. Mellows me out. As you've come to learn, I have an edge sometime." Both ladies smiled silently, not wanting to agree and hurt my feelings. I added, "Mom always told the nuns I had ants in my pants, to give me a swat if the critters got too active." The ladies giggled.

Now that they were looser, I thought it a good time to start the victim calls. Earlier, I verified with Merlano that he spoke to all, they would talk with Chloe, were eager to help. I told Chloe to use the group support angle, that they would probably respond to that.

She nodded, "The truth is always the best approach." That sounded like something my mom would say, made me like her more. I listened quietly as she made calls to these unfortunate ladies. She added my involvement deftly. Spoke how much I'd helped her. I welled up as I heard her narrate their shared tragedy. Marveled as she spoke with such compassion and dignity. Behind my wet eyes, I got more infuriated at the monster that ruined so many lives. Knew I had to regain composure before she ended the calls. A crying weenie wasn't helpful. Chloe needed my strength to push on. I breathed in through my nose, held the air as long as I could, exhaled slowly, settled down.

When she hung up, Elaine summarized the performance eloquently, "You sounded like a courageous victim asking for their help, asking for a miracle. That was beautiful." I kept quiet but thought: for someone who wasn't religious, she gave an inspirational sermon.

When home later, I opened the Bulletin, read the sports page. The Phillies were improving, but still weren't a threat to win the Series. Mike Schmidt was a bright spot, maybe the best third baseman in baseball. At least the diehard Phil fans thought so. Then remembered to turn the game on the radio. They were playing the Pirates, were winning two-zero behind a stellar performance from Steve Carlton. I liked listening to Richie Ashburn and Harry Kalas kid each other. You could tell they really liked each other, best friends busting chops. That reminded me how lucky I was to have Nut. Not many people would drop everything to protect someone they rarely saw anymore. For the second time that night, I started to well up. I shook my head. Better get my shit together, as they said in the army. Funny how some phrases never left you. I heard consistently in Nam that "my shit was packed tight." Translation was, I stayed focused in tough times, could be depended upon. I hoped that was still true.

After completing the sports section, I turned to the obituaries. My lawyer buddy Gator got me started with that weird habit. Although he wouldn't admit it, Gator did it early in his career to look for potential clients. Struggling to get his law practice started, he trolled for whatever he could find. I'm not sure why I did it. Sometimes you read something funny, like "My dad hated going to funerals, so pretend he's still alive and just doesn't want to see you anymore." Other times there were sappy eulogies that would make you puke. "My uncle Seymour was a giant among men, he trod the earth like a Titan." All I could think was: who would name their kid Seymour? And that made me chuckle. Done with the obits, needing more distraction, I turned to the "weekly crime" section of the Delaware County News. One of my childhood goals was to never be mentioned in the weekly column. So far, I succeeded. I spent the rest of the night recalling all the things that should have gotten me listed. Was glad putting dog turds in kid's pockets wasn't worthy of publication.

♦

Next morning, I called Gator. He had an unusual mind. I wanted his input on my strategy to catch this sadistic bastard. His new secretary answered on the first ring, "Attorney Light's Office, my name is Hilda, how may I assist you?"

Figuring I'd break her in, "Oh, hi. I'm glad Mr. Light got out of prison so soon. Didn't think he was paroled till next week. I was calling to see if he needed a ride from the slammer. Guess he made it home already; won't need that ride anymore. Can you tell him that Dylan's on the phone?" I heard her start to stammer. I bailed her out. "Only kidding, I'm a childhood friend who never really made the leap to adulthood. Mr. Light's never been in prison." Paused, "That I know of."

By now, Gator had arrived, explained to Hilda that I was a mentally challenged friend who would call periodically, and shouldn't be taken seriously. That he acted as a guardian for me at his parent's request, kind of a "pro bono" service. And then Gator started his unique howling form of laughter and that got me chuckling. When we calmed down, Gator told me to drop over before lunch.

I was thinking about the name "Hilda" as I approached Gator's office. Should I start with that or leave her alone? I opened the door, spotted Hilda at the file cabinet by her desk. She was a big, severe looking woman with a Dorothy Hamill hairdo. That haircut seemed somehow off, with her blond hair and bulky frame. Gator's last secretary Janice was the polar opposite, a sultry sex bomb. I got disarmed as Hilda gave me a nice smile.

"You must be the nutty friend I talked to this morning. Mr. Light warned me not to take anything you said seriously." She walked over, shook my hand. "I'm headed out to lunch while you visit. Mr. Light said it was for my own protection." She giggled; her sense of humor proved appearances are deceiving. But she was getting off too easily.

I shook my head. "Mr. Light has become very cautious since getting out of the witness protection program. He did warn you about that, right?" She chuckled louder, grabbed her purse and left.

Gator stood in the doorway, nodding his head. "You really are a douche bag. Leave Hilda alone, she's an amazing secretary, don't scare her off." He gave one of his snorting laughs, loving his own wit. We spent the next half hour reviewing the facts I compiled. I decided to consolidate Chloe and Miriam's list, even without answers from the other victims. It would give us a place to start. Gator shook his head in amazement when he saw my map, the circle of attacks. "Jesus, it's right in our old backyard."

I looked at him, "That's what has me worried." We continued. He liked the idea of completing a list of people the victims frequently encountered.

He grinned, "Pretty good idea for a numb nuts like you."

I let the jab go, was now in a pissy mood from thinking about these perverted crimes. Didn't want to waste time with more inane quips. Looked at Gator, "Anyway, after we meet all the victims individually, I was planning to gather them together, get them talking. Go over the lists they compiled, show the overlaps. See if something occurs to them they'd forgotten." Thinking of another angle, "Or maybe something they'd buried, not wanting to think about because it was too painful. That work for you?"

He nodded his head. "That's a ploy of mine in court when I talk to a jury. Encourage them to say if something that hasn't been mentioned or asked about is bothering them, even if it seems obvious. A lot of times, a person mentions something obscure, then that gets the others thinking. Something always crops up."

We looked over the lists Chloe and Miriam completed. We wrote them on a flip chart that Gator used when planning a trial strategy. We circled any overlaps from each other's lists. I was surprised that the doctor, gynecologist, dentist, grocery store, UPS truck, pharmacy, gas station, hoagie shop, hardware store, department store and butcher shop were identical. Gator said he expected it. "It's a relatively small area, there's bound to be overlaps." He added, "Plus there are multiple subunits in many of these. Like in a grocery store, there must be a dozen sections that have employees that could be our guy. We might have to break those down further." I hadn't thought about that. What he said made sense. But it just compounded our suspect list ten times. I asked if I'd overlooked anything obvious. He didn't answer right away. Put his hand to his chin, "Both of them are Catholic but don't practice. Does that mean anything?" I had no response but added that question to the column: are they all non-practicing Catholics? I don't know why but that bothered me. Was this some twisted religious vendetta?

The lunch hour was over. I thanked Gator, made my way to his office door. "Do you mind if I drop in after I get all the lists? That way I can show you what I get and tell you what I found as I snooped around the places. That twisted mind of your will be useful." I knew Gator enjoyed helping me. It gave him a break from chasing crazy clients. He didn't show it with his rumpled sartorial appearance, but he had a meticulous eye for detail. He'd spot anything I missed. Plus, he enjoyed our ball-busting nonsense.

He smirked, "Only if you promise not to pester Hilda. She's a gem and I don't want you spooking her with your weird sense of humor. Everybody doesn't get it, you know."

I threw up my hands. "So, I can't ask her if being named Hilda, and looking like a blond Amazon, was she from a Viking background? You mean that's off the table?" He gave me the finger as I left his office. I noticed Hilda had returned. As I shut his door, I told her Mr. Light said I couldn't talk to her anymore, that I was a bad influence. From now on I'd speak to her in sign language. She hesitated, and then gave a crisp salute.

NUT

The MP's watching Dylan had split into teams of two, each taking twelve-hour shifts. The strategy was to be always moving, never sit still in a car for long, never just waiting for Percy to show up. Stay in Frazier's area, but keep mobile and look for a wiry, black killer. Percy was cagey and experienced, would spot a stationary set of guards. The teams had to know Dylan's itinerary for that day, be ahead of him, not behind. They knew this would leave short gaps of coverage. It was the weakness in the plan, and they knew that. It was judged the lesser of evils. That ran through the MP's minds while waiting for "Captain Nut" to arrive for a briefing. It had been three weeks already, no signs of Percy Price. Today, the two teams got together to compare notes, trying to stay sharp, or face the wrath of their stalwart leader.

They knew Dylan Frazier called him Nut- but he was the formidable Captain O'Hanlon to them. Despite being in his mid-twenties, the young captain had attained legendary status. Rumor was that he led an elite special forces team trained for assassination. One wary MP said, "I heard he was dropped behind the Ho Chi Minh Trail whenever a key North Vietnamese Military leader got close to our lines. They said he killed at least three of their bigwigs."

The wide-eyed MP added, "With his bare hands. No wonder Frazier calls him Nut." The other three shook their heads, said nothing. Each knew that Dylan Frazier was important to this fearsome soldier, and they weren't about to let anything happen on their watch.

Like a storm cloud, the brooding Captain O'Hanlon entered the office. Without pleasantries, "Report."

The big-eyed MP said, "Sorry, Captain, but there's been no sight of Percy Price, or anyone even slightly resembling him. In fact, we hardly see any black faces in the area."

Nut looked at them sternly, "Any other comments?" No one spoke. He looked at the foursome, "Stay vigilant. This guy was Special Forces in Nam, is trained to be unobserved. He had lots of time in Leavenworth to plan this. He's not about to make obvious mistakes. Even if you don't see anything, look for anything in the environment where it would be a good place to hide or attack. Try to think of this exercise as, 'How would you attack Frazier' and then look again to see if you missed something. He's out there." The MP's stared at the massive Captain O'Hanlon, as he added, "I can smell him. He'll be laying quietly like a snake in the grass." His gaze softened, "I thank you for your help. As you already figured, Frazier is important to me. What you may not have known is that Frazier has saved my life on more than one occasion. This is personal. Frazier is family."

Nut dismissed the MP's, took a few minutes to assess. In his personal reconnaissance, he noted the most obvious time to attack Dylan was at night when he was doing something repetitive. Like going to McCormick's Deli or visiting Chloe Zubrisky. He knew his zany pal had a big heart. Even if he deflected any praise by saying it was part of his job, Nut knew Dylan liked fixing broken things, especially defenseless people. Both hated bullies. Nut smiled suddenly: Dylan could always make me laugh. Usually, the worse the situation the funnier he got. Nervous habit maybe, but who cared, it helped. But his mood changed suddenly. He banged his fist violently. He said aloud, "Where the hell is Percy? I know he's here. Where and when will he strike? What are we missing?"

With that sobering conundrum, he went to his car. He never let Dylan, or his MP teams, know he was also out there hunting. Time to cover the territory again, look for the kill zone. He shook his head: I have to think on a different level. How would a lethally trained sociopath do it?

DYLAN

Was just about to grab my morning coffee at McCormick's Deli when the phone rang. A perturbed Hoban was on the line. "That damned lunatic struck again. He wrote Harley Burns with another crazy letter about him being a spy. This made me laugh, but I could tell immediately Hoban was pissed. "Nothing funny about this anymore, Dylan. Burns is furious. He thinks if his boss finds out this it will hurt him. He's a workaholic and doesn't want anything in his region that reflects badly on him."

I promised to drop over right away. With Chloe's case absorbing my thoughts, I hadn't spent any time on the Nudleman caper. Besides not thinking it was too important, I had to admit it was a world-class prank. Who in their right mind would spend all that time writing nutty letters to strangers? It had to be someone very smart- the letters were so zany. I pondered that some. Was it someone with a high-powered job who did this to break the tension? Got a better thought: show it to Chloe to get her laughing again.

Speaking of stress relief, this would be a good distraction for me. I was starting the meetings tomorrow with the other attack victims. Wasn't looking forward to seeing these broken souls. I shook off that dour thought, as I realized this might be the start to stopping the maniac. Was thinking about this positive outcome, as I circled the Voyager building hoping a parking spot would surface. No luck. Drove down the Parkway toward the Art Museum, found a remote corner. A soft pretzel stand was on the corner. Figured a mustard-smeared pretzel would fuel my hunt. The chatty vendor opined, "How about them Phils? Ya think they gotta shot?"

I shook him off, "Not this year. Carlton's the best in the game, but after him, Larry Christensen is all they got. Need some more arms, right?"

He shook his head, "And that Ozark's got his head up his ass. Fuckin' cracker makes some dumb-ass moves. Needa change." I nodded approval. Kind of felt sorry for Danny Ozark, everybody in Philly was an expert baseball coach.

I made my way into the Voyager building. Hoban was still wound up when I got in his office. His look was intense. "This has got to stop, Dylan, so none of your quips, okay? Let's get this wacko. My boss has a zero sense of humor."

Since it was hard to take these letters seriously, I restrained myself. "Got the message, boss. Let me get a copy of the letter and I'll snoop around."

The normally happy Hoban gave me the letter, pointed to the copier in the corner. "Use my conference room if you want to stay awhile." As he walked away, "Sorry, I'm being such an asshole, but Burns is really busting on me."

I waved it was okay. Thought I'd read the Nudleman missive first to see if it was funny enough to amuse Chloe.

I wasn't disappointed. I called Chloe at work to warn her I'd be dropping by. She gave me the green light. Said she'd be home in a couple hours.

I did mundane disability investigations to kill time. One funny guy lived in Fishtown, was unable to operate his tool and dye machine because he had hammertoe, claimed it hurt too much to stand. Before I could ask a question, he pulled off his slipper, pointed at his swollen big toe, "Look at that sucker. Looks like it belongs on King Kong, right?" It wasn't easy, but I stifled a laugh. Hard to believe I got paid to do this work.

♦

Later that night, I sat with Chloe and Elaine, took the part of Bernie, reading aloud. As per the past letters, it began as follows:

C/O Harley Burns, Big Boss

Voyager Insurance Company

Hartford, Ct.

P.S. Mail Guys- Don't read this before giving to Harley or face consequences

Dear Harley:

    Double check the mail guys didn't steam this open. Use your training kit that Fielding gave you- gooey globules is a dead giveaway. If you suspect foul play, take them out. Maybe they get accidentally run over by a sloppy mail truck driver? The irony would be a nice deterrent for other snoopers. You heard me, rendition protocol. But I wander off the point. Back to business, Fielding sends his regards. He said the documents from your Philadelphia office were received. Etna is delighted!!!

    Fielding says you can receive the five thousand at coordinates 4753-2295 (use the Sunoco Map). Once there, you start by telling the ticket taker that Morrie sent you, followed by the recognition signal, "I tossed a salad during Toledo's first snow fall this year." The ticket taker will counter-signal with, "Have you invited the Schechter's to your son's bar mitzvah?" You will then nod twice, and he will pass the envelope to you. And don't worry, it's all in circulated tens and twenties.

    Fielding wants assurances that you will split fifty/fifty with Hoban. Hoban intimates that you held out on him on the last drop, and his payment is overdue on the Datsun 240z. Fielding seriously recommends that Hoban scale back with the glitzy car; he's getting too showy. As you know, Fielding has no sense of humor or style. In many ways a putz.

    Anyway, of most importance, Fielding has reason to believe that you are being watched. It is confirmed that Voyager has a mole planted at Etna, and some suspect it is that tasty morsel you have on the side. (Not to worry, your hausfrau has no idea; we have her under surveillance.) But time for action. As you know, your lovely tidbit's a secretary at Etna. Coincidence? Time to end the dalliance, non-negotiable! Not to worry, security has not been breached thus far. However, to insure your cover, you are directed to discontinue the use of the code name, "Pork Hocks" effective August 1ˢᵗ. Thereafter, respond only to communications directed to "Liver Sausage."

Under no circumstances are you to contact me by telephone unless you suspect that your cover is blown. Should that occur, call 313 455 8865, ask for Kishka and simply say, "Mendoza has a hernia." I will contact Fielding so as to relay further instructions. Listed below are code name changes that will go into effect on the first of each month. This may seem an overreaction, but this mole is wily.

Former Code Name	*New Code Name*
Stromboli	*Ponte Vecchio*
Doctor Death	*Der Fledermaus*
Bratwurst	*Scrapple*
Chi Chi	*Lupe*

These will take us to the New Year. If the mole is uncovered, the rapidity of code changes will revert to normal spy craft. Mozeltov!

If you get a sec, call me at the store. You have the number.

Best Wishes,

Bernie

The ladies were laughing out loud after a few sentences. My tension break idea was a winner. I didn't think it possible, but they were happier than a tick on a fat guy. I left a copy, heard Elaine reading, "I tossed a salad during Toledo's first snow fall…"

I closed the door to new howls of laughter. In that instant, I made up my mind not look for Bernie Nudleman—the girls were having too much fun during a time of little joy. I slept well that night. No dreams haunted my subconscious.

MEETING THE VICTIMS

Chloe agreed to set Saturday aside to meet all the victims. I liked the idea of doing this quickly; get the painful sessions behind us. Gillian Bender was our first stop. Was again struck by the physical similarity to Chloe. I watched Gillian eye me cautiously. Chloe noticed that, introduced me as the person who helped her, and who would catch this sadist. On cue, I smiled hello, said that we were meeting everyone today, would get the group together if all were willing. Gillian stood a little straighter, in a drone-like monotone, "We'll never find him. He's too smart. He's long gone by now."

I didn't react, looked at Chloe, hoping she would respond. Chloe said nothing right away, seeming to have an internal battle. She moved toward Gillian, took her hand. "Gillian, we've all felt the same way, but we have to find a way to fight that negative thinking. I'm still doubtful, but with Dylan's constant prodding, am starting to feel hopeful. By Gillian's grimace, I could tell she wasn't sold. We pushed on, chatted amiably, found out she'd gone back to work, but still lived in fear. She liked the idea of the group getting together. I think the therapy approach sold her. We bid her goodnight, promised to stop by next day to get the list of common places or people she encountered weekly or monthly.

On the drive to Cynthia Sutter's home, Chloe said, "It's eerie how similar Gillian and Miriam are with me. I know you've said that, but it really hits when we meet in person."

Nodded, "It can't be a coincidence. I'll bet the others we meet today are the same. Whoever this bastard is, he has a specific kind of women he's attracted to. What we have to figure out is where he met you. There has to be a common thread." We finished the drive to Cynthia's house in silence. Chloe knocked on the door, identified herself. Introduced me.

As we walked inside, Chloe gave me a look that seemed to say: Cynthia could be my cousin. The only difference was Cynthia had jet-black hair, was a few years older and a bit taller. Sure enough, she was convinced we'd never find the attacker. He was too careful. I asked Cynthia to describe the man, noticed the change in tone as she outlined a vastly dissimilar assaulter than Chloe. When I told her each victim said the same thing it seemed to throw her. She got visibly agitated. Chloe again recoiled momentarily, but reached out, gently pressed her hand. Softly, "I felt the same way when I heard that. But now I believe Dylan can help us." I saw Cynthia exhale, but she didn't look convinced. As we walked away, Chloe said, "She's going to need more time." I thought: we don't have more time.

The meetings with Margot Palmieri and Ginger Spellman were carbon copies of the others. With slight differences, each woman was the same body type and attractive. All were around the same age when attacked. All were divorced. I let that percolate. Where do you go to meet divorced women of the same age who are built alike? I scratched my head. Each woman repeated the impossibility of finding the attacker. Each liked the idea of meeting the other victims. It had to be comforting to know you weren't alone with this misery. I gave my list of questions to each, said it would be critical to fill it out accurately. Told them I believed their list would point us to the person or place they had in common. Secretly, I worried in such a bustling geographic area there might be too many overlaps. But it was our best chance; my gut said these encounters were not random.

I gave a specific time next day when I'd pick up the list, not wanting to worry them about a surprise visit. Could sense they were still jumpy around men.

VIGILANCE

I dropped Chloe off, walked her to the door. She was tired but seemed pleased with our meetings. Heading to my car, spotted Nut's security team for the first time. Two bulky guys parked at the end of her street couldn't be a coincidence. Before I could mess with them, they took off. Nut's plan was to anticipate where I'd be but keep mobile. Although that was pretty smart, I resolved to form my own plan. I stood still, looking around. The sun was setting. This was a spot I'd been frequently in the last few weeks. Chloe's front yard was pretty neat, but still had some dark places. I hadn't even thought to check my surroundings. It was the perfect time to attack. I returned to my car, sat back, exhaled. Wondered when this would be over. Smacked the steering wheel. Yelled, "You have to be more damned careful." Shook my head, disappointed in myself. I recalled the miserable times in Nam when Percy was chasing me. I was vigilant for months. It was just a few weeks and I was already careless.

I called Jimmer Sunday morning, asked if he could give me a good ass-kicking. Told him of my recent lapse, wanted to stay sharper. He chuckled, "That's music to my ears. An opportunity to kick your tail and you're volunteering? You promise not to whine?" We would meet after I went to church and had breakfast. McCormick's Deli made a mean egg, cheese and bacon sandwich. Washed it down with some bad coffee, one of the few things McCormick's didn't do well. I sat on my couch, read the Bulletin sports column. Mike Schmidt had another big night. The Phillies beat Cincinnati, a rare event against the talented Reds. While I let my mind drift, I felt something gnaw at my subconscious. What had I seen in the last day or so that wasn't right? It was vague but was drifting around. Something I noticed but didn't follow up on? Nothing came. Maybe when I consolidated the women's lists it would be come to me. Or maybe my nerves were winning the battle.

Jimmer had a new approach. "I'm going to blindfold you, and make you walk through this gauntlet. When you feel contact, or even an unusual pressure, I want you to react the way I taught you. Ready?" Jimmer had assembled a series of heavy bags, sparring dummies, cushioned chairs, etc. in uneven patterns. I walked to the entrance of the practice area. Let him blindfold me. Jimmer put both hands on the back of my shoulders, told me to walk where he led.

He spun me around. For the next hour, I circled aimlessly, crashed into his obstacle course, pounded at whatever brushed me. His goal was to train to strike what I "sensed" rather than saw. He said it would heighten my defensive skills. For the first half hour, I hit wildly at the air, hitting nothing. By the end of the session, I did better, made more consistent contact. Finally, Jimmer spoke, "Enough for today. Not great but you got better. See you tomorrow." I stood for a couple seconds, pulled off the mask. Jimmer was nowhere to be seen. I shook my head: why did I have creepy friends?

VINCENTE

Vincente consoled Mrs. Stump. He had given bad news, pretended to empathize. Long ago he mastered the acting skills needed to fool the world. No one, except Rosa, realized he was devoid of any human feeling. He pondered his prowess as he turned a benign gaze on the sad woman before him. She was nice looking, but tall, a little too young, not his type. If she were shorter, he might overlook the age, and select her for future grooming. Her differences in appearance made him think of dear mother, the woman who had inspired the ritual life. He glanced at his mother's picture on the desk, as he guided the stunning Mrs. Stump out through his office door. He looked at his mousy wife sitting rigidly at her desk, a vision of efficiency. He shook his tiny head thoughtfully: things would have been quite different if the meek Rosa had been his mother.

Vincente sat in his office, thought of his bewitching mother. She still haunted him after all these years. He still bristled that she never saw him rise to success. Would she have been proud of him? Or would she have berated him for not making more money? Even when he got great marks and scholarships, she found fault. Her criticisms still stung. He could hear her vividly, "You have no friends. It's no wonder you get good grades. All you do is study. Why can't you have friends like a normal boy? And what girl will go near you? Odd little Vincente, who looks more like a troll than what you see in comic books. I still can't believe I gave birth to such a creature." Next, she would berate his missing father, and how having Vincente had ruined her life. These outbursts always precipitated a call to one of her endless lovers. She never tried to hide her wild fornications on the living room couch. Vincente watched it all. Those bitter condemnations and memories were like fresh wounds that wouldn't heal.

And his mother always had final say. His brilliant marks from prep school won him a full ride to Georgetown University. Because this was such a prestigious school, there were many foreign students and eggheads from all over the U.S. His gnomish appearance wasn't so unusual in a class of different looking kids. Living away from his derisive mother freed him from the daily abuse that marred his existence. It was invigorating to be surrounded by other smart people. Vincente was thriving in this academic environment. But then came the knock on his dorm door. A policeman looked at him dolefully. "Sorry, son, there's been a death in your family."

When he returned home he found his mother had died, a suicide caused by barbiturate overdose. The police told him she left a letter for him along with the suicide note. When the policeman left him alone, he opened the letter. It was only one sentence. He got chills as he mouthed her last taunt: *I WILL SEE YOU IN HELL!*

These lurid reminiscences had worked Vincente into a full lather. He shook his misshapen head violently. He tried to rid his demons. Suddenly, he paused, and realized things had changed. He was now controlling the beautiful, voluptuous women. Now, he would choose whom to torment. He no longer needed mother's approval to get what he wanted. He was master. Vincente's breathing returned to normal.

Once again under control, he began to think of final preparations for Angelique Bevilacqua. Her time was drawing near. She had an appointment later this week. He would make certain she would be home for the ritual visit. As he pondered the final steps, a thought occurred: Angeligue took great pride of her beautiful smile. Should he knock out those perfect teeth as a new part to the ceremony?

PERCY

It was time to get on with it. He already observed Frazier was being followed. But the two guards never stayed around for long. That puzzled him. Why did they leave him unprotected? At first, he thought they were trying to sucker him. Maybe another team was hiding nearby? On the last few nights, he positioned himself close enough to Frazier's house to see any activity after the guards drove off. Nothing. What was going on? He determined it was probably too risky to attack Frazier at his house. It was too obvious. The patrols always returned but didn't have a set pattern. Sometimes it was half an hour, sometimes it was five minutes. Other times, they sat around for an hour or more. Other times, they left after ten minutes. It was too unpredictable. Was that their plan?

Percy thought back to one of his most creative murders. When he killed his MP partner Ben Burton in Nam, he caught the bastard returning from the latrine. Who would expect to get fragged when you just left the shitter? That's what he needed to do this time. The only places Frazier seemed to visit consistently were McCormick's Deli, church and the white woman's house. The church murder was tempting. Who would expect that? But something about doing it at the bitch's place appealed to Percy. And then Percy had an idea. Kill Frazier in front of his whore? Have some fun with her afterwards? Maybe have the fun while Frazier watched? Kill him after? He would visit her neighborhood a few more times, start to finalize the attack. Percy got happy weighing both approaches, started to whistle.

DYLAN

I had enough of waiting around. Called Nut last night to meet. I was frustrated Percy remained elusive. I was just a lure, not an active part of Nut's team hunting this maniac. We agreed to meet at Nut's house after his mom left for work. Nut opened after one knock. My big buddy waved me in. I frowned, "I saw you peeking through the blinds. Better work on your super spy techniques, a little sloppy."

He reared back a fist, like he was about to punch. Grinned, "I'm glad you're finally staying alert."

I sat down, told him I'd been doing some thinking, wanted to run some thoughts by him. "Nut, I spotted your teams almost immediately. They're good, but if I see them, I know Percy has." Nut started to argue. I waved him off. "I'm not complaining; it was a good plan. I just think it's time to go on the offensive, flush him out."

Nut sat back in his chair, interested. I forged on, "You've talked before that the technique of the Green Berets was to think like and become your prey. That strategy served you well in Nam. You thought like the Viet Cong. What were the places they would hide? Conversely, where were the best places to attack? I'd like to use that approach here. Drexel Heights is a completely different battleground. I've already determined McCormick's Deli, my apartment, and Chloe's house were the most likely target areas. Where else? I'm sure I've missed something, because I stupidly think they're too obvious. Anyway, I've come up with a few more but want you to confirm. That's what we should talk about." Nut was almost smiling, as I finished, "I know you think you've fooled me, have been tracking me yourself, but it's pretty hard for a silverback like you to stay inconspicuous." Nut shook his head, rolled his index finger to go on, "I want you to follow me the next couple days, see if I've missed any likely spots, double check me." After a few minutes, a full smile came to his sculpted face.

♦

Later that afternoon, to distract dour thoughts of Percy, I plowed through the victim lists. Seemed to be on a run of bad luck. All the women shopped at the local Food Fare, which was one of the biggest food stores in Philadelphia. There had to be over a hundred employees, most of them men. All went to Haybridge and Clothier to shop. The store was huge, loads of employees, a mix of men and women who worked there. That intrigued me. A man would be able to size up these buxom women as they tried on dresses. I decided to visit the store this Saturday, the probable day the victims were likely to shop, since all of them worked. Each had the same gynecologist, dentist, and family doctor—none other than my own Dr. Powers. That was expected, the listed docs were about the only nearby medical options. All victims had the same UPS deliveryman, post office, police station, fire company, bakery, hardware store, hospital and dry cleaners. All rode some form of public transportation to work. They were raised Christian, but none considered themselves religious. Rather, they seemed hostile about religion. They must have asked themselves the toughest question facing all religions: how could God allow such a thing? I pondered whether their lack of religion had anything to do with this? As I thought about religion, realized my friend, Monsignor Pugh, would not be useful. Too early, he wouldn't get a fair hearing. Maybe later.

I reorganized all the list information onto a new flip chart, adding new observations. Fran Philips had agreed to hold the group session tonight. I wanted to review the lists with him before showing it to the ladies. Needed his guidance for the best way to present the material. Called Fran, told him I had everything in order, asked if I should simply present the information and make observations, or shut up and listen.

Fran was quiet. "You should show them the information but offer no conclusions. It's best if they comment individually. Maybe, that will get them talking collectively, and something you hadn't thought of comes up. Sometimes a group dynamic gives the meeker ones the strength to voice their opinion." He was quiet again, thinking. Finally, "Or, they may say aloud what they were afraid to even think about, even subconsciously. I see that occasionally in these settings." Another pause, "We are hoping for a miracle." More thoughtful quiet, "But miracles do happen." Not wanting to jinx that notion, I was silent.

♦

Our plan was for Fran to meet with them by himself, counsel them on the different ways victims dealt with traumatic events. He would prompt them to be forthcoming, express how each was feeling now. Ask if they thought they were healing. I wasn't allowed to be in the room or overhear what was said, fearing another male presence might stifle them. Fran was going to explain that my investigation was solely focused on catching this monster, and once caught, the final step in their recovery would be more possible. With the criminal behind bars they would feel truly safe. After his session, Fran would invite me in to review the lists they compiled, see if a new fact or observation might surface. Fran would announce I uncovered a pattern; that it was likely another woman would be attacked unless we stopped this sadist.

Being true to professional ethics, Fran made it clear he would not tell me what went on in the group meeting. Naturally, that didn't stop me from prying. Fran smiled as I pushed. "Only if it is something they're willing to have known. I have to foster their complete trust. If they think I don't respect their secrets, they'll never divulge their true feelings. Trust takes time to build." He hesitated, "Kind of like a great friendship."

I understood, agreed with him but couldn't restrain myself. "How about if I give you twenty bucks. Will you spill the beans?"

Fran frowned, "I think that traumatic stress you got in Nam is surfacing again. You're getting more and more delusional." He turned more serious, "Anything new on the chase for Percy?" Before I could answer, "Just like what these women are going through, I don't see you fully healing till Percy is put away for good."

I filled him in on the bad news but told him Nut was on the job. Fran raised his eyebrows, "Well, at least you're in capable hands." He said, "Oh, by the way, I'm having a session with other Vietnam vets with adjustment problem next week." He looked intent, "You need to be there." I nodded, but my focus for now was these ladies.

♦

While Fran was meeting with the ladies, I sat in his outer office, thought about that earlier discussion with my friend turned psychologist. My hunt for this sadist had occupied my attention so much that it did distract me from Percy. That had become a problem. I was not as attentive as I needed to be. I didn't delude myself that Percy had gone underground forever, could almost feel he was close by. Hard to explain, but it was like a chilly wind. The feeling was primal, nothing logical. My recent discussion with Nut jolted me, made me more alert. I survived Percy in Nam by being super-vigilant. I vowed to recapture my watchfulness. I did trust Nut but knew somehow this would end up with me facing Percy alone. And that both excited and terrified me. Could I defeat him once more, be lucky twice?

Fran opened his door abruptly, shook me from my

reverie. "You're up, Dylan." I took a deep breath, grabbed my flip chart. Went inside. Looking at the women side by side was chilling; they were so similar in size and shape. I watched them stare at me. Was it hope or mistrust on those weary faces?

I set up the flip chart. "Now that you've all met each other and had a chance to talk with Dr. Fran, can my first point on the chart be more obvious? You all look like you could be sisters or cousins." I stepped back, pointed. "Take a few minutes and look over the information you gave me. Does anything strike you? Is there anything you think has been overlooked? What I want you to reconsider is where this bastard could have met such a similar group of women? None of you knew each other existed till recently. How could he have found you?" I thought of the sweet or minty smell. "A couple of you noted a sweet or minty odor after the attack. Is that something anyone else recalls?" No one reacted, so I said nothing. For the next ten minutes, I watched them scan the list of facts. Nothing new came up.

Per my agreement with Fran, I didn't voice my opinions, ended the session that they should keep the information in mind and let it percolate. They should call if they had a revelation. Finally, the aggressive Miriam raised her hand. "Dr. Fran said you found a pattern. Can you tell us what it is?"

I looked at Fran. He nodded to go ahead. "All of these attacks seem to occur almost nine months apart."

I could see them wondering at that, so Chloe filled them in on what I had already told her. "It's almost like he's on a pregnancy cycle. It's like the attacks are some form of birth."

Fran chimed in. "I believe this predator has severe issues with his mother. That he was either abused or unloved by his mother, and that somehow he twisted this rage onto other women who either resembled or were somehow like his mother." When Fran said that aloud, a bell went off. The same idea had occurred to me, but I hadn't focused enough on that point, got too distracted with other possibilities.

Before I could chase it further, Miriam said aloud, "How long has it been since the last attack?"

Not wanting to put the spotlight on Chloe, I was about to give a vague reply when Chloe said simply, "It's almost nine months from the day of my attack."

That dreadful comment ended the session. Fran asked if they wanted to meet again. There was unanimous agreement. The next meeting was scheduled in a week. Before they left, I reiterated my plea to let the facts stew, to call if something new came to anyone. Chloe's roommate Elaine had agreed to pick her up, so I stayed to chat with Fran.

I grinned, "I know we agreed to keep your confidentiality but is there anything you can share that might help?" He hesitated, seemed to weigh options before saying, "All of the women have a striking physical resemblance, we already knew that. But, except for Miriam, they also have a similar manner. Miriam is more aggressive, tries to project that she has put this behind her, and moved on."

Fran said nothing else. I asked, "Do you believe that or is she just acting strong?"

He seemed surprised by my question. "I think Miriam is the most severely traumatized of the group. I think she's always been an extremely strong person, but this trauma might be the only time in her life that she's lost control. I think she's devastated." And then quietly, "I'm going to call her tomorrow to see if she'll meet with me separately."

My childhood friend was not only observant but was an exceptionally nice person. Was thinking how lucky it was to have such good friends, when Fran interrupted. "Dylan, I know we've talked about it before, but the other noteworthy thing is the robotic response from each woman when they say we'll never catch this guy. I did it as a test tonight. The response and tone were almost verbatim. It was like they rehearsed it together." He rubbed his chin, "It was eerie hearing such hopelessness, such a complete acceptance of their fate."

I nodded. That control also had me puzzled. The predator terrified them to such a degree they couldn't force themselves to believe he'd be caught. Almost like some form of brainwashing. This wasn't new information, but I needed to consider it further. I told Fran to keep thinking. To make what he thought were obvious observations. It's so easy to ignore something right in front of you. He agreed, would give it more thought, see if anything came to him.

As I walked out, Fran said, "Make sure you come to

the Vietnam group session next week." He handed me a card with the date and time. "I think you should talk about your Vietnam flashbacks. Some of the other vets have been reluctant to talk about their feelings. Listening to you might open them up." I waved agreement. Owed Fran a lot for helping these ladies. But knew it was a waste for me till Percy was put away.

HAYBRIDGE AND CLOTHIER

Whenever I had an unusual scouting assignment, Gator was always my first choice. Besides being observant and curious, he was funny as hell. After I reviewed my list with Merlano a couple days ago, he sent detectives to reconnoiter the Food Fare and other local businesses. He laughed when I said I was bringing Gator to poke around the famous clothing store. He met Gator when he got involved in the Sylvan Skolnick case. Merlano grimaced, "Don't go peeking in the ladies dressing rooms, okay? Last thing I need is some wild goose chase for two perverts sniffing around the ladies' underwear department."

He laughed when I said, "We'll be wearing disguises, I'm going as Linda Ronstadt, got the black wig all picked out. Gator's going dressed as Connie Stevens in her character, Cricket Blake, on 'Hawaiian Eye.' No one will ever suspect we're men." Merlano shook his head; "Maybe I should just arrest you now."

I picked up Gator at his office. He often worked Saturdays to catch up with paperwork. He was at his desk reading the Bulletin when I walked in. By way of explaining why he wasn't doing real lawyer work, "I just got done, wanted to scan the obituaries before we left. Reading about dead people always cheers me up. You know, glad I'm still alive, fighting the fight. Not like some poor schlub biting the dust prematurely. Get me?"

I shook my head, "Maybe Merlano was right, you are just a short hop away from the funny farm. Maybe today's the day."

He snorted his ebullient laugh, "Look who's talking. You have the sickest mind in Drexel Heights. Only that altar boy face keeps you protected. Me, I got your number, old friend." He had a point. Despite my innocent appearance, the good nuns at St Tim's had me pegged years ago: fire ants in my pants. I liked to stir the pot.

I waved at Gator, "Let's get going. I want to be there well before lunch. The ladies on my list said they usually went Saturday morning after breakfast." I gave Gator the newest details by telephone the night before, wanted his insight as we prowled the store.

The exuberant Gator sprinted past me. "Let's beat feet." That made me laugh, Gator was hardly ever still, was like a whirling dervish.

I followed, "Don't go sprinting inside Haybridges, the customers will think you're a shoplifter." He gave me the finger, continued trotting to my car. When he sat in the passenger seat, I told him to put his seat belt on. Before he could protest, "I don't want you hopping around while I'm driving. I'll feel safer if you're restrained." He drummed the dashboard like Ringo Starr in response. Off we went.

As we entered the store, Gator asked, "What's our strategy?" I didn't have a clear plan, wanted to ad lib things when seeing the environment. After all, I never shopped in the ladies department.

Said to Gator, "Let's poke around first, see if anything jumps out as odd or unusual."

Gator gave me his classic grin, "You mean like spotting a dude walking around with his zipper open and his ding-dong dangling?"

I chuckled, "Don't get me laughing, we have to avoid getting security chasing after us." It took some doing but we gathered ourselves, ambled around. The ladies' department was huge, covered about three-fourths of the whole floor. We eliminated the "girls" and "petite" areas as unlikely. The attacker liked smaller women, but they were all full-sized. The place was busy. Not wanting to be too conspicuous, we separated, stayed within sight of each other, but appeared to be solitary shoppers, like two clueless men probably shopping for their wife or girlfriend's birthday.

The only thing I noticed was almost all the sales clerks were women. I reversed course, finally spotted a man helping a woman with an arm full of dresses. Getting close enough to inspect the guy, I immediately eliminated him. He was probably in his sixties but was obese, could barely maneuver behind the counter to operate the cash register. But not wanting to be too impetuous, I got in line behind the shopper. When this older male clerk spotted me, he got a big grin, said in a high-pitched voice, "Well, lookie here. You look like you should be shopping in the strapping men's section. I'll be with you in a jiff."

The woman turned to me, eyed me up and down. She winked at the clerk, "Bruce, I think he's out of your league, sweetie. My bet is this one only dates Main Line girls with lots of money." She winked at me, "Isn't that right, sugar?"

Playing along with them, "Actually, I'm thinking of

entering the priesthood." The clerk, giggled, waved his hand, "What a waste."

Sure this wasn't headed anywhere, I asked, "Are you the only man that works in this department?"

Bruce shook his head, "I'm the only male they let serve the ladies. As they say, 'Old Brucie knows more about dressing the fairer sex than Professor Higgins knew about refining Eliza Doolittle.'"

Now the lady started to giggle. While both chortled at their inside joke, I crept away as rapidly as my feet would move.

Gator had witnessed the discussion but wasn't close enough to overhear. "What was that about? You three looked like you were having a good old-time gabbing."

I grinned, "I learned that old Brucie over there would be far more interested in dressing up in a moo-moo and serenading you with Broadway show tunes than molesting buxom women." While he puzzled that, I stopped at another counter, asked the lady about other male clerks.

She looked at me funny, "Not unless you count Bruce." I decided to let it go.

As we walked to our car, two shady looking teenage kids, both husky, were messing around my car. Gator, "What the fuck are they doing?"

I didn't respond, ran ahead. "Hey fellas, can I help you?"

The biggest one said, "Yea, ya can give me yer keys so I don't have ta break yer window. This piece of shit ain't worth much as it is. A broken window will hurt resale." The other punk laughed at the resale quip. Maybe it was pent up rage over the women's assaults or maybe just my lingering Vietnam anger, but the wise-ass response set me off.

I opened my hands, "Or, I could place my right foot up your ass, and then wipe it off on your ugly buddy when I'm done. But either way, this isn't going to end well for you unless you get the hell away from my car." The two punks stared at me.

Gator walked up close, said nothing, but I could feel his adrenaline pumping. The big lummox growled, "Fuck ya say?" He ran at me. In hindsight, it was sort of fun having a real opponent after endless hours of practicing for Percy. I let the punk charge, but at the last minute ducked under his outstretched arms, got him on my hip and body-slammed him into the concrete. You could hear the "whoosh" as air expelled from his lungs. Gator was grappling with the other knucklehead as I came up and kicked the back of the punk's thighs, collapsing him to the ground, in agony from the vicious blow. The first moron was trying to get to his feet as I closed, sweeping his arms, his jaw smashing into the unforgiving macadam. Blood oozed from his useless mouth as he waved surrender.

Gator moaned in mock anger, "Why'd you interfere, I had him right where I wanted."

We got in my car, leaving the wounded assholes to wonder how everything had gone to shit. Gator grinned,

"That was the most fun I've had since I got out of the navy and spent the whole summer in Margate trolling for babes. Remember the fights we used to get in at Mahoneys?"

I had a different recollection. "What I recall is you getting your ass beat most of the time. Like that time you kept calling the girl 'snake woman,' and thinking she liked it, but her boyfriend didn't and punched your lights out. Funny how age causes you to color memories into such a rosy picture."

He gave one of his raucous laughs, "Ain't that the truth, Dylan, ain't that the truth. That snaky girl was kinda sexy, right?" We spent the rest of the drive home comparing notes. Both agreed it was unlikely the attacker picked his victims at Haybridges. At least one from the list of common places was crossed off. I tried to stay positive.

PERCY PLANS

Percy silently reviewed what he knew. For the past two weeks, Frazier had visited the white bitch on Wednesday night, around seven-thirty. Every Saturday, he played basketball after lunch, dropped by to see her on the way home, around four. He went to church the last couple Thursday mornings and did laundry Monday early. They were the only patterns in an otherwise random schedule. After thinking more, he shook his bushy head. Except, most nights he went to McCormick's Deli for late night meals. He never ate there, always carried it home. The Deli location was mostly dead to traffic after nine. A few people, like Frazier, seemed to eat at odd times, the Deli stayed opened till eleven. But the Deli fronted a busier main street and cars routinely drove by. Even though Frazier always parked on the quiet side street, the traffic bothered him. What if a car pulled down the street as he was attacking? No car had done that yet, but was that worth the risk?

Percy ran other options through his troubled mind. He shook his head, trying to get a clearer picture. As taught in the army special forces, he visualized his attack. He saw himself committing the murder and retreating to safety. He exhaled deeply, returning to the present. He couldn't shake off one thing that made the white bitch's house so appealing: not only satisfy his uncontrollable revenge; he could humiliate Frazier. Doing it there offered that extra attraction. He thought more, mentally walked each step. After killing Frazier, kill the bitch. Make it seem like Frazier did it. Did a crime of passion go to hell? Ruin golden boy's reputation and keep me from suspicion. Percy squinted, liked that. Almost instantly a grimace creased his brow. He mumbled, almost growled, "Ain't the bitch's place where they'd expect me? Maybe Frazier's apartment is the better option?" That idea was starting to settle into his disturbed thinking. He closed his eyes, began to picture it happening.

But typical of his mercurial nature, he soon jumped to other worries. For the last few days, he followed the local UPS driver, studying his schedule. The guy was in Drexel Heights every day, usually till late at night finishing his route. And the driver was black, the only dark face you saw consistently in this lily-white neighborhood. That irregularity emboldened him; sparked an idea that he acted on yesterday. Percy had gotten up early, parked on busy State Road, and waited till he saw the UPS truck. Pulling out behind him, he followed for a while until the driver parked and hauled packages up to a candy store. Percy stopped nearby, got out and waited for him to return to the truck. As the driver neared, Percy walked by on the pavement, nodded, "What's up, brother? Nice ta see another black face around here. Gets kinda lonely."

The driver smiled, "Know what ya mean. But these white folks are paying the bills. This be one fine job."

Percy continued, "How'd ya get such a plum job? I'd a figured they'd just be hiring whitey fer deliverin' round here."

The driver grinned, "My old man drove a truck, taught me how since a kid. Got me some good credentials. The unions in Philly be screamin' for more black jobs. Just good timin' is all."

Percy spent the next few minutes telling the driver he just got out of the army, told some Nam war stories, got the driver comfortable, hinted at being a decorated war hero.

Half thinking out loud, Percy said, "Maybe I outta apply fer a drivin' spot. Did lots a truck work in Nam myself, mostly deuce and a half. Knows my way around vehicles. Can repair 'em an shit. Can ya tell a little more about how things work at UPS?"

The friendly driver, anxious to help a brave vet, gave a thorough description of his job, where his warehouse was, the whole works. Percy asked if he could look inside the truck; see if the boxes and packages were too big. Percy added, "Kinda outta shape, ain't had a job since I left the army months ago. Time ta get my black ass in gear."

The driver chuckled, "Me, I been married forever, had to go to work serious like after kids started comin', no layin' round." He chuckled, "My ole lady cracks the whip."

Percy grinned, "Knows how that goes. My ole lady gots her own deal, but still likes ta fuss. Percy asked if he could follow him around sometime; get a real feel for the job. They made plans to meet.

BERNIE NUDLEMAN

Dylan picked up the phone early Monday morning. Without identifying himself, Hoban ranted, "That asshole is writing me again." I bit my lip; let him rant. "But the good news is he's done with my boss. He claims that Harley can't be trusted anymore. Anyway, can you swing by and get this latest letter?"

I said I'd make it my first stop today. He hung up. I finally got out my belly laugh. I'd been so preoccupied with Percy and hunting the sexual attacker that a good Bernie Nudleman laugh was just what I needed. Before leaving the apartment, I remembered Nut's plea for vigilance. Looked outside my front door before heading to the car. Nut said my apartment might be a better spot for Percy than we first thought. I hadn't argued, lots of shrubs and bushes, easy to hide. But it was a bright, sunny day in beautiful Delaware County. What more could I ask for? Oh yea, I was being hunted by a maniac and a sadistic pervert was assaulting my neighborhood. I shook off sour thoughts, headed into the city of brotherly love.

Hoban was on the phone when I arrived, held up the latest letter, pointed to his conference room. I grabbed the missive, sat down. This was another comic gem to share with Elaine and Chloe. Only the other day, they asked if Bernie had struck again. I was laughing seconds later.

Dear Hoban (or should I say, Goldfarb? ha, ha):

Don't worry… Bernie forgives you. I was a little irked having finally contacted Fielding, the guy makes us an offer to make us lots of money and it falls apart. But it turns out your tiff with the Big Boss Harley was well founded. A bigger putz has never lived. Fielding finds out from his other mole (code name "Nachtmusik" —he's got over thirty agents at Etna alone), that Harley was trying to throw us to the wolves, so he could be the "go to" operative. When Fielding tells me, I say that you and me are a team, like Napoleon Solo and Ilya Kuryakin or Kulp and Cosby. So, Harley is OUT! It's back to the old days, just Hoban and Nudleman. More details on code names, (a Native American theme—but nothing like Tonto, too obvious.) and drop spots to follow shortly. Before I dispatch Harley for good, please settle this argument we've had. When you make potato kugel, which makes better? White or red potatoes? Expert that you are in Jewish haute cuisine, I will respect and abide by your opinion.

But I digress. What great news! To learn that you got married, and who would have guessed Sylvia Goldfarb? A real sweet potato, that Sylvia. (Personally, but as an old friend I can ask, how can you stand her brother Melvin? About six years ago he cheated me on six gross of shoestrings of which about ninety percent were frayed, but he blamed Louie Fein in Newark who brokered a discount shipper with rough wooden pallets. I prepaid like a dummy. One look and I knew they were made by that Herschl Esterman; a weaver that no self-respecting shoe merchant would employ). Let's hope the Goldfarb apple tree only dropped Melvin as the rotten one.

But hey, what's with Sylvia these days? I hear she's too

proud to switch names. Hoban is too goy. That she wants you to change your first and last name to Hercule Garfarb? After her rich grandfather. Is she bucking for sole inheritance? I hear he's big in scrap iron and custom carpet cleaning. Word has it she thinks the name Hoban can be easily confused with Hobo. She's got a point. Something to consider. Anyway, did you hear about our old pal Bennie Jacoby? Well, Bennie doesn't have that horrible harelip anymore. Papa Jacoby shelled out fifteen thousand to send Bennie to Dr. Ruben Zellermeyer in San Diego. Remember we used to call him "Bugs," an obvious rabbit allusion. It was cruel. I admit my guilt. But remember watching Bennie eating a carrot in elementary school? How we got revolted when the chunks of carrot got kind of caught in the crease? Well, a happy ending. Hoban, you wouldn't recognize him anymore. A Robert Redford with curly hair. Zellermeyer told my brother if Bennie corrects the overbite, every girl in Chicago will make goo-goo eyes at him. Are wedding bells for Bennie in the wind?

I have to sign off now. Lupe Sanchez is just walking in the front door to pitch me a new Afro-Latino shoe line, which he says will set Chicago footwear on fire. When you get a sec, call me at the store... you've got the number.

Bernie Nudleman

I was almost crying. It was the first time in days I stopped thinking about my problems. Bernie had grown tired of Harley Burns and that would let the pranks continue. Hoban only cared because of his boss. I noticed Hoban was off the phone.

I wandered in. Straight-faced, "I didn't know you got married. Why wasn't I invited?"

He finally grinned, "Can you believe that guy? Who in their right mind would spend that much time writing such nonsense? It's just so stupid."

I was going to remind him of the dictionary executive who wrote gadfly letter a couple years ago but shrugged, "Just someone with a bizarre sense of humor and maybe someone who has a stressful job that needs to do something so ridiculous that it's actually relaxes him."

He wrinkled his eyebrows, "You mean someone like you." I shook my head, "The answer is yes, someone like me. But it isn't me. I'm in awe of Bernie. He's taken this art form to new heights. He's my hero."

As I left, Hoban frowned, "It doesn't sound like you want to catch him." I waved my hands, didn't look back.

DYLAN HUNTS

Merlano's team visited most of the businesses on the ladies' lists- came up dry. I volunteered to check the post office, gynecologist, dentist and doctor. Since I couldn't walk in and ask, "Do you have any psycho employees," my ploy was to drop by randomly, poke around. See if anything or anyone looked off. The post office in Drexel Heights was a beautiful old stone building next to the trolley tracks. I went there first, thinking maybe the victims might make a weekly mail drop or pick up packages, hop the convenient trolley to go shopping or complete other chores. People did that stuff on Saturdays, so I mimicked that routine. I patrolled the ornate post office, looking for oddballs, glanced at the Wanted Posters—glad my buddies were absent- watched the postal employees dispense stamps and weigh packages. I spotted lots of interesting people but nothing abnormal. I noticed a postal employee staring at me eyeballing the Wanted Posters, remembered Hoban said I looked menacing, exited quickly. No need to draw attention.

I wandered to the trolley station, grabbed the News of Delaware County to read, sat and watched the action. There was creative graffiti, carved initials and sayings to read and amuse. Looked hard at the initials for one I carved years ago. Couldn't find it but found something better. My favorites graffiti was, "Wear a raincoat if you piss in the wind." You never knew when good advice would surface. I continued reading the newspaper, turned to the Obituaries, found only one odd eulogy: "Willy

Harter wanted a big, Irish blow-out wake, but didn't leave enough money, even after going for the cheap, wood casket. Bottoms up, Willy!" After an hour of amusing myself, only two trolleys came by. No one got on or off. I scratched the shopping/chores theory, after remembering buses and trolleys ran a limited weekend schedule.

Since I knew Dr. Powers already, I would visit him last, mentally eliminating him but not wanting to cut edges, even if obvious. The gynecologist visit would be tricky. How to explain a large, menacing guy wanting to see the gynecologist? I drove down State Road, got an idea as I passed McCormick's Deli. Also made a note to stop back for a late lunch after reconnoitering. There was a phone booth on the next corner. I stopped and called Chloe, told her I needed an alibi for visiting her docs. After a little thought, she gave me dates of recent visits. I hung up, finished my drive. I parked on a side street, meandered to the gynecologist office. Since I was an insurance investigator, my ploy was to say I was verifying bills Chloe submitted but were lost by Voyager. But my conniving was for naught. Another strikeout, Chloe forgot to mention the gynecologist was a woman.

The dentist was my last stop. It was almost noon as I entered the office. A couple older women were in the waiting area, I said hello. They smiled back as I moved toward a woman hanging up the phone. She looked puzzled, asked if I had an appointment. I told my lost bills story, asked if she could get new copies. Before she could ask, I told her to call Chloe to verify. The small lady nodded professionally, looked at her Rolodex, called Chloe immediately, got the okay. Just then her phone rang. She listened for a minute or so, got up, knocked on the dentist's door. She said aloud, "Mrs. Bevilacqua is calling, wants to know if you do a whitening procedure she read about in The Times. I told her you were busy but she insisted."

While that was happening, I glanced around. Like Dr. Powers' office, there were magazines galore. I spotted the National Geographic, forced myself to concentrate. Noticed an old picture of a woman in an ornate frame on the receptionist's desk.

My concentration was broken as the dentist cracked open the door, "Tell Angelique I will research the procedure and get her in next week." I never saw the dentist, but he had a distinct, powerful voice. I liked hearing him pronounce the lovely name, "Angelique."

The tidy receptionist turned to me, "Mrs. Bevilacqua is very particular about her teeth." She rolled her eyes, retrieved copies of Chloe's last couple visits. "Please let us know if we can be of further assistance."

I pointed at the picture, "Your mother?"

Got an odd look back, "No, the doctor's mother." She turned, started typing. I guess my visit was over. Another dry well.

NUT

Tracking Dylan the last couple days was an eye opener. How did he miss these other patterns? He shook off his anger, would need to revisit his previous thinking. He was angry Dylan had more patterns than he knew about. In less than a week, found two more. He slammed his bunched fist onto the desk. Thought over the new information. It was a surprise to find Dylan went to mass every Thursday morning at 6 am, total darkness, few people around.

When he mentioned that, Dylan gave a characteristic response. "Trying to cut down jail time in Purgatory. If I don't do something drastic, I can see myself doing a shitload of burn time."

His last habit was equally disturbing. Dylan did his laundry Monday morning at 7 am. Last week, he was the only person in the cavernous laundromat, a noisy place that could easily mask an attack. His cleanliness explanation was typical. "Why do you think I smell so nice?"

Nut's guard duty just got more complicated. There were too many places Percy could strike. He rolled his eyes: how do you manage the unmanageable?

DYLAN

Nut called last night to say I needed to warn Chloe about Percy. Since that was a place I went routinely, her house might end up in the crosshairs. He had a point, but I was hesitant to lay more worry on Chloe, she was progressing so well. Nut had been relentless. "She'll be a lot safer if she knows Percy is after you, and keeps her eyes peeled."

Reluctantly, I agreed. After a little noodling, I had a better idea. I called Chloe's house, fortunately Elaine picked up. When I asked if Chloe was nearby she said she was taking a shower. I spent the next ten minutes filling her in on the Percy problem, told her I didn't want to spook Chloe, but maybe she could be the eyes and ears for me. Without hesitation, "You can count on me, Dylan. I agree this might cause Chloe a setback. She's really healing, we can't have her reverting back; she's still too fragile."

I gave Nut's number in case she couldn't reach me. "Nut's phone is manned all day and night. The military never sleeps. If Nut doesn't answer himself, they'll get him by radio." I described how big Nut was, what he looked like, so she wouldn't be spooked if they met. I heard Elaine take a deep breath. Feeling bad about that, "You can trust Nut completely. He's been protecting me his whole life. Chloe is in good hands." She mumbled something, hung up quietly. I hoped she'd never have the misfortune of meeting Percy.

♦

The next morning, I dropped by the police station to debrief with Merlano. He told me his policeman had found a few leads but nothing substantial. Sitting in his office, the hairy detective frowned, "You don't always get the cream of the crop working in grocery stores. Especially the butcher shop, guys that like to butcher meat got to be a little off, right?"

I hadn't thought of that but agreed, "Wouldn't be my first career choice. Hacking off wings and legs, dealing with blood and guts all day. Can't be a positive profession if you're on the dating scene." I feigned a pensive look, "How about working with fruit. Nothing weird about that, is there?" I paused, "Unless you started hanging around the melon bin too often, fondling them, or making odd noises and breathing too deeply. That could scare off co-workers, right?"

Merlano shook his head, "Sorry I brought it up. It wouldn't be safe having you working around anything that breathes."

We got down to business. I was frustrated, looked at Merlano, "What if your guys showed some of the ladies' pictures around the Food Fare, see if it rattles anyone."

The husky detective shook his head, "We'd need to get their approval and that ain't likely. Plus, what if the picture put one of them in danger. Got them attacked again. We can't risk that."

I knew he was right, "Dumb idea. Forget about it. It's just so infuriating. I feel we're so close to another attack and I can't stop it."

Merlano raised his eyebrows, "That's the worst part of this job. Pieces of shit like this guy walking around free as birds." After a few seconds, "These bastards always make mistakes. We'll nail him, count on it."

Walked to my car hoping he was right but having a sense of doom. What if he was wrong? I was an optimist by nature, shook myself, vowed to work harder, find some elusive connection.

It had been a while since I'd been to the basketball courts. Most of my free time was spent with Jimmer, working on reacting to blind attacks. I needed a change of pace. Throughout my life, the rhythmic basketball drills always freed my mind. The summer was unusually warm, I returned to my apartment, changed to shorts and t-shirt, made the short drive to my favorite place. This slanted court befuddled most newcomers. The elevation changes from side to side made you rely on constant repetition, locking in muscle memory. Over fifteen years of practice, I didn't have to think anymore. It was the perfect therapy.

As always, I started in close, made five in a row and moved farther out. By the time I got to twenty feet, my touch returned. On this court I was a great shooter, totally confident. Draining long shots, listening to the soothing swish calmed me. I relaxed. My mind drifted.

PERCY

Per their agreement, Percy met the friendly UPS driver, Walter Davis, near the warehouse after the truck was loaded. The driver commented on Percy's new haircut. "Cut down the Afro, huh, bro?"

Percy's new hairdo wasn't about style. It was to mimic the driver as best he could. His bushy Afro had to go. "Got's tired of it, too much work pickin' it out. When I gots out the army, thought I needed a change after all those years bein' shaved close for Uncle Sam. But my shaggy bush gots ta be too much work. Figured I'd cut it back some, kinda like yours. If I apply fer a job, gots to be lookin' sharp." Percy grinned before adding, "Started doing some sit-ups and shit, gotta get my fat ass back in shape. UPS don't wanna be hirin' some lazy-lookin' fat brother, right?"

The driver smiled, "Ya gots a point." Looked down at his ample belly, "Not like I'm Mr. Universe or anything."

Percy punched him playfully, "More ta love, right?" Both men rubbed their bellies, had a good chuckle over that one.

Percy learned Walter always worked Saturday but had Sunday and Monday off. That schedule was important since Percy wanted to hit Frazier on a Saturday or Thursday. He thought that would be more unexpected, being a rest day or near the end of a long workweek. They drove all over Upper Derby and Drexel Heights. Percy helped to carry heavier boxes to gain the Walter's appreciation. This delivery job reminded him some of the army, very neat and organized. The olive brown colors of the UPS uniform eerily like what he wore in the military. Percy commented, "Kinda like the spit and polish, can see myself fittin' in here nice."

The driver said, "Ain't as much fun when ya have to wash this big sumbitch when yer done each night." He explained that his truck had to pass inspection each morning before leaving for the day. The driver added, "Me, I do the job at night, some drivers get in early. Me, I likes my sleep."

Percy got excited when they pulled up the white bitch's street. Walter stopped the truck in front of her house, grabbed a mid-size box and started to exit. Percy said, "Need ta stretch my legs, can I give you a hand?" Without asking, he took the package from Walter, scanned the addressee, Chloe Zubrisky.

Walter shook his head, "Better not, Ms. Zubrisky had some bad shit happen to her last year, gets kinda jumpy. Till a month or so ago, she wouldn't even answer the door. Took her a while ta get used ta me. Nice lady, though, once ya get her trust. Had to be some bad business ta be that scared."

Percy shook his newly shorn head, as if in sympathy, stayed behind in the truck as Walter knocked on the door, got no answer and wedged the package inside the screen door to give some protection. It was Percy's lucky day, now he knew the bitch's name. Might be useful.

His good fortune wasn't done. They drove down Frazier's street, and sure enough, stopped in front of his apartment. He looked at Walter, "Who lives there, looks like the only apartment on the street."

Walter agreed, "Looks like they converted an ole house a whiles back." He added, "The guy Frazier gets packages all the time, some kinda investigator. He caught some famous murderer last year. I think these are files fer him to investigate. They's all come from big shot insurance companies. Don't see him much, though, always be out."

That bit of information was invaluable. Walter hauled a large manila envelope to Frazier's door, totally unaware he helped Percy plan a murder. Frazier was used to getting deliveries from this driver, wouldn't be surprised to see a black man walking to his door. Just like that Percy finalized his attack. Smiled as this last detail fell into place: it would work.

DYLAN

Fran was relentless about getting me to attend his veteran therapy sessions. Since we already concluded I wouldn't improve until Percy was caught, I begged off. This time, my cagy friend had a different tactic. He asked to meet at his office. My empathetic friend looked at me intently, said sincerely, "Dylan, do this for the other guys. Most of them are really damaged. I think it will help if they hear your story. Do it for them if not for yourself."

I waited a few seconds, smirked, "Are you saying that after hearing my pathetic story, they'll say to themselves, 'Gee, maybe I don't have it so bad. Sorry ass Frazier is a total burn-out.' Then they'll undergo some miraculous cure."

Fran shook his head, "We'll that actually wasn't my plan, but now you mention it, that does sound like a solid strategy." He was kidding me back but had my attention. I told of my recent nightmare being attacked in the airport after coming from Nam. About being hated as a "baby killer." He listened solemnly, said each of the vets felt the same way, embarrassed they went to Nam, feeling despised at home, that somehow, they had failed everyone. I shook my head, agreed to return that night.

♦

I came back to Fran's office with low expectations. There were four Vietnam vets at the session. Fran started the meeting, said to take a chair in a circle, just use first names to avoid worry about being recognized. He scanned the circle, looked at us individually, "Later on, if you feel comfortable you've made a connection with someone, go ahead and tell them your name. For now, let's keep this as five guys who shared the same experience of going to Vietnam and just want to talk how it affected them. Okay?" Everyone nodded. I looked at my companions, realized immediately that my wise friend was right. Just based on body language, I was much closer to healing than these fellas. They slumped in their chairs, squeezed their armrests for support, fingers fidgeting. Like hanging onto a life raft after your ship went down, still not certain you were safe. Watching them, I had a hard time catching my breath. I teared up.

It seemed like forever before I could compose myself. Embarrassed, I lowered my head, rubbed my wet eyes, waited for my breathing to slow. When I lifted my head, all these broken souls were looking at me. No judgment in their sad eyes, just understanding. One of them introduced himself as Joe, "That happened to all of us in the beginning." He smiled, "It gets better." The other vets, Walt, Vic and Andy introduced themselves. Said they broke down just like I had, that they were there to help me. I shook my head back and forth, fighting back a new set of tears. Here I was thinking I'd be some big savior. These guys I'd judged as worse off were now consoling me. What an arrogant bastard. I breathed out slowly. Made up my mind and proceeded to tell my tale. They listened attentively. I could almost see them understanding my situation, looking for a way to help catch Percy.

When I was done, Fran spoke. "Dylan and I have been friends since we were ten. I've never heard him ask anybody for help. He was always the strong one, someone who could fight through anything. As tough a person as I've ever met." He paused for what seemed like an hour before adding, "But now you've seen what Vietnam can do to even the strongest of you." He let that sink in, "Now it's time for all of you to get better."

I spent the next two hours listening to Joe, Walt, Vic and Andy telling their stories. They were all infantry grunts, spent their tours fighting in the bush, walking the impenetrable jungles and mountains of South Vietnam. They tramped through that dense vegetation week after week looking to kill Charlie or some rogue Viet Cong outfit. They explained after a firefight, there was no sense of victory, no elation you had been in some glorious battle for freedom. It was just the numbing, inexorable hunt to kill whoever dared get in their path. All had seen buddies die. You made friends fast in the bush. When you needed someone to keep you alive, you got attached instantly. You didn't judge them by color, education or religion. Everyone was the same when they crawled through the bush. Mourned the same when they died, just men trying to survive.

Vic and Andy told how they stood by as their lieutenants got fragged. The rookie officers had carelessly led the platoon into near death traps once too often. The fragging murderers were burned out soldiers who had enough. They were trained to kill. They hadn't discussed the bloodthirsty plan with the rest of the platoon. They just acted, saying afterward, "Ain't no place fer dumb shits in the bush. Woulda got us all killed. I ain't even bullshittin'."

Joe and Walt talked of friends strung out on drugs, too wasted to go on duty, unable to function. Joe said, "They were good guys when they arrived. Went to college and all. Nam just fried 'em." Joe wasn't looking for an answer. He had a wounded look as he spoke. The common question was why we made it home safely. Why us? Each wondered why so many people back home seemed to hate us.

Fran explained there was a sense of public guilt about Vietnam. So many men fled the country, gotten bogus medical deferments, did anything to avoid being drafted. Fear made people do unexpected things. He told us it wasn't something that would ever make sense. Just something we would have to live with. "War doesn't play by fair rules." I watched each of them walk out a little straighter, more in control. I did feel better. Agreed to come to the next meeting. My childhood friend was in the right job. He made an incorrigible cuss like me face memories I wanted to bury.

VINCENTE

The time had arrived. It was hot and humid, a blistering August day in Philadelphia. Everyone grumbled about the Phillies. Another mediocre season, but most believed hope was on the way. Larry Bowa was the best defensive shortstop in baseball and could finally hit more than his puny weight. Mike Schmidt had a breakout season, leading the National League in home runs, and showing Gold Glove defense at third. If Greg Luzinski played the whole season, they might have made it interesting. But something happened every year with the Phils. Most people didn't mind much since it gave them ammunition for Philly's favorite pastime—second-guessing their baseball team's manager. Every fan in Philly was an expert. Just ask them. They'd spout volumes on the intricacies of hitting the curveball. All this athletic wisdom would spew as the beefy fan downed a cheesesteak. Slurped a cold Ortlieb.

None of this inane trivia mattered to Vincente. He put down the Bulletin, didn't like baseball, but followed the results to converse with his clients who were fanatically loyal to the hapless baseball team. His diminutive size precluded him from playing sports. To appear more normal, he watched sports to fit in better. Oddly, Rosa was obsessed with the sport since coming to America. He tolerated her jabbering about the Phils, so he could get insights into what his patients might bring up. Today, she was questioning whether Danny Ozark could ever get them to the World Series. When Vincente put down the sports page she said, "To me he doesn't seem intelligent. When you have Steve Carlton on the team, don't they need some other pitchers? He's the best in baseball but can't do it alone." The look she got from Vincente chilled her. She could judge by recent behavior, he was near his cyclical boiling point. She quickly rose from the kitchen table, began clearing dishes.

The rest of the day was a blur for Vincente. He saw less than his normal amount of people, instructing Rosa yesterday to free his schedule in late afternoon. He never ate dinner on the night of his "rituals." It wasn't nerves. It was an all-encompassing focus on the pleasure to come. Over and over he rehearsed his routine. Everything had to flow, just as he had groomed Angelique during her past sessions. She was a willing patient, very susceptible. His other victims required manufactured visits to get them fully controlled. But not Angelique, her obsessive personality had her in his office every three months. Not that she was just vain or stupid. Angelique was a successful CPA, was partner in one of the most successful firms in Drexel Heights. But just as Angelique prized an orderly spreadsheet, she also insisted on appearances. She was a textbook perfectionist.

It was almost ten o'clock. Rosa was in the den watching the end of the Phillies game as he prepared his materials. Satisfied everything was in order, he stowed them in the trunk of his car, a brand-new Plymouth Satellite. Vincente wasn't normally interested in cars but had to admit this sporty car was fun to drive. He even burned rubber sometimes to feel the power of full acceleration. It gave him chills, all that horsepower. And the black vinyl roof made the metallic blue paint look jaunty. He always envied the cool kids in high school with their flashy cars. Now, he was just like them, on top of the world. But his joy was momentary. His eyes flashed: he would never be like the beautiful people. The beautiful people were the ones that tortured him. His life was a torment because of the beautiful people, especially the women. Now he was getting even. Now he had control.

Rosa went to bed after the Phillies game. She bid him goodnight, said the Phillies lost to the Pirates. "That moron Ozark should have left Lonborg in. That closer Farmer has nothing left."

Vincente didn't respond, watched her amble upstairs. He waited an hour, crept the stairs softly, opened the door; peeked in. As usual, her heavy snoring signaled deep sleep. Vincente envied her ability to sleep so soundly. Since childhood, nightmares haunted his fitful attempts at rest. As he walked off, Rosa opened her eyes, checked the time, thought to herself: off again. What is he doing? She shook her head, tried to nod off, actually more relaxed when he wasn't in the house, her strange wanderer. Downstairs, Vincente looked at the clock: still too early, a few minutes to kill. He always left the house at exactly midnight. The "witching hour" was supposed to be myth, but Vincente didn't believe that. He believed midnight was the time when evil took over, that devils and spirits walked the darkness. Vincente felt a pact with these spectral creatures. It was their time.

He always called from the same telephone booth, part of the ritual. It took a few minutes, but a sleepy Angelique eventually answered. Altering his normal voice, he told Angelique to turn off the outside light, that he would be there shortly, would knock three times. Her voice was now alert. She hung up agreeing to do as told. The lush vegetation in Drexel Heights made it easy to conceal his car. Vincente removed all internal lights to remain invisible when opening the doors, gathering his satchel from the passenger seat. As with past victims, he parked a few blocks away. Even though Angelique lived in a wealthy area, with very few houses on spacious lots, he wanted no surprise walkers. She had been divorced for over five years, had no children, but still wanted a large home to announce her fortune. Vincente thought about that success as he loomed in the shadows, whispered in a feral tone, "Your smug, perfect life is about to change."

He stood still in the gloom, savoring these last moments of anticipation. It would be another nine months before he indulged his hunger. That saddened him. He hated such a long wait. But the morose thought passed rapidly knowing he would begin the selection process anew. Vincente brightened. He continued his hunt. Angelique had done as requested. The enormous house was dark as he trudged from the massive side yard to the front door. After three distinct knocks, the lovely Angelique appeared in a flowing nightgown. She looked at him wordlessly, opened the door to let him enter. Vincente took his time as he gazed at the stylish furniture, a clear display of opulence. Angelique liked nice things, had been privileged for most of her life. Vincente breathed deeply, altered his riveting voice. Turning to the motionless Angelique, "Go up to your bedroom." He pulled out the candy cane, placed it in his mouth, and breathed the aroma deeply as he ascended.

NUT AND DYLAN

Rather than getting frustrated by Dylan' chaotic schedule, Nut called his mercurial friend, explained his angst. Without hesitation, Dylan said, "I was thinking the same thing. We need to go back to the drawing board." They agreed to meet at Nut's house since his mom was at work. Ten minutes later, Dylan walked inside, pointed at Nut, "We need to simplify the variables."

Nut lifted his chiseled jaw, "Unless you agree to be more routine, managing you is like herding monkeys."

Dylan smiled, "Or as the nuns said about Maria, in The Sound of Music, 'how do you keep a moonbeam in your hand'?"

Nut wasn't amused, "You just confirmed my worry."

Dylan shook him off, "I'm just funning with you. Believe me, I'm deadly serious, was just trying to lighten the mood." Nut just stared, so he proceeded, "In the last few days, I've given this a different look, think I have a better plan." Nut started to argue but Dylan shushed him. "Listen to what I have first. If I'm off base, I'll do what you say." Nut waved him on.

Dylan took a breath. "I decided to whittle the places of attack to a top five. If you agree with my choices, it will narrow the odds of being surprised. Plus, you can focus my guards easier." Nut remained quiet. Dylan opened his loose-leaf binder, stated the following locations:

1. *My apartment*

2. *McCormick's Deli*

3. *Chloe's house*

4. *Early morning mass*

5. *Laundromat*

Dylan paused for comments, but Nut rolled his hand. "Although other places were possible, these were most likely. For each location, I asked: when was the best time of attack? For the apartment and deli, night was most likely. I rarely go to the deli except later in the evening. In addition to the cover of darkness, I would be more tired at night after a full day of work. And late-night snacking leaves me nice and content, less alert. For the laundromat and church, only early morning works. It's the only time I go there. And that leaves Chloe's house. I check on her occasionally after work and on Saturday afternoon."

Nut rubbed his chin, "Night-time would be better for an attack. Saturday afternoon is still light outside, much trickier."

Dylan let that sink in and got another worry. "Elaine is usually with Chloe, another variable to overcome. Hmm. But would Percy know that Elaine lives there? She adds another complication." He decided quickly, "I'll stop going after work or at night, too dangerous for them. That might take them out of the crosshairs." Nut gave the thumbs up.

Dylan watched as Nut remained eerily still: was he thinking about weak points or just annoyed? He plowed on. "I thought about the specific approach for each location. How would he surprise me? But rather than imaging the attacks, let's go look at them right now. We should eyeball them together; say out loud what we're thinking. Make sure we miss nothing." Nut was already moving toward the door without a word. Dylan yelled, "Hey Lone Ranger, wait for Tonto." Nut never broke stride. They went first to Dylan's apartment. It was broad daylight. They had to visualize the scene as if it were night. Large maple and oak trees were everywhere. Mature shrubs lined the house, partially hid the walkway. There were numerous attack points.

They agreed that Percy would probably strike when Dylan was walking from his car. Once Dylan got inside, he was on the second floor, with no access except through the locked door and up the stairwell. Nut said, "What's the possibility of you opening a door to someone late at night?"

Dylan, "Slim and none." Added, "Only for someone I know. That leaves the outside, an attack walking from the car is the winner." They jotted more notes, went back to the car.

As they drove to McCormick's Deli, Nut started talking as if he were Percy, "He'd follow you, let you go inside to order your food, figure you'd be off-guard, jump you on the return to the car." They pulled into Dylan's normal parking place, on the side street near the entrance.

Dylan looked more carefully at the surroundings, saw a murky place about fifty feet away, thought about that. "I should park in that specific spot from now on. Those large rows of hemlocks would provide perfect cover. Percy would see that immediately, be drawn to it. You could have your team nearby, already in place, perfectly obscured by the hedge of mountain laurels only twenty feet away. Your team could be on Percy on seconds." Dylan added, "Percy would want to toy with me a while before finishing. Sadists like to see their victims terrified." Nut frowned, didn't argue. They made more notes, got in the car.

Chloe's house was on a nice residential street. Although there were large sycamore trees lining the street, they were spread apart, not clumped together. The impression was people wanted you to see their beautiful home, didn't want the view blocked by too much vegetation. Chloe had some shrubbery, but they were well maintained, kept trimmed. They considered that neatness factor. It would be harder to hide except at night. Since Dylan came mostly on Saturday afternoon, it would be broad daylight, good visibility. But what would a meticulous hunter do? Dylan looked at Nut, "We should leave nothing to chance. How would you do it, even in daylight?" Dylan watched as Nut stepped away to get a clearer view. Standing perfectly still, he locked-in on the neighbor's side yard. There was a clump of bushes that might work. He walked to the spot. You could almost hear him thinking aloud: if Dylan were at her front door, he wouldn't be able to see me. But then I'd have to run about a hundred feet noiselessly.

Nut turned to me, squinted, "Tough but feasible." That is what they planned for.

They drove to St Tim's, their former grade school

and church, to study the early mass situation. They sized up the church area. Both agreed attacking Dylan at church presented problems. Although it would be dark and early morning, there was no place to hide. There weren't too many churchgoers at six o'clock mass, so Dylan parked out front, a short hike up the steps. Because there were lights on the street and church entrance, it made hiding impossible.

Dylan started talking out loud, "Maybe the unlikelihood of this spot would make it appealing. I would have my guard down, not be as attentive." He was quiet as he turned and walked to where he normally parked. There were houses across the street, but no trees on the sidewalk to hide behind. Dylan continued his brainstorm, "After mass, I would be looking in that direction as I returned to my car. It would be tough to surprise me."

We were about to rule this one out, when Nut said, "Did you leave your car unlocked? You're always joking about what a piece of crap the car was, that no one would steal it." Nut balled his fists as he finished. "No way you lock it. Percy could sneak into the backseat, garrote you in seconds."

Dylan watched the slight sag in Nut's massive shoulders. They had a lot to ponder.

MORE PLANS

Nut dropped by next morning with more thoughts. There was a smile, a kind of self-satisfaction on Nut's face as he explained. "Let's talk about how to maneuver 'in the kill zone.'"

I shook my finger, "Let's call them something more pleasant. How about 'windows of opportunity'?"

Nut chuckled, "I know you're nervous when you joke more than your normal irritating level."

He was right; I was trying to distract myself. I looked at my hulking pal, shrugged, "I'll behave, let's get back to what I should do at each spot." Nut had drawn a diagram of the five locations, pointing out the weak points that Percy would notice.

I must have flinched because Nut raised his palms, "Nothing to worry about, I'm way ahead of him. Percy has no idea a shit storm is coming down on him." I looked at my best buddy's grim expression. It was frightening, even to me. He was going to war. I had no wise-ass retort. It was time to fight.

♦

Next morning, I called Jimmer to fit me in. All he

said before hanging up, "I'm waiting for you. See you in a few minutes."

I guess my voice gave me away. I was nervous. This was coming fast. Jimmer was standing at the door. "I gather you got some bad news." Nodded, explained our plan, how Nut was preparing me for each likely weak point.

Jimmer frowned, "That Nut was always prepared, even as a kid. I guess having a psychopathic old man makes you hate surprises." Walking into the dojo, Jimmer said, "You're about as prepared as can be." Paused, "Now we have to go over it again." We spent the next couple hours walking the gauntlet blindfolded. I practiced sliding away from contact points, using feet and hands to counter. The goal was to get a momentary advantage, deliver a lethal blow. We practiced again and again striking the vulnerable points on the human body. I walked away exhausted but somehow more confident. Jimmer's words stayed with me. "Look for the opening. There's always a soft spot. When it appears, crush him."

Before I left he reminded me of the major worry. "What are you going to do if everything we trained for doesn't work? That he surprises you and disables you. That might be the most important thing you'll need."

He made me recite the obvious. "I'll be off-guard, maybe in shock. Fight or flight. The tendency is to shut down, almost be paralyzed. My adrenaline will be running wild."

He asked, "How do you calm yourself? You must

have a routine, something physical to shake the nerves back to earth." He had given me a few suggestions before.

I told him what I thought would work best for me.

Jimmer said, "This Percy is insane, so logic won't be in play. You know him, make certain you find something to throw him off balance. What you must do is regain control of the situation. Throw a curve he can't hit."

♦

I spent the remainder of the day retracing the five vulnerable areas. Assuming that Percy was following, I made certain not to linger, or make it apparent what I was doing. I mixed in multiple spots to mask my real motive. Over the course of four hours, I completed my mission. It helped to see the places with fresh eyes. It was still daylight as I parked out front of my apartment. The late summer sky was getting dark earlier. I wondered if Percy had waited so long just to terrify me. Or was he waiting so I'd start to feel safe, get careless? He probably counted on being underestimated. I remembered years ago being on patrol with him in Nam when he said, "Peoples think ole Percy's a dumb ass." He'd laugh his maniacal way, "Then, them people look surprised when I fucks em up." I scanned my front yard, vowed not to let that happen as I walked upstairs.

◆

Next day got much worse when I answered the phone, heard Merlano say, "We got another attack. Same MO, same vague description, and same damned certainty we'd never catch him. I'm telling you, its eerie." Merlano was a tough guy. I could hear the dejection in his voice.

In a sympathetic tone, "Is she still there at the station?" He told me she was so shook up she stayed overnight, was with a policewoman and social worker going over the details again and again, looking for some small clue. I could tell it surprised him when I asked, "Can I come over, maybe talk to her? There might be something fresh she might forget in a day or so. You can kind of pretend I'm a cop, so she doesn't think it odd. Even you say I look like one."

Merlano snapped out of his funk. "You look more like a hit man for the mafia than a cop. Kinda look like you're slightly off, like a fuckin' loony." After he finished chuckling, "It's against my better judgment but I'll talk to the social worker, get her okay. Come on in, we've got to try every angle to nail this prick."

◆

Shortly thereafter, I sat at Merlano's desk reviewing the file. The name Angelique Bevilacqua struck me immediately. Looking at Merlano, "I've heard that name before." Shook my head, "Just can't place where."

He nodded, "It's a distinctive name, kinda musical almost. It would be one you might remember." And then he gave bad news, "The social worker freaked out when I said I wanted you to talk to the victim, said it's way too early to introduce another male cop into the interrogation. She's way too fragile still."

I worried about that reaction on my drive there, was prepared. "Can I talk to the social worker? And maybe get a look at the victim? I know I've heard the name before, maybe seeing her will jog my memory."

Merlano frowned, "You are one pushy son of a bitch." He got up, walked out to plead my case.

The social worker was tough. Her name was Bertha Limcus, looked ex-military, short but with impressively square shoulders, built like a bulldog. Her opening salvo didn't bode well for me. "How come I've never seen you around here before? I thought I knew all the cops." She eyed me up and down, "Especially the macho boys." Before I could react, "You look like a CIA spook, but you're dressed like a bill collector. What am I missing here, why should I let you talk to that poor lady?"

She put her arms akimbo, defiant. Unexpectedly, that made me laugh. I smiled, "You nailed me. I'm not a cop but I think I can help Angelique." Paused, "And the six other women who had their lives ruined by this heartless piece of shit." Bertha's eyes opened wide as I told her the whole tale, all the other women who had been assaulted exactly the same way, and what I'd been doing to catch him.

When I was done, Bertha said, "Well if that isn't some shit on a shingle." She agreed to let me talk to the latest victim but only with her present.

Walking in the room, I was no longer sure I'd seen her before. She looked like the other victims, same type. Maybe I was jumping to conclusions. While I was trying to recall, Bertha introduced me, asked me to explain whom I was, why I was involved. I spent the next fifteen minutes giving Angelique the sad story. You could see her analyzing the information, had learned from her file she was a CPA. She looked composed but maybe just an act. I purposely didn't mention how each victim believed we'd never catch the attacker.

Testing my theory, I asked Angelique. Her voice changed, "You'll never find him, he's too intelligent, he's long gone." Bingo.

Before we went into the room, I told Bertha about this unique reaction, that I would test this with Angelique, but wanted her approval. Bertha had agreed. I turned to Angelique, "Let me tell you something very unusual." She held her breath as I explained that was verbatim, tone and all, what the other ladies said. I could see on her face it was too early to convince her.

She looked at us blankly, "But he never will be caught."

I changed gears, "Do you remember tasting or

smelling anything afterwards?"

Her eyelids lifted, inhaled as if trying to recall, "I think I remember smelling peppermint."

CLEARING COBWEBS

Walking to my car, I felt like a failure. Another woman attacked as I sat by, useless. Felt I should have worked harder, and it could have been stopped. Shook my head hard, "It's a puzzle, stupid, think!" More determined than ever, I drove to my apartment in a fury. While parking, tried to gather myself, knowing rage would cloud my focus. Percy popped into my muddled thoughts. Blinking rapidly, I hammered the dashboard, "Get your head out of your ass." I scanned the street, no signs of Percy. Looked more carefully, no signs of my guards. Were they screwing off or just well concealed? Got a twisted thought. Had Nut gotten tired of my horseshit and decided to let Percy blow me away? That made me chuckle, snapped me out of my gloom. Slapped the dash again, "Stop feeling sorry for yourself numb-nuts, and get after this psycho." Caught myself, blinked before realizing I forgot to add, "Both of them." Looking around once again, with the coast clear, I headed to my pad.

I pulled out my recent notes, started adding them to the flip chart. It was a welcome break from worrying about Percy. Had to admit, I was getting jumpy. On a separate sheet, I wrote *ANGELIQUE BEVILACQUA*. Under that, *"Where did I hear the name?"* And then, *"Did I meet her?"* She looked exactly like the other victims, wrote that on the page. Went back to the first page on the flip chart, read all my notes. When the pugnacious social worker, Bertha, gave me clearance, I'd ask Angelique to complete the chart of people and places she frequented. Wanted to make sure they matched the others. I had no doubt they would be identical. Staring at the facts, I realized there was a missing question. "Why does this monster hate this particular type of woman?" I scratched my head, "There must be something in his past that made him hate attractive but small, voluptuous woman." I let that sink in, "Was it a mother or maybe a girlfriend who jilted him?" It seemed unlikely that a guy with this rage was married. "Or was it?" I would call Fran Philips later to ask his expert opinion.

The intense concentration turned my mind to mush. No coherent thoughts or questions came. When I did hard word jumbles and puzzles, I had learned to look at things from different angles, used other parts of my noodle. When this approach worked right, the incoherent string of letters became a word; they just came together. Maybe I was trying too hard, needed a distraction. I looked at my front window, still light outside, said screw it, headed to the closet to grab a basketball. Always liked the Voit basketball, nice grip, especially on asphalt courts. Nut would probably flip out by altering my routine, but I dashed down the stairs, looked over the terrain for an all clear, and jumped in my sad excuse for a car. The basketball courts in Drexel Heights had always been my safe haven. No one was there. Better to have the place to myself. I ran full court drills, laying the ball up full speed. The trick was letting the ball kiss off the backboard softly, somehow neutralizing how fast your body was moving. It took time, but I found that perfect rhythm, the ball drops cleanly through the net. My mind settled.

Shooting jump shots came next. Starting five feet out, I made ten shots in a row before moving in a semi-circle.

That precision got harder as I got to foul line distance. Part of the routine was grabbing any missed shots, not letting it hit the ground. The farther away, the longer the rebound, the more you needed to hustle. Soon my mind went blank. I concentrated on keeping a high arc to my shot. That made any miss hit the rim softer, a more manageable carom. I was now at twenty feet, swishing the ball consistently: such a beautiful sound to a basketball player. When I was about to move out farther, it came to me:

I had heard Angelique Bevilacqua's name at Dr. Candido's office, the dentist on each victim's list. I recalled him hidden behind the door, pronouncing her musical name. He had a distinct voice, but I never saw him. I remembered that picture of a beautiful woman on his wife's desk. The frame was quite old. The woman was full-bodied. Heard the wife's words, "No, the doctor's mother."

I felt that jolt, when a riddle starts to clear, gears starting to engage, the engine purring to life.

I hustled to my car, thoughts racing, piling atop each other. It was still light outside as I parked and ran up to my apartment. The grueling basketball drills left me exhausted but with growing clarity. My apartment was muggy, no air conditioner from the stingy landlord. I turned on a fan to get some breeze. Sat in front of it to cool down. The fan reminded me of my dad, and his theory that air conditioning was bad for you. I could hear his litany, "Clogs the pours; doesn't let your skin breathe." Dad would get an intent look, "And that can lead to all sorts of problems, rashes, chills, sinus problems and fever if you let it fester. There's nothing wrong with a little hot air." His theory also extended to fans. He gave the same rationale, just not as vehemently. What he was really concerned about was the expense. My frugal dad was thrifty to the extremis. When I got my first job, I bought myself a fan for my room. I can still picture him walking by, looking at my fan; shaking his head as if to say, "My son is a profligate."

The fan was nice background noise as I put together the random pieces. The humming noise helped me think. Listening to that rhythmic sound gave me the last part of the puzzle. I recalled Dr. Candido's strong, soothing voice. Dr. Fran and I assumed the victims were traumatized, created a similar narrative as protection from reliving the horror. But I believed that Dr. Candido hypnotized these helpless women, probably during their dental sessions. Why had it taken me so long to see this? He was the dentist for all the victims. I thought again about the picture. It was his mother. Was she the source of the sick rampage? Maybe she died at an early age, left him motherless? Was he trying to get back at any woman who looked like his mom? Rather than getting myself worked up, I called Fran Philips, asked if he could see me right away. I told him what I was thinking.

Heard his, "Oh my God," as I hung up.

Fran listened to me without commenting. His face got tighter as I unveiled each connecting thread. I mentioned Dr. Candido's distinctive voice. "Fran, he has that syrupy, deep voice, very soothing. Would be perfect for a hypnotist, right?" I looked at him, "Kind of like yours, now that I think about it. Hmm."

Fran finally grinned, "Let's stay on track, I know you

like to tease to break tension, but get back to your facts, tell me more." He was right; this breakthrough had me excited, in overdrive. I made an effort to breath slower, iterated my final list of connections. Fran was especially interested in the picture of his mother. "One of the classic causes of mental problems is a boy's relationship with his mother. Freud made a career studying that dynamic." He ran his hands through his hair, "If Candido had a turbulent mother/son connection, it could explain the victim selection process." He was quiet for a few moments. "I'd have to get him in therapy to learn exactly what went wrong."

I looked at him sternly, "Fran, what I want to concentrate on is how can we prove he's the attacker, and how can we put him away forever. The last thing I care about is how to solve his mommy issues."

Fran didn't respond. Realizing that was harsh, "Sorry, I know that's your job, but I need your help nailing this down before I go to Merlano." For the next hour we brainstormed. We decided to get all the victims together immediately, to review our suspicions, and to see if identifying our suspect would shake any memories loose. We called Chloe first, told her we had a breakthrough, didn't tell her any specifics, but got her help connecting with the other ladies. Within an hour, the entire sad train-wreck of women marched into Fran's office. Looking at the worried faces, it took me a while to compose myself. I gathered my wits, started, "This may be hard for you to believe, but I think that…"

♦

Beforehand, we decided to use Fran's video camera to tape this session. He told me before my Vietnam vet meeting that he taped most of his appointments. Many patients had no idea how downtrodden they looked and sounded. By taping them, he could demonstrate how they changed as they healed, carried themselves more upright, appeared stronger and more confident. He showed me a few tapes where the patient truly looked like a different person after therapy. It was a powerful visual. Even though we discussed this tone change with the group at the last meeting, seeing it would be more effective. When I delivered the punch line about their dentist, I stopped talking. Immediately, the group tilted their head up, simultaneously said robotically, "It couldn't be Dr. Candido. He's such a gentle man." If I had any doubt, that eliminated it.

Fran took my place before the group. "Ladies, I want you to see what just happened. We said last time that somehow this attacker had either traumatized you or scared you into believing he's invincible." Fran had their attention. "But what really happened is that he's hypnotized each of you. He probably did it over a period of time as you had dental visits." I watched as all their eyes widened, jaws dropped. "This is probably hard for you, but I'm going to show you how you reacted to Dylan's message about Dr. Candido." Fran replayed the tape on a large screen on the side of his office. Each of them watched in silence, shaking their heads in disbelief. They started to squirm in their seats. Fran summed up, "That ladies, is a classic hypnotic response."

The lively Miriam Keller broke the tension. "If this is true, I'm going to strangle that little coward." That galvanized the crowd, others chimed in their intent to march over and throttle the bastard.

Fran said, "I wish it were that easy. He still has you under his thrall." He explained that he had some hypnotic training as part of his psychology education but was not an expert. "He would have planted a posthypnotic suggestion that only he is aware of. If you went over now, he'd get you back under control in seconds, maybe just by one word or expression that appears meaningless. A gifted hypnotist might use multiple planted suggestions to maintain his spell. There is no way of telling unless we hear how he's done it. He probably used the same approach with each of you. Most hypnotists have a specific technique. It might be one word or how he says the word." Fran let that sink in. "We don't have a shred of evidence, just a theory. Unless we can undo this command over you, your memories will be either blank or so totally dissimilar as to be useless. We have to crack his code." I could see the look of dejection on their faces. It seemed hopeless. But I had an idea after seeing Fran's arsenal of video equipment.

"Ladies, don't despair. I have a plan, but it will take one of you with enough courage to go back into his office to do something that might trap him." After a few seconds, Miriam's hand shot up. Fran looked concerned, he had mentioned to me that Miriam acted strong, but it might be a coping mechanism.

I looked from Fran to Miriam as I said, "Hear what I have to say before you volunteer. This will take some guts and also some acting skills." I had their attention. "You saw that Dr. Philips has some cool audio/visual equipment. He mentioned we have to get the exact suggestions he's planted to erase your memories. Plus, it would be even better if we taped his voice giving the commands." They looked expectantly, still not understanding.

I asked them to show me their purses. That brought surprised looks from all. Slowly they raised their bags. Large, cloth purses were the new rage. I then told them how I could modify a purse so the small recording device would not only record sound, but also videotape Dr. Candido delivering the message. Smiles appeared for the only time that night.

I knew from a previous case the cops couldn't tape a suspect without his knowledge—that would be entrapment. But, there was no legal issue with a private citizen taping someone if worried about security. I learned from the ladies that Dr. Candido had a table and chair for patients to bring pocketbooks, coats etc. into his office while he worked. Most people liked to keep track of their things. I explained the volunteer only needed to place the bag at the correct angle. We could simulate the height in Fran's office to make it foolproof. The hard part was getting a brave lady to enter the office and spinning the tale I concocted to push Dr. Candido into using his hypnotic technique. I told them my approach. At the end, I asked if we had a volunteer. This time a quicker reaction, all the brave women raised their hands.

Getting this done right was vital. I asked the ladies to nominate someone else. To my surprise, Chloe was the unanimous pick. Miriam was upset she wasn't chosen, but the group told her nicely she might be too intense. I hadn't anticipated Chloe. Shaking my head, "We only have one shot, can't afford him smelling a rat." It scared me a little, but Fran and I finally agreed Chloe was the best fit. She had progressed in recovery, had a quiet strength that would help sell our charade. And she trusted me. I told Chloe I would be outside the office while she gave her performance. "I'll be in there in seconds if I sense anything off track." She smiled, liking that. We spent the next two hours modifying her purse, practicing her lines and simulating the height of Dr. Candido's desk. We agreed the shorter her playacting the better. Didn't want it to appear robotic, fake. After just a few tries Chloe was perfect, delivered her short lines flawlessly. And the video and sound were clear. Rather than delay, and add time to worry, next morning was our target to see Dr. Candido.

♦

Not wanting to piss him off, I called Merlano that night, told him my theory. Told him about the session with all the victims, and how they responded robotically in Fran's office. He was silent, thinking over the facts. "It hangs together, Frazier." After a couple seconds, "That little fucker."

I continued, "Fran Philips told me if we could undo the hypnotic suggestions, the ladies would probably remember Candido was the one who assaulted them." Just for protection, he agreed to have a cop car nearby if something went wrong while Chloe was in the office. I explained we would review the tape back at Fran's office. Hopefully, get back to him with substantial evidence. I told Merlano, "If all went as planned, we would get the victims to his office later that afternoon to give statements."

In typical Merlano style, "Frazier, I got one piece of advice." I heard him breath through his large nose, knowing this wouldn't be a pep talk. "Don't fuck this up."

I chuckled. Merlano would never be a motivational speaker. But he had a point. I was worried about Chloe: lot of pressure for a wounded soul.

THE VISIT

Rosa had just settled at her desk to review Vincente's schedule. He always wanted to see who was coming that day, what work was necessary. Yesterday, he asked for files on two female patients. Rosa knew all the patients well. Both women were divorced, small but curvaceous. It was always the same, his interest in these types. Years ago, she wondered if Vincente was having affairs with them. She soon stopped worrying about that. Vincente had no interest in sex, never consummated their marriage. He was a sad man, devoid of love or passion. However, she knew these types of women were important to him. Over the years, Rosa kept files on each of them; instinct telling her it was wise to track. A rare smile crossed her severe face: she had taken other precautions. Rosa had one persistent fear: having to return to her village destitute, it terrified her. The telephone rang, stopping her reflection. "Hello." It was Chloe Zubrisky asking to see Vincente, an emergency. Rosa remembered gossip about this woman being viciously attacked and was especially accommodating. Looking over the morning schedule, "How about eleven thirty, we can fit you in before lunch."

Dylan was with Chloe as she made the call that morning. As planned, he drove with her, hopped out a couple blocks short of the office. Chloe looked frightened, but Dylan explained, "Just in case he happens to look out his window, it wouldn't look right coming together. I'll be in a minute or so later." Added, "Inside, I'll be twenty feet away." Her shoulders relaxed a little as she drove on. As

Dylan neared the office, he spotted Chloe's car.

Entering, he wasn't surprised to see no other patients: it was lunchtime. Mrs. Candido's head rose, looked surprised. Could see her recalling Dylan's name, "What can I do for you, it's Mr. Frazier, right?

He wasn't sure she would be there but had planned a good excuse. "Having trouble with the insurance carrier again. They called saying they lost the records from a few of your patients. Was wondering if you could maybe get me some copies, help me resubmit? It's embarrassing for the insurance company to lose bills." I gave the list.

Her eyes blinked rapidly, processing. Finally, "Do you need this right away or can it wait?"

Wanting to hang around till Chloe emerged, Dylan shrugged, "If it's not too much trouble, I'd like it now. I'd be more than happy to wait."

Without answering, she rose, went into another room, the file room. Dr. Candido's office door was closed. Dylan inched closer, hoping to overhear. The wait began.

CHLOE

She was very nervous but knew Dylan was just steps away. Dr. Philips told her the previous night to find something calming, a memory, a prayer, or anything that would bring a sense of peace. She needed to be in control, to deliver a convincing performance. It took a while, but it came. No longer religious, she thought back to childhood, remembered learning the Psalm 23, the soothing words. She kept whispering to herself, "… thou preparest a table before me in the presence of my enemies; thou anointest my head with oil; my cup runneth over. Surely goodness and mercy shall follow me all the days of my life…" Chanting these beautiful words relaxed her as she entered this monster's lair. She placed her handbag at the proper angle, and sat in the dental chair, inches from the evil man who defiled her.

She forced herself to look at him, breathed in quietly. "Dr. Candido, I've been having terrible dreams." He looked at her with no expression, shook his head to continue, but started clenching his hands when she added, "In these dreams, I see you standing over me. It's you, but you're wearing a mask." She hesitated before adding, "And I start to scream."

Chloe watched his eyes widen. Dylan had prepared her for this moment; it was crucial. "But I know that doesn't make any sense. Why would you be wearing a mask?"

The ploy seemed to work. Dr. Candido stopped

rubbing his hands, his dark eyes softened. He finally spoke, "Perhaps, it's an unusual reaction to our new treatment protocol, where we used relaxation techniques instead of gas or Novocain." He rubbed tiny fingers on his chin. "Perhaps, your subconscious is confusing that pleasant experience with something more troublesome from your past."

It was difficult, but Chloe forced a smile, "I think that must be it. But these dreams are so vivid. I just didn't know what to do, so I thought you could help me. I always feel so good after I leave here."

That was the hook Dylan hoped would connect. Chloe watched as Dr. Candido walked to his desk, pulled out a shiny chain with a crystal orb dangling on the end. He walked toward her, told her to relax; adjusted the strong dental light toward her, and then raised the sparkling necklace. Chloe heard him say something and then...

DYLAN

Mrs. Candido was far more efficient than planned. I heard her footsteps, returned quickly to a nearby chair. She came back to her desk, had a few files open. "They've only been here twice in the last year. I'm not sure why the insurance company would be bothering them. We submitted the charges and got back what we expected." I expected that, asked if she could go back a couple years and see about those. Maybe those hadn't been paid? She grimaced but returned to the other room. That bought some time. In a few minutes, she came back, "Those bills are also in order. Everything is paid appropriately."

I really didn't have a logical response, winged it. "You know how insurance companies are. Must dot their I's and cross those T's. I remember when I worked there, they were always worried about surprise audits. The manager freaked-out if their internal audit wasn't squeaky clean. Would ream out the poor processor, like they just broke into Ft Knox, like they were part of Jesse James's gang. Isn't that nuts?" The look on Mrs. Candido's face said she thought someone else was also nuts. I threw up my hands, "Anyway, can you make me copies, and I'll walk them in myself. Make sure their files are nice and tight." She was back in a few minutes, handing me the paperwork.

The dilemma was how to make another excuse to hang around and risk making her suspicious. It had only been about twenty minutes. Figured Chloe would be there at least a half hour. I looked at Mrs. Candido, thanked her for the help. Said I'd let her know if anything else went wrong.

As I was about to go outside, turned to her. "Do you have a good deli nearby that you like for lunch? I'm craving an Italian hoagie, and you being Italian and all, thought you might be discriminating, maybe be an aficionado." The dour woman recoiled. I kept digging. "Like, if you were German or something, I wouldn't bother you. Know what I mean? Unless, of course I was on a sauerbraten binge."

Her eyes crunched so close together I thought she might pop a blood vessel. Her face returned to normal, "No self-respecting Italian would eat a hoagie. That is a purely American concoction."

I hesitated, as if I forgot something, but heard voices and beat a retreat from the befuddled Mrs. Candido.

Outside, I worried I went too far with Mrs. Candido, was too odd. Chuckled to myself: I needed to worry about that almost every day. I glanced back, was relieved to see Chloe exiting the office, cheered silently. Chloe seemed fine. The plan had worked. I moved fast toward her car.

As she turned the corner, I approached. My thumbs-up signal was met with a blank stare. "Dylan, what are you doing here?" I noticed the benign look on her face. She had no idea why I was there. Had she forgotten her mission? It got worse. I noticed she didn't have her purse.

My mind raced: had Dr. Candido outsmarted us, sensed the trap? It didn't seem likely, but... I said the first thing that came to me, "Chloe, did you lose your purse? You always have it with you. How about your keys? You'll need those for the car."

She shook her head, trying to place what she had done with it. Smiled at me, "I must have left it in Dr. Candido's office. I'll be right back." I tried to remain calm, waited for her to return. Had this just gone to hell?

Chloe seemed puzzled when I asked for a ride to Dr. Philips office, but smiled her agreement. The ride to Fran's office was quiet at first. I didn't mention our mission to convict Dr. Candido of these horrific crimes, just said we had agreed to meet Fran and the other victims. She didn't remember this appointment, but soon started to chat amiably, seemed oblivious to what had recently happened.

The good news was she retrieved her purse from his office with no trouble. For fear of interfering with Fran's plan to de-hypnotize her, I restrained from looking to see if the camera was inside. Finally, I asked, "How'd your dental visit go, I always hate those."

I watched her cheeks crinkle upward, "Dr. Candido's such a gentle man. I never worry about that visit." Silent for a few seconds, "I always feel so peaceful afterwards." I looked out my window, not wanting her to see my dejection.

As we arrived, told Chloe I wanted to talk to Fran alone for a little bit. She was still very mellow, nodded it was no problem. She sat in the reception area, grabbed *Good Housekeeping*.

Fran took one look at me, "What went wrong?" I narrated what happened, explained my worry. He agreed, "You did right not discussing what she was sent there to do. He obviously hypnotized her again, making sure he erased any worry of dreams." When Fran saw me about to explode, "Don't worry, that was what I expected. Let's bring her in, look in her bag, and hope she got what we needed."

I went out, brought Chloe back. Fran spent the next ten minutes slowly recreating her traumatic past, and that of the other ladies. She looked perplexed when he explained she had just filmed her session with Dr. Candido. While he talked, I fished through her bag. Let out a deep breath when I saw the video camera perfectly lodged in the peek hole, still running.

I waved at Fran, "Got it." He completed his narrative with Chloe as I rewound the film.

When Fran was done, she looked bewildered. Turned to me, "Oh my God."

Fran, his kindest voice, "This may be a bit painful, but I think you should watch, Chloe. If it shows what I think, it will probably help us erase the hypnotic suggestion, and allow you to remember that night." He smiled at her, "Then you will heal"

She squeezed her fingers, lowered her head, as if in struggle, but as her eyes rose you could see resolve. She nodded, "I'm ready." We watched the evil man put Chloe in deep sleep. He told her to forget seeing him in her room that night. That was all in the past, she needed to always see him as her savior, a kind man who takes care of her. The man who did those horrible things would never be caught, was smarter than the police, had disappeared forever. The malevolent Dr. Candido lowered his voice, recited a phrase that would awaken her, and make her forget ever discussing this. The secret phrase: IRMA, said slowly, elongated for emphasis.

Chloe stared, shaking her head, eyes ablaze before saying, "I never thought I could ever kill someone, but if he were here, I'd strangle him." Seeing and listening to the tape had worked. For a few minutes, her eyes blinked rapidly, but soon stilled. She looked at me, reliving that dread assault, "I got a call that night. He said he would be over in minutes; that I should turn off all outside lights. And then..." We listened as Chloe reiterated the details. Fran was jotting notes the whole time. He was making sure there were no other suggestions within the tape.

He looked up, "I think that's all there is. He got them to sit in the chair, used the dental light and sparkling orb to relax them till they fell asleep. Then he planted their instructions. He must have done it over and over till he was satisfied with their obedience."

I was getting excited, "Let's call the other ladies, get them here, see if this snaps them out of it when they see the tape." Set my jaw, "If it does, we get it to Merlano and nail the prick."

The ladies got there quickly. Fran went through how Chloe had gotten the tape successfully but had been hypnotized again to the point she completely forgot going there. Chloe spoke, "But watching the tape, listening and seeing what he did brought it all back."

Before she could continue, Fran raised his hand, "But it might not be as effective with each of you. I don't want you to be discouraged if it isn't as immediate."

The spunky Miriam spoke, "Run it. I don't care if it takes all night. I can't live with this anymore." Heads nodded. Fran had the projector set, ran the film. I watched the anxious faces. They were all pinching fingers together, shoulders hunched, nervous. The body language changed as the film rolled. Expressions started as apprehension, went to a rapt attention, nostrils flared in alarm, but finally changed to recognition. When done, I was still uncertain until heads bobbed up and down. They all remembered their dreadful night. The worry on their faces was now pure anger. And just like Chloe they wanted revenge.

I didn't want to screw this up by overlooking some legal detail, called Merlano. Told him of the tape and the unanimous recollection of the attacks. All victims could identify Dr. Candido as the assailant. His first comment was, "Holy shit, Frazier, ya did it." He paused, said to bring the ladies in for statements. After that, he'd decide how fast to pick up "the sick fucker," as he put it.

♦

We were at his office in twenty minutes. After making introductions, and doing paperwork, Merlano led our sad procession into a large conference room.

There sat the pugnacious social worker, Bertha Limcus, who looked at me, "You don't shit around do you, Frazier." She turned to the ladies; a warm look came over her sturdy face. "I want you all to know I've also been attacked before, that's how I got into this line of work." Bertha's face kept its warmness but became resolute. "Now we put this motherfucker behind bars." I saw six lovely heads nodding approval. Payback time.

THE ARREST

But my brilliant plan didn't work out so well. Merlano called later next morning to say the arrest had gone smoothly, but Candido denied everything. "He was cool as a cucumber, Frazier. You won't believe the balls on this twerp, said these women were all lonely. Had made passes at him that he rejected. That this was just spurned lovers trying to get even." Before I could go ballistic, "It gets worse, Frazier. His lawyer was here, said he'll ask the judge to throw out the tape, its classic entrapment." I listened to Merlano fight back rage, "Don't blow a gasket, Frazier, but our in-house counsel says he might be right, might not be able to use it."

Too stunned to speak, I mumbled, "You got to be shitting me." Merlano tried to calm me down, "Don't give up. We still have six women's testimony saying the same thing, so it's not hopeless." Added, "But if the tape's out, we don't have any hard evidence. Just their word against his." He gave more bad news. "Candido's lawyer will try to get this heard before a judge, not with a jury. The lawyer will argue a jury'll be too easily swayed by emotion. A judge will stick to evidence. He's got a chance winning that argument, and a judge could go either way."

I hung up, dejected. Needed to do something to get back my mojo. Flipped on a rerun of "Star Trek," watched an episode where Spock returns to Vulcan, and is reprimanded by his father, Sarek, for becoming too human. Naturally, that was a high insult in his home planet

Vulcan, a race run by pure logic. Later in the show, Spock was speaking to Captain Kirk as they worked out a sticky problem. Spock said simply, "Insufficient facts always invite danger."

I never heard Kirk's response as an idea sprung loose. In solving the case of serial killer, Sylvan Skolnick, I learned these predators liked to keep some reminder of their kills: "trophies." I knew that Dr. Candido wasn't a serial killer but wondered if he was prone to the same hunger. Since our ace card video probably wouldn't be admitted, we needed more proof. I stood up, walked to my window, looked to see if my bodyguards were visible. As I scanned the street, another idea hit me. The next hour I planned my next step. Then called Merlano to tell him my idea. He said nothing at first, probably worried I'd get him canned, but then offered sound advice.

I ran to my car, drove slowly, trying to find my best words. Parked my green excuse for a car around the corner from Dr. Candido's office. It was past lunchtime, didn't expect there would be anyone in the waiting room, since the good dentist was in the slammer. I didn't want his wife to see me coming, she might decide to lock the door, or just slip into the back room, ignore me till I left. Hard to predict how she'd act. It was pretty obvious I was involved in his arrest. I walked up the lawn to avoid noise, popped the door open quickly, and went inside. Mrs. Candido sat at her desk, like the good soldier not deserting her post even in times of peril. If she was angry, it didn't show. She said calmly, "What can I do for you, Mr. Frazier, I assume you know the doctor has been detained."

Approaching slowly, I pointed to the chair beside her desk, "May I?" She nodded, seemed surprised. Started my rehearsed speech, "Mrs. Candido, this is going to be painful, but I need to explain exactly what your husband has done."

I laid out years of unsolved assaults, all with the same sordid abominations. Told her each victim was their patient and had been subjected to hypnosis and could not identify the attacker afterwards. Mentioned that all victims had similar sizes and shapes: almost identical to the picture of Dr. Candido's mother. We might have a hard time proving it this time, but eventually he would be caught, and put away forever. I ended with, "I need your help to put your husband away. We can't let him hurt more women."

She hardly moved or blinked during the recounting of her husband's savagery. I watched the wizened face, her eyes active, like a cornered animal deciding fight or flight. She relaxed slightly, "I thought originally he was having affairs with them." Eyes hardened, "But Vincente was incapable of love or passion." Looking dead at me, "He is a man with no heart, he's empty inside. He hid that from his patients, but I knew, watched it every day." Pausing again, "I do think his mother mistreated him, although he never talked about it. Maybe that caused his attraction to that type?" She seemed to ponder, "Maybe we'll never know." Her head lowered, seemed to be weighed down. Was it overwhelming grief that her husband was a sadist? Before I got an answer, she stood, shuffled passed me, went to the front door, locked it. "I don't want us to be interrupted, there's something I'd like to show you."

She unlocked the adjoining file room. Not a pin out of place, the three file cabinets all in a row alphabetically. She moved to a small desk in the corner. Turning, "This is my area." With that, she took a key from her purse, opened the lower drawer, and pulled out a manila folder. Handing it to me, "This might help. I started compiling these files when I first suspected he was having affairs. I wasn't sure what I'd do with them but wanted to keep track. I like order." As I paged through it, she said, "It's alphabetical, not chronological." With that clue, I found Angelique Bevilacqua's file first. All her appointments were noted but a red line appeared about a year ago with the simple note, "special interest started." After that line, the appointments became more frequent, all lasting an hour and a half. Rosa saw me note that, "Vincente never allows more than an hour, that's when I first took notice. He's a very precise man, it stuck out."

I found files on the six other women from Merlano's list of similar, unsolved cases. But no incriminating evidence in the folder. Nothing like the "trophies" or other details I hoped to find.

It then hit me there were a dozen or so other files in the folder. Looking up, "Are these women also look-alikes for his mother?"

No emotion on her face, "Almost identical."

I paged through the entire folder, noting dates. Had a hard time saying aloud what I suspected, "This has been going on for over twenty years." I sat still, thinking. Tried not to let the horror of this overwhelm me. It took a while to compose myself, "Mrs. Candido, I need you to think if there's any place where your husband might have kept secret papers or files that might help us. This information isn't enough. I believe he's guilty, but we have to convince a judge and jury. Please think."

The tiny women sat, small hands tented under her chin. Lifting her gaze, "It never occurred to me as strange, but he has a wood shop in the basement. He keeps it locked, calls it his private retreat. He often goes there to putter with his woodworking. He's built a number of pieces for our house." An afterthought, "They're quite nice." Seconds later, "Maybe there's something there."

We left the office, entered the house, and went directly to the basement. The workshop dominated the north corner, foundation walls on two sides. A substantial door guarded the entrance. A large padlock hung ominously. Before I could ask, Mrs. Candido said, "I don't know where he keeps the key, probably with him, with the car and office keys. He always opens up in the morning. It's one of his rituals. I never learned to drive. No need for me to have keys." All I could think was: I know that's where he keeps the trophies. God damn it, so close. A thought popped to my puzzle-solving brain: look for a solution differently, see the answer then work backwards. Don't be traditional. It came instantly but I had to sell it.

Looking at this stoic little lady, "Mrs. Candido, I think something spilled in his workshop, maybe varnish, I can smell it. We better clean it up or the house will stink, might even catch on fire." I looked at the heavy tools neatly hung on the wall, "Do you want me to use that sledgehammer to break the lock and check out the problem?"

Perplexed at first, she caught on, "That's exactly what you should do."

When Merlano heard I was going unorthodox, he coached me not to contaminate the crime scene. The ornery cop had sneered, "Don't get your meat-hooks all over the place. A smart lawyer will say you planted evidence. More entrapment shit." After his elegant pep talk, I bought cheap cotton gloves on the way here. I slipped them from my pocket, donned them before I broke the lock with two swings. Asked Rosa to open the door and look around. Asked, "Do you want my help? It looks like that varnish or paint thinner can is open."

After she nodded, I entered and soon found a shelf full of stains and paint thinners. Twisting off the cap, I showed it to her, "This is the culprit." I spilled a healthy dose. Being careful not to touch too much, I looked for the likely hiding spot. There was a large workbench in the center of the room, two drawers on each side. I turned, "It's better if you search the drawers." I hadn't explained that if we found something, I wanted her to call Merlano. Didn't want to spook her with too much, too early. Wanted to spoon it slowly.

The drawers on the right were full of pictures, mostly tables, probably ones he made. The top left drawer was more interesting. There was a jar full of candy canes. As I was remembering the mint connection, Rosa pulled out a Polaroid camera, looked quizzically, but said nothing.

Next, she pulled out a large satchel. She slowly pulled out rope, evenly cut in six-foot lengths, and dark scarves. Finally, she lifted a ski mask and gloves. I inhaled sharply.

The poor lady looked at me, alarmed. Said with resignation, "Oh, no."

Not wanting to lose time or her help, I said gently, "Open the bottom drawer, see what's in there." I leaned in closer as she pulled it open. In the front section, there were more woodworking photos. But tucked in the back was a large manila envelope with a string to bind it shut. Rosa opened it slowly. She pulled out a series of files, with a picture of his mother attached to each. Opening the first file, there was a Polaroid picture was of a nearly naked Angelique Bevilacqua, tied to her bed with ropes, mouth bound with a scarf. You could see she was still dripping with urine, but appeared oblivious, still hypnotized. Rosa opened on the next file. It was my dear friend Chloe in the same sordid pose. I couldn't take it anymore. "Mrs. Candido, stop. You have to call the cops to say what you found."

As we walked to the phone, she remained silent, probably in shock. She was married to the maniac who had done such horrific things. I coached her on what to say to Merlano. It was very important to the case that she was the one who found the incriminating evidence, and she was the one reporting it. No entrapment. Just a bewildered wife who discovered she was married to a psychopath.

Minutes later, Merlano and his team arrived. I greeted him, showed him my gloves, "No meat-hooks to worry about." He just shook his head. Rosa said she felt ill, asked if I would show them what she found. The evidence was far more detailed than I had thought. Beside the sordid pictures, there was a detailed description of what was labeled, "the hypnotic grooming." There were nineteen files dating back twenty years. With minor variation, all had the same profile and sequence. Dr. Candido had improved his skill over the years. He bragged in the files he could get them under full control more quickly.

Merlano looked at me, "He's toast."

TRIAL

The judge agreed to rush the case to trial. The evidence was so overwhelming, and there was an outcry from the community when news leaked to the press of the atrocities. My buddy Gator was the lawyer representing the seven known victims. Merlano decided not to contact the other women who had never come forward. He wisely said, "Maybe they've buried it, moved on with their lives." Then added, "Or maybe the newspaper coverage will jolt their memory, but at least they'll know the bastard is gonna be put away forever."

Preparing for court, Gator asked me to dig around about the mother. He might be able to use the information to explain why Candido became a sadist. Merlano gave me the address where she lived with Vincente years ago. It was a beaten-up row home street beside the trolley tracks, near commercial space long abandoned. I knocked on all the nearby doors, talked with a few without any luck, but finally met an elderly couple that remembered the sad family. Got a succinct message from both, "Mother was probably a whore, got by that way I guess, cause she never worked. The ugly kid took care of hisself, never said much. They was trash. Pretty sure the mother killed herself. Never saw the kid after. Musta moved."

Two weeks later, Dr. Vincente Candido went to trial. His lawyer dropped the innocent plea after Gator masterfully grilled Vincente about his mother. Got him to blurt out, "All those women were whores, just like my mother. They deserved what they got."

Candido's lawyer jumped in; tried to switch the plea to insanity but Vincente screamed, "I knew exactly what I was doing. I planned each detail. I wanted them to know who was really in control. That I was the master."

The judge reached an easy decision, sentenced him to seven consecutive twenty-year terms in prison. He would be in jail till he died. But that didn't make me feel better. The sentenced pissed me off, too soft. I wanted him executed.

When I said that to Merlano on the way out of court, he made me feel better, "Bastard won't last a year. Perverts don't survive long in prison. They tend to hang themselves." And then winked, "Or maybe get a little help."

The seven victims were in court with Gator the entire time. Fran Philips sat nearby, worried Vincente would try to re-hypnotize them and blow the case. Fran had spent hours with the ladies preparing for that, coaching them on the planted suggestion: IRMA, spoken in a drawn-out fashion. IRMA turned out to be the mother's name. But Gator didn't give Candido the chance to play games. Whenever Vincente looked in their direction, Gator hollered, "Look at me, only at me." And it worked. It was late Friday afternoon as the trial ended. Fran and I walked over to the ladies. Fran told them how brave they were, asked if we could get together again in a group session.

He summed up, "It will take some time to process this. It will help the healing if each of you expresses what you're feeling."

The seven had become close. Almost simultaneously, they said, "We'd like that." And then giggled. Nervous laughs but it made me happy.

As we parted, I said to Chloe I'd stop over the next day for my Saturday visit. With a nice smile, "Elaine and I will make a cake to celebrate."

PATROL DUTY

Nut got to Chloe's house around two in the afternoon, enough time ahead to find an observation post. Dylan usually showed at four. The trial made it easy to watch Dylan because he spent most of his time preparing with Gator and Merlano. Once the trial started, his friend was inside the courtroom for the past week. Once the trial was over, it was time to resume reconnaissance. Chloe lived on a nice street, so he altered his watch position each time to avoid snoopy neighbors getting worried. He was aware his size drew attention. He had parked a few streets over, grabbed his backpack, planning to act like a civilian out for a summer stroll. His Green Beret uniform would act like a flashing sign, so he wore jeans, a t-shirt and Phillies cap. Before he left the car, he checked his walkie-talkie. The command post answered immediately; came in loud and clear. He was getting anxious, wondered if he had overestimated Percy's vengeance. Maybe Percy spotted the guards and split. Even Colonel Lynam was pushing to get his men back. Nut didn't know how long he could stall.

As he settled into his post, Nut thought about his elite training. He was among of handful of Green Berets selected for the "Rendition Team." That implied abduction of military targets but the true assignment in Nam was assassination. His fighting prowess and strength made him an incomparable weapon. With his 20/10 vision, the weapons training was just repetition. He shot BB guns as a kid, was a gifted shooter. He could have gone to sniper school but that didn't interest him. Hand to hand combat was his forte. Most of his targets had been Viet Cong leaders. The VC wreaked terror in South Vietnam villages. Therefore, if you eliminated these lead recruiters and organizers, the VC became ineffective. Some could be turned as double agents, if you were persuasive enough: especially those who didn't like pain. Those who resisted were "sanctioned." His code name was Panther—partly because of his face paint and dark camouflage uniform, but mostly because of his lethal skill. His kill rate was one hundred percent. His reputation amongst the VC was legend. Just the rumor he was in the area wreaked havoc. Was Panther on the prowl?

Nut shook his head, forcing himself back to the present. No time to dwell on the past. He could let nothing happen to Dylan, his best friend, one of the few people he loved. Was about the only person who could make him laugh. Their bond went back to childhood. Long ago, he confided to Dylan that he planned to kill his abusive father.

He still chuckled at Dylan's reply, "Remind me again why I'm friends with a crazy kid?" He exhaled, enjoying that memory. Now it was time to refocus. More importantly, now it was time to repay his debt. Nut wasn't proud of his ability to kill without guilt. It was a skill learned while coping with childhood beatings. He would pretend it wasn't happening to him, he was simply watching. The gift of compartmentalization was how he rationalized being a member of the Rendition Team. There was no clean way to destroy evil. Percy Price was a ruthless killer who had Dylan in his sights. He would have no regrets punishing him.

PERCY

Percy followed Frazier to court the past week. He read in the Bulletin that Dr. Vincente Candido was found guilty on seven counts of sexual assault. It infuriated him to read Frazier getting so much credit for solving the case. He growled, "Fuckin' hot dog is what he is." That rage motivated him. He growled again, "Today's the day, motha' fucker."

He'd been shadowing his UPS pal, Walter Davis, for the past two weeks. Walter liked getting the help. He never picked up on Percy avoiding helping him at either Frazier or Chloe Zubrisky's houses. At those locations, Percy used the safety of the truck to watch for unfriendly eyes. He hadn't spotted anyone lately but was playing it safe. He got dressed and left his apartment to meet Walter. This part would be tricky. He checked the gun multiple times each day, kept it clean, a bullet in the chamber, set on safety. Practice sessions in the deep woods of rural West Chester kept him sharp. His trip to the Army/Navy store in West Philly got him some extra firepower—a KA-BAR knife, just like the ones he used in Nam.

Percy figured Frazier would have his antenna down after winning the court case. He mumbled, "Big hero, all puffed up. Gonna deflate that motha' fucker right quick."

The thought passed as he saw Walter drive up. Putting on a big grin, "How ya doin', Bro Davis. Lookin' sharp as usual." Like always, they exchanged the army dap handshake Percy taught him. It made Walter feel like he and Percy were pals. They spent the morning doing deliveries in Upper Derby, would work their way to Drexel Heights after lunch. As he did his whole life, Percy ran on instinct. As they drove down City Line Avenue, Percy made up his mind where to attack. It felt right. All his planning was done. There was one last detail to take care of. "Hey, Walter, where ya wanna eat? How's about that diner comin' up? Pretty good chow there, huh?"

Always amiable, Walter said, "Sure nuff. Let's do it."

City Line Diner was a popular joint. It had a big parking lot to accommodate the large clientele. Walter pulled the truck towards the rear of the lot as usual, easier to get out if it got too crowded. Percy rose from his seat, walked to the back of the storage area. "Hey, Walter, take a look here. I think we delivered the wrong box last stop. Been eatin' at me, take a look."

Percy stepped aside to let Walter bend down to inspect. Walter said, "Looks okay…" as Percy jammed the KA-BAR in the back of Walter's neck, just where brain and spine meet. That was how he was taught to kill with a knife, if you didn't want a lot of mess. Percy pulled the rag from his pocket, withdrew the knife and stanched the wound to soak up the blood. Walter had died instantly.

The demented Percy talked to him like he was still alive, "Nothin' personal, bro. Jus' part a the plan." He quickly stripped Walter and changed into his UPS uniform. He stashed the body between the rows of packages. Percy went into the diner and ate a cheeseburger and Coke, was in no rush.

NUT

From his secluded vantage point, Nut spotted the UPS truck down the block from Chloe's house. He watched the driver amble up to a neighbor's front door, a few houses away. He'd seen this UPS driver multiple times on his stakeouts, hard to miss the chubby black man, one of few you saw in the area. Chloe apparently had lots of urgent mail from her job as distribution manager, which was code for resolving union/management conflicts. Having listened to Dylan talk about her, she was good at her job. Dylan said she had a disarming way with people, made you want to help her. That was probably why his softhearted pal got so involved. Dylan liked hopeless causes. Nut shook his head at that, thought: just as he did with me when we were kids. Very few of Dylan's friends were what would be considered "normal." But Dylan was the most eccentric, or as he said himself, "I'm paranormal." Nut fought off a laugh, got back to the mission.

Right on cue, he saw Dylan drive up, and park outside Chloe's house, a predictable two minutes early. Pleased to see Dylan look around before exiting the car, he mouthed, "Good boy." Roommate Elaine answered the door, and let him in. Dylan normally stayed about a half hour but warned of a cake to celebrate the trial victory, that he might be longer. They had spoken last night, compared schedules. Nut was firm, "Don't go winging it, Dylan, stay boringly on track so we can be there."

The other team had been with Dylan as he played basketball after lunch. They reported by walkie-talkie that Dylan returned home, got showered, and was on the way to Chloe's. "No problems to report."

Nut watched as the UPS truck drove up and parked behind Dylan's car. He noted the contrast between the spotlessly clean truck, and Dylan's green mess. Thought: my boy is not UPS material. He watched the chunky, nimble driver carry a small package to Chloe's door. After a brief exchange, the driver walked inside. A few minutes passed. As Nut looked down to check his equipment, something struck him: why did the driver go inside? He was moving when his walkie-talkie buzzed.

DYLAN

I parked in an open space near Chloe's house. Looked around to see if Nut or his team was visible. Nothing. I relaxed. Elaine greeted me at the door, "Well, if it isn't the prize guest, come on in, Dylan." She added, "Chloe's finishing the cake, we'll have it with tea in the dining room."

Chloe peeked her head in from the kitchen, "Elaine, will you finish the tea, I want to talk to Dylan." They exchanged places. Chloe was wearing an apron, some vanilla icing smeared here and there from her labors. She came close, gave me a big hug, held it a few seconds before, "I've never been so happy, and I owe it to you. My job is going great, and Elaine has brought meaning back into my life, she's the best friend I ever had." Could tell she wasn't done, kept quiet. "And with Dr. Candido behind bars forever, I can now put that horrible night behind me. What seemed like a hopeless future now seems so wonderful." I was getting embarrassed, was relieved when the doorbell rang. Chloe went to answer it.

No matter how much you prepare, sometimes you mess up. I saw the familiar black UPS driver as Chloe opened the front door to take the package. That wasn't unusual, you often had to sign for important deliveries. I was confused when I heard, "Oh, no." Thought she had gotten bad news as I walked over to help. And got a jolting shock to see Percy Price with his hands on her neck, and a Colt 45 pointed at her head. He was wearing a

UPS uniform, but I immediately recognized the dead, feral eyes. But the formerly lean mean fighting machine of Vietnam had gotten fat. He was a little shorter than the real UPS driver, but now had the same meaty build.

He seemed to read my thought, "Fooled ya, huh, white bread? Ole Percy gained a few pounds but don't let that fool ya. I still got plenty left ta put ya in a world a hurt. Big fuckin' hero, my ass. Time fer me to settle up."

He pushed Chloe into the room. Despite the extensive preparation, I was frozen with shock, unable to move. Goose bumps ran up my neck. Remembering Jimmer's advice, I breathed in through my nose, exhaled slowly through my mouth, tried to stop my adrenaline rush. After a couple breaths, I started to think more clearly. Part of Jimmer's training over the last weeks was preparing for being surprised, and suddenly helpless. His words echoed, "First get yourself calm. Then try to get him off balance. You must regain control. Look for an opening and strike instantly."

I remembered Elaine was in the kitchen. Making sure she didn't barge in, raised my voice to a near shout, "Well, if it isn't my old pal, Percy Price. Hadn't gotten word of your pardon. Must be nice being back on the outside."

He squinted his muddy eyes, "Fuck ya yellin' about. Shut up or I'm gonna shoot this sweet thing right now." He tightened his grip on Chloe's neck, pushed the barrel in her right ear." Elaine didn't appear, so she must have heard my warning. Hoped she would run for the police. Now, I had to get closer to Percy, get Chloe from the line of fire. No ideas came.

Percy stood grinning. "Cat got yer tongue, Frazier? Never thought you'd see me again, did ya? Thought Leavenworth could hold ole Percy, huh? Don't ya remember me sayin' I be comin' one day? Think that some idle shit?"

As Percy rambled more venom, I got an idea. Shook my head real slow, "What I am surprised about is you using a girl to hide behind. You always said you could whip my ass, but in Nam I could have killed you, but took it easy, kind of felt sorry for you." I watched Percy's eyes bug. Went for the punch line, "What I really thought was you'd want to use your bare hands, not shoot me like a pussy."

He pushed Chloe aside, came at me. "Who ya callin' a pussy?" He was still a few feet too far away. I put up my hands as a peace offering, "Fair fight is all I'm asking for."

His eyes darted back and forth. I could see he was tempted. Maybe I'd get a shot at him. Finally, he decided, "Turn around, look at the wall." I thought: still too far away. As I turned, he suddenly slapped the side of my head with the pistol. I saw stars, but it was only a glancing hit. As Jimmer trained, I blinked rapidly, my eyes wide open, still woozy but quickly felt better. By then Percy was right behind me, gun jammed under the left angel bone of my back, ready for the kill shot to my heart.

Jimmer preached that people always veered left when startled. We trained as if that would be their reaction, and I would move right. All I would need was a split-second distraction. Jimmer taught a specific countering technique he learned from magicians who mastered the ability to shift people's focus. Once your opponent was distracted, you counter moved. As I felt the Colt 45 push me forward, I raised my head suddenly up and left, as if gazing at something unexpected.

Trusting and hoping Percy would look up, I fell to the right, pivoted backward with my right foot slamming into Percy's arm, the follow-through landing a solid blow to his jaw. The Colt 45 roared, I didn't feel any pain, but had no time to check. Still on my back, I saw Percy lying nearby, clutching his face. His gun was a few feet from him, toward the kitchen. As I moved to the gun, Percy revived. As he scrambled for the Colt, I realized there was no way to beat him.

But then the unimaginable happened. Like the Archangel of Death, Nut flew from the kitchen. His massive hand karate chopped Percy's forearm. The gun fell. All I heard was a sickening crunch, and Percy's howl. Without hesitation, Nut moved nearer, and viciously axed his speared fist into Percy's throat. I heard sickening gurgling noises as Percy struggled to breathe. When I reached out to help, Nut stopped me. He held me motionless, whispered, "He'll choke to death in a minute or so."

LOOSE ENDS

From Chloe's house, I called Merlano, hoping he would smooth out any police concerns. He knew about Percy, wasn't surprised when he learned what happened. His comment made me laugh, "Some people are shit magnets, Frazier. And you are the biggest one around." He was there with a squad car in twenty minutes.

Nut coached me on what to say, "Tell him exactly what you did, the kick knocked the gun away, but was discharged. I'll say I got the call from Elaine, came through the back door, heard the shot, and struck Percy as he went for the gun." He looked to make sure I understood. His intensity was riveting. He continued, "Apparently my blow broke his windpipe, caused him to choke to death. It happened fast, we didn't have time to get medical help."

And that's what I said. Merlano listened carefully, looked at Nut, shook his head, "Not many people would survive a shot from that guy." Then he looked at us, smirked, "One less asshole in the world."

After the police left, I got more details on why Nut showed up. Elaine knew I was sending her a message that Percy broke in. She kept Nut's number beside the bulletin board in the kitchen. The telephone had a long extension cord. She dragged it into the pantry, so Percy wouldn't hear, made the call. Nut was watching outside, and already on the move when he sensed something off with the UPS driver. That was how Percy ended his lifetime of brutality. Chloe was shaking, but overall in fairly good spirits. I felt

TOM FAUSTMAN

terrible, like she didn't have enough trouble already.

She smiled, "Now you can heal, Dylan. Just like Dr. Fran said to us." She looked at Elaine, seemed to draw comfort from her friend, turned to me, "Maybe you should come to our therapy group. It will help to talk it out." Such a gentle lady, worried about me now. Her thoughtfulness touched me. I just nodded, had a hard time catching my voice.

Nut and I walked to my car. Something was bugging me. Wasn't the type to let loose ends dangle. I turned to him, "Is that true about the windpipe? That he choked to death?" He said nothing, seemed uncertain how to respond. My large friend said in monotone, "Actually, I broke his hyoid bone, just below the jaw. That bone controls swallowing. He couldn't breathe so he choked to death."

I wanted to ask if he did it on purpose but knew the answer. My buddy Nut was on a lifelong crusade against bullies. Had been since his childhood. I didn't miss the real meaning of his actions. He knew Percy would chase me till he killed me, or until he was killed. Nut wasn't taking chances. His decisive action turned my life from endless uncertainty to normalcy. How do you thank someone for saving your life? I started to well up for the second time. Said quietly, "Thanks." He waved me off, walked away without looking back.

♦

I slept like a baby that night. Woke up realizing the phantom haunting my dreams was dead. Wondered if Fran was right, that my flashbacks would end. Another thought popped up. Maybe I was the kind of guy who wandered into trouble, always too curious. Or as Merlano said, "a shit magnet." That got me laughing.

During breakfast, I thought about Rosa Candido. Her testimony solidified the verdict. I began to worry about ruining her life. What would she do now? Walked to my car, started to scan my surroundings on reflex. Smiled, whispered happily, "That Inspector Clouseau shits over."

Rather than go to Rosa's front door, I went to the office door. Saw lights on, opened the door. I spotted the tiny women at her desk, just like normal. She looked up, "Well, I didn't expect to see you here again. What can I do for you?"

There was no strain in her tone, she almost sounded happy. "Checking in to see if you're okay." The next hour I heard an astounding tale.

Rosa Candido sounded joyful because she was. When she suspected Vincente was having affairs, she kept those files in case she went to divorce court. After realizing Vincente was incapable of sexual relationships with other women, she worried it was something else. Rather than wait for a surprise, she made plans. The first move was to buy business insurance that paid fifty percent income levels if one of the partners was unable to work. There was no exclusion for felony or misdemeanors. Rosa said innocently, "Vincente signed whatever I put in front of him, he didn't care about the business side of the practice. I've already filed the claim and was told my checks would start next month." That wasn't all. "I filed for divorce. My lawyer said Pennsylvania is an equitable distribution state. Even if Vincente contested, the Common Pleas Court will distribute the funds, with him in jail there is no contest." She had a smile on that once weary face as the punch line was delivered, "I will be return to Puglia a rich woman, buy a small villa near the sea."

I laughed aloud walking to my car, no need to worry about her.

I drove to meet Nut, he was leaving today, would return to Parris Island, already had a new assignment. It was nice having him around but wouldn't miss his daily grilling. Wasn't used to being managed, and he wasn't used to having a knucklehead to control. Could tell I was getting on his nerves, and sort of enjoyed it. I noticed he was done packing his car as I parked.

To irritate him, "Do you need help finishing up?"

He knew me well, shook his head, "Thanks for nothing."

Not wanting a sappy display like yesterday, I added, "Next time you come to town, give some warning. I'll make sure I'm at the Jersey Shore."

He got in the car, was about to close the door when he said, "This new case I have is very odd. Someone is killing retired army officers. Apparently, it's been going on for years, but they just spotted the pattern." He shut the door, rolled down the window. "All the murders are in the Greater Philadelphia area. Maybe I'll give you a yell if I need help." He rolled up the window, drove off without another word. A few seconds later, shook my head. I guess I wouldn't be getting a goodbye hug.

I spent the rest of the day organizing the insurance files I'd neglected. Hoban would be happy I'd get some shaky Voyager claims resolved. He was the gravy train. I needed to keep him happy. As I put the files in my briefcase, realized I hadn't called Jimmer to give him the gory details.

Picked up the phone, dialed my judo instructor and friend. He recognized my voice. His gruff answer was typical, "This better be important, I was just about to take a crap." When I told him how his training saved me, he got more serious. "You had me worried, glad it worked out."

He hung up without another word. I laughed again, thinking I really did have odd friends. I was having a hard time relaxing, decided to grab a ball, and head to the courts. Doing shooting drills, I started thinking about Bernie Nudleman. Was glad I hadn't figured who he was. Believed that some mysteries should remain unsolved.

THE MISADVENTURES OF DYLAN SERIES:

Dylan's Chase

High school senior Dylan Frazier's relentless hunt for the city championship takes a turn when he is compelled to uncover the demons his two friend's, Nut and Truck, have been battling. Can he solve their problems in time to capture the elusive basketball title at the Palestra?

Dylan's Nam

Dylan is drafted into the Vietnam War and is assigned as an MP to one of the most dangerous areas of the front. He quickly learns the ropes of life in a war zone and begins making friends with his unlikely assortment of fellow MP's. His curiosity leads him into a dangerous predicament where he is investigating crooks within his own unit. He is torn between doing his police duty and getting home safely.

Dylan's Monsters

Dylan Frazier has returned from the Vietnam War and finds himself employed in the only unlikely job that will have him—an insurance investigator. His hysterical on-the-job antics are challenged when he pokes around what appears to be a related series of unexplained deaths. Dylan is pulled deeper into the workings of a sinister mind. And the monster is watching.

Dylan's Devils

Dylan, fresh with the success of his first famous solved crime, his investigation business is booming. His new case involves a gruesome attack in the Philly suburbs. The beautiful victim puzzles Dylan with her inconsistent details and odd belief her attacker will never be caught. While chasing this psycho, Dylan learns that Percy Price, a villain from his Vietnam days, has escaped prison and vowed revenge. Will the hunter become the hunted?

ALSO BY TOM FAUSTMAN:

Chameleon Skills

Learn the unwritten rules of Corporate America that are not covered in business school. Funny, true to-life, proven examples of how to get ahead in business today. A must-read for all college grads and those stuck in a business rut. The book outlines the dramatic transformation of Tom Faustman--from overwhelmed rookie to Senior Vice President of a Fortune 100 Corporation where he managed over 6,000 people that included lawyers, doctors, MBA's and actuaries. Without the benefit of a business education, advanced degrees, mentoring or outside training, his career skyrocketed. What he did to prosper is outlined in this book. Through observation, acquired skills and wily techniques, a "chameleon" was born.

No business school will give you what lies within! An invaluable gift for college grads!

ABOUT THE AUTHOR

TOM FAUSTMAN is a retired Senior Vice President from a Fortune 100 company. Born in Maryland, Tom spent the rest of his youth in Drexel Hill, PA where he divided his time between playing pick-up basketball on the neighborhood courts and making the Catholic school nuns shake their heads. An English Literature graduate of West Chester University, Tom is also a Vietnam Veteran, a lover of family, fine wine, books, humor, and sports, He pens a monthly newsletter, WineLore, and is the author of *Chameleon Skills, Dylan's Monster, Dylan's Nam, Dylan's Chase and Dylan's Devils*. He lives with his wife on an orchard farm in South Glastonbury, Connecticut, where they are surrounded by their three children and six astounding grandkids.